Her life would ...
be the same aga...

Elizabeth snuggled down under the blanket. She could hear Sam moving around in her living room, hear the quiet sound of the telephone as he dialed, the murmur of his voice. Probably checking up on her, she thought muzzily. He wouldn't find out anything interesting. To all appearances, she'd lived an ordinary life, with a family, friends, even a fiancé.

She shivered. Her family was dead now, her friends scattered. No one knew where she'd gone after Alan died. She'd disappeared, unable to accept their sympathy, unable to accept the fact that she could have stopped it from happening.

It wouldn't happen again. She wouldn't care for someone so much that it clouded her visions. As soon as this current mess was cleared up, as soon as Sam Oliver left, she would pull her defenses back around her and not let anyone near again.

She only hoped it happened soon. Before Sam Oliver kissed her again. Before she made the mistake of kissing him back.

Dear Reader:

February has a reputation for being a cold and dreary month, but not at Silhouette Intimate Moments. In fact, so many exciting things are happening this month that it's hard to know where to begin, so I'll start off with *Special Gifts* by Anne Stuart. Anne is no doubt familiar to many of you, but this is the first time she's done a novel for Silhouette Books, and it's a winner. I don't want to tell you too much, because this is definitely a must-read book. I'll say only that if you think you know everything there is to know about love and suspense and how they go together, you're in for a big surprise and a very special treat.

Another name that many of you will recognize is Linda Shaw. In *Case Dismissed* she makes her first appearance in the line in several years. If you've been reading her Silhouette Special Editions, you'll know why we're so glad to welcome her back. This is a book that literally has everything: passion and power struggles, dreams of vengeance and, most of all, characters who will jump off the page and into your heart. Don't miss it!

Award-winning writer Kathleen Creighton treats a serious subject with insight and tenderness in *Love and Other Surprises*, the story of two people who never expected to find love again—much less become parents!—but are more than capable of dealing with such unexpected happiness. Finally, welcome bestseller Naomi Horton to the line. In *Strangers No More* she gives us a whirlwind romance and a momentary marriage between a heroine you'll adore and a hero who is not at all what he seems. Figure this one out, if you can!

No matter what the weather's doing outside, February is hot at Silhouette Intimate Moments!

Leslie J. Wainger
Senior Editor
Silhouette Books

Special
Gifts

ANNE STUART

Silhouette Intimate Moments

Published by Silhouette Books New York

America's Publisher of Contemporary Romance

SILHOUETTE BOOKS
300 East 42nd St., New York, N.Y. 10017

ISBN: 0-373-07321-6

First Silhouette Books printing February 1990

Printed in the U.S.A.

ANNE STUART

was first published at age seven in *Jack and Jill* magazine. She wrote her first novel in 1974 and has since published in a variety of genres, including Gothic, Regency, suspense and contemporary romance. She particularly likes the spice of danger mixed with the emotional turmoil of romance. She currently lives in the mountains of Vermont with her husband and two children.

Chapter 1

There was a red shoe lying in the dust. The leather was shiny, new, with a few scuff marks marring the satiny sheen, and the heel was broken off. There was blood, old, brown and dried, but unquestionably blood. On the shoe, in the dust, on the splintery wooden steps of the deserted building. Too much blood for one person to lose and still survive.

They were in the mountains. Elizabeth could see the jagged peaks of the Rockies behind the deserted building, could sense the snow that lingered in the air, ready to strike like a predatory hawk. A car, no, a truck was off to one side. It was blue, and fairly new despite its beat-up condition. It had gold stripes on the side and a smashed-in left rear fender....

Elizabeth stopped abruptly. It was cold. So very, very cold, making her shiver to the depths of her bones, a frigid sheet of ice that nothing would melt. She could feel the pain start in her shoulder blades and radiate outward, rigid shafts of pain spiking through her muscles, shattering her head, making her cry out. And then sweat broke out, a cold, terrified sweat that left her drenched and shaking and too weak to even fight it.

She squeezed her eyes shut, ignoring the pain, trying to concentrate on the truck, on the cargo in the back.

But the smell of blood lingered in her nostrils, dried blood, fresh blood; the cold pierced her heart, and the agony in her head threatened to burst it. With a cry of hopelessness she sank back against the metal chair, releasing the vision as she opened her eyes.

"What did you see?"

They weren't in a mountainside camp in the Rockies, and there wasn't a drop of spilled blood around them. Elizabeth Hardy sat in the least threatening interrogation room of a Denver police station, the metal folding chair hard and solid beneath her clutching fingers, the half-skeptical, half-sympathetic eyes of Police Detective Phil Grayson opposite her doing little to bring back her peace of mind.

Her breath was coming in shuddering gasps, and the cold sweat that covered her too-thin body made her shiver in the warm room. "Nothing much new," she said finally, her voice husky and strained. "The shoe, the blood, the front steps, were pretty much as I described them. It was in the Rockies, but we'd assumed that anyway."

Phil nodded, his broad, middle-aged face creased in thought. "It's good to have verification, though."

"Such as it is." Elizabeth was able to breathe more evenly now, and the ice around her had dissolved under the bright lights. "I know you have your doubts about how much I'm able to help."

Phil had the grace to flush, his red face darkening. "We've worked together long enough, Elizabeth. I can't deny that you see things no one can explain. Things that have proved helpful time and time again. It's just that I'm a practical man—I've spent twenty years in the Army and another ten on the force here, and it's hard for me to accept the fact that I need help from a . . . a . . ."

"Psychic," Elizabeth provided glumly. A stray shudder racked her body beneath the thick wool sweater.

"Why do you do it?" Grayson questioned, leaning forward across the narrow metal table that separated them. "When it tears you up so much, why do you volunteer for this work? Why don't you just turn it off, forget it?"

"Don't you think I would if I could?" she said in a weary voice, pushing back a strand of thick brown hair that had escaped the bun at the back of her slender neck. "I'm afraid it doesn't just turn off and on like that. The visions would come, whether I wanted them to or not. I might as well put them to some use." She let out a long, pent-up breath. "I did see a truck this time."

"Terrific." Grayson pulled a notepad in front of him. "I suppose a license plate number is too much to hope for?"

"No license plates. It didn't have them," she said, her voice sounding more solidly assured. "It was a late-model panel truck, blue with gold stripes, beat-up, with a bashed-in left rear fender. It had...it had..." She struggled to crystallize the thought. "It had writing on the side of the door. Or it used to. I think it had been painted over, but I can sort of see it." Her dark brown eyes closed for a second. "The Spandau Corporation."

Grayson's pencil broke. "You're sure? The Spandau Corporation?" His voice was almost as strained as hers.

Elizabeth stared at him. "I'm sure. Why? I've never even heard of them. Have you?"

"I've heard of them," Grayson said in a grim voice.

"Do you think they have something to do with Mary Nelson's disappearance?"

"I never would have thought so. The Spandau Corporation shouldn't have a damn thing to do with the disappearance of a thirty-two-year-old suburban housewife. It'll be up to us to find the connection." He looked more than dubious; he looked deeply troubled. "Did you see anything else?"

Elizabeth shook her head. "Nothing. Maybe later." She yawned, then stretched her cramped, aching muscles.

"Maybe later," Grayson echoed. "You want a ride home, Elizabeth?"

"No, thanks. I drove, and the snow's not bad yet. I can make it home if I leave now."

"You'll call me if something else comes up? If you...see something new?" Grayson was clearly still uncomfortable with the notion that vital clues could just materialize from Elizabeth's brain, but he persevered.

"Of course. But there shouldn't be anything for a few days. You know I need a little time between sessions." She watched him out of steady eyes. Phil Grayson was nervous, agitated and positively anxious to get rid of her. Usually he offered her coffee, lunch, or they just sat around and talked while he smoked his incessant cigarettes. She was his daughter's age, and she knew that he felt protective toward her. But not today. Something more important was riding him, and if Elizabeth had had any more energy left she would have wondered what it was.

But her last reserves of energy were fading fast. Which was just as well—no answers would be forthcoming, no matter how hard she probed, from the man opposite her or her own mysterious mind. Grayson was too stubborn, and her mind was too weary. She'd simply have to wait until he was ready to talk to her.

Grayson had risen, and she could see the tension and impatience radiate through his body. "Drive carefully, Elizabeth. You'll be home this weekend? In case I need to talk to you?"

"Yes."

Phil Grayson's eyes were troubled as he watched her leave. She was too thin—he'd told her that time and time again. That slender neck looked too fragile to bear the weight of the heavy coil of dark brown hair, and her eyes were too large for her pale, oval face. It always amazed him to see how much these sessions took out of her. She would come in looking pale but energetic, and when the sessions were over she would look as if she'd run a marathon. Sweating, ashen, breathing hard and completely exhausted. Whatever his doubts as to the legitimacy of her peculiar gifts, there was no question in his mind that they were very real and very traumatic for her.

But he couldn't worry about her right now. The words she'd spoken so innocently had brought back an anger ten years old, a fear and determination that wiped out any minor consideration. He reached for the phone in front of him, dialed a handful of numbers, then went through four deliberately vague departments before tracking down his quarry.

"Oliver here."

"Sam," Grayson said with a sigh of relief. "I thought I was never going to get to you. Since when has Army Intelligence been so inaccessible?"

"Since you left, Grayson," Sam Oliver replied instantly. "They keep me locked away from temptation—they don't want me running off to the Rocky Mountains like you did."

"I'd had enough, Sam. I'm surprised you can still stomach it."

There was a long pause on the other end of the line. "So am I," he said softly. "You didn't call on a social matter, Phil. I know you too well. What's up?"

"Still the same. We've got problems. Or, more specifically, you've got problems. It's out of my jurisdiction, and I don't know how I'm going to explain it to you without you thinking I'm out of my mind."

"Try me. You've never steered me wrong before."

"Sam, it's about the Spandau Corporation." Dead silence on the other end of the line. "Did you hear me, Sam? We've got this woman here..."

"Don't say anything more, Phil." Oliver's words were short, terse, his tone dangerous indeed. "I'm coming out there. You haven't said anything to anyone yet, have you?"

"Sam, we worked together long enough for you to know me better than that. When can you get here?"

"Tonight. Don't tell anyone I'm coming—I'll just show up at your place. You still live alone?"

"Marge has the girls," he said glumly. "Yup, I'll be alone. You still drink Johnny Walker Red?"

"No, I've switched to white wine," Sam drawled. "Of course I drink Johnny Walker. See you, buddy."

"See you." Phil Grayson stared at the phone in his hand, then slowly replaced it. His instincts, such as they were, had been correct. The moment Elizabeth Hardy had said "Spandau Corporation" they'd been in big trouble.

He shouldn't be so uncomfortable with her. Those visions of hers—those near trances that had produced information over the past two years that had saved lives, recovered hidden bankrolls, even found lost pets—were probably nothing more than simple human instinct gone haywire. But damn, he'd feel a lot better if he were able to find some concrete explanation for them. And he was going to have a hell of a time explaining all this to Sam Oliver without sounding like a gullible fool at best. Sam could be blisteringly frank on occasion, and he had little time for metaphysics.

Phil would have to warn him, of course. Elizabeth Hardy wasn't the type to stand up to his browbeating tactics, and if he knew Sam, he'd try to shake her story. It would be a cold day in hell before he'd believe it. Phil would have to run interference between the two of them—there was no way he was going to stand by and let Sam make mincemeat out of her.

Though Elizabeth had more grit than he sometimes realized. She might very well be able to stand up to Sam better than anyone imagined. He reached for the phone, almost tempted to warn her, then thought better of it. Sam had told him to keep his mouth shut, and that was what he'd do. The Spandau Corporation was too important to mess with. If Sam said he'd be there tonight, he'd be there, and even a raging blizzard wouldn't stop him. Phil thanked God it would be out of his hands in another few hours.

* * *

She should have taken the offer of a ride, Elizabeth thought as she squinted through the rapidly falling snow. The roads were absolutely horrible, with just enough icy snow to make them a skating rink. They'd be better in another hour, when the snow had accumulated enough to give her some dubious traction, but at this point they were treacherous indeed. And she barely had enough energy to devote her full attention to the weather.

But if she'd left her car she would have had to go back for it, or be stuck out at her house with no transportation in the midst of what the weather report had assured everyone would be a nice little winter snowstorm. Typical for January, but in two years she still hadn't gotten used to the weather. She had no intention of venturing out during the thick of it, but she hated the feeling of isolation when she was without a car. It was a psychological, rather than a physical, deprivation, and therefore even worse. For reasons she didn't care to examine she needed an escape hatch before she could be at peace.

But what she needed *right now* was home, as fast and as safely as she could make it. She would have just enough energy to dump wood on the fire, take a hot shower and then fall into bed and sleep through the blizzard.

She always slept like the dead after one of those sessions. It drained her body of life and energy, and the only way she began to recover was to sleep the clock around. Only to face the start of the cycle once more.

But she didn't have to think of that. All she had to think about was the calm and peace of the house hidden in the woods. And hours and hours of sleep. And then maybe she could try again to find Mary Nelson's body.

Because Mary Nelson was dead. There was no doubt at all in Elizabeth's mind, no hope still clinging. But as Phil Grayson had pointed out, that had no bearing on the necessity of finding out just what had happened to her. One day she was a pretty young wife and mother from Golden,

Colorado, the next she was gone. Dead, and no one knew why, or how, or where. Or, apart from Elizabeth Hardy, whether she was dead at all.

She was the fourth young woman to disappear in the past few months. The other three bodies had turned up before long, raped, their throats cut, with no clue to the random killer who'd just happened to choose them.

But Mary Nelson hadn't been found. In every other way she fit the pattern, but she'd been missing for almost a week, and her body still hadn't turned up. And the tension in the area around Denver had mounted to almost vigilante pitch.

Her driveway was nearly obscured by the heavy snow, and Elizabeth skidded as she turned sharply, the Subaru sliding into a snowbank and then back out again. It was lucky she had enough food in the pantry and the freezer, she thought as the wheels spun and she careered the quarter of a mile up her twisting drive to the house Alan Spencer's money had bought for her. She wasn't planning to go anywhere until the roads were clear and the western skies were blue once more.

And maybe the damnable, haunting visions would give her a few days' respite. She didn't want to have to think of Mary Nelson's fate, didn't want to suddenly envision where her body might be lying, her face battered beyond recognition....

Now how did she know that? Her palms were sweating through the heavily lined gloves, and the pounding in her head increased. The Subaru slid to an abrupt halt against another pile of snow, and she turned the engine off and stumbled from the car, not even bothering to get it into the dubious protection of the carport. The snow was already past her ankles this far up the mountain, but she ignored it as she made her way with blind desperation into the shelter of her snug little house.

She didn't turn on the lights; she didn't bother with the fire; she didn't head for the shower. She turned up the electric heat, kicked off her shoes and walked blindly toward the bedroom, tumbling onto the unmade bed with a moan of pain as she burrowed under the covers. With the electric blanket hovering between nine and ten, she shut her eyes, both against the pain and the visions, and willed herself to sleep. And in this small matter her body obeyed her.

Sam Oliver sat in the small jet, his long legs stretched out in front of him, silently thanking God he didn't have to cope with public transportation and the narrow little seats and aisles in most commercial airplanes. And he didn't have to give reasons. All he'd had to do was call a number, order a plane, and half an hour later it was at his disposal at a private airfield outside of Langley. He had the best pilot the U.S. government had to offer to steer them through the thickening snow that blanketed Denver, and if he had to rely on his own flask of Johnny Walker, instead of one dispensed by a long-legged stewardess, it was a small enough deprivation. He was in no mood to appreciate long legs.

All he had to do was sit back and think. Think about the sudden, ominous reappearance of the Spandau Corporation, and what it could have to do with a possible kidnapping in Golden, Colorado.

He figured that part out before the plane even left the ground. His secretary had provided him with a week's worth of Denver papers, and the disappearance was front-page news, with Phil Grayson quoted as saying the police were working on several leads. One of which appeared to be the Spandau Corporation.

Sam would have to put a stop to that. Word of the Spandau Corporation wasn't supposed to have gone beyond a few tightly restricted rooms in Washington. For them to have turned up in Colorado suggested all sorts of possibilities, none of them pleasant.

And most unpleasant of all was the possible connection with the disappearance of Mary Nelson, a pretty, thirty-two-year-old blond housewife, and the terrorist kidnapping of Shari Derringer, the blond, thirty-year-old daughter of the secretary of state.

So far they'd been able to keep that one under wraps. She'd been snatched three days ago, and word from the kidnappers was ominously vague. It had been with a real chill that Sam Oliver had looked at the picture of Mary Nelson's pretty face and recognized the resemblance to the kidnapped Washington socialite.

He hadn't had time to brief his superiors. There was a task force working on the Derringer case, and he wasn't really involved. This might turn out to be a wild-goose chase, and then again, it might not. In the meantime, the less said the better. Kempton and his boys were busy enough following a thousand red herrings—Sam could follow his own lead in peace.

Provided they landed in one piece. Sam looked out the window of the small Army plane into the swirling snowstorm and shrugged. It had been years since he'd felt something as mundane as human fear. If the pilot didn't make it, there wasn't much he could do about it. If he did make it, then it would be time for Sam to get to work. Either way, it was out of his hands. Leaning back, he shut his eyes, emptied his mind and promptly fell asleep.

Chapter 2

Sometime during the night Elizabeth had thrown off her clothes, rather than turn down the comforting cocoon of her electric blanket. When the first sounds began to penetrate the thick wall of sleep that surrounded her, she resisted them, burrowing deeper, pulling the pillow over her head with a muffled groan. The pounding persisted, penetrating the thick feather pillow, penetrating the determined mists of sleep, penetrating all of Elizabeth's natural protective instincts.

Slowly, in a sleep-drunk daze, she climbed out from under the pillow to peer at the clock. Three-thirty—she'd only slept nine hours when she needed a good fifteen or sixteen. She listened for a long moment. At least the damn pounding had stopped. If she didn't have to get up to go to the bathroom she might be able to recapture sleep.

But she did have to get up. She was reaching for the thick flannel robe that lay on the chair next to her bed when she heard the new sound. The unmistakable noise of someone moving around in her living room.

She sat there, the flannel robe tight around her chilled body, and listened, with her ears, with her mind. Had she been too weary yesterday afternoon to lock her door? She couldn't have been that careless when a serial killer was out and about, could she? Delicately she probed her mind for tendrils of fear. Had a burglar invaded her house? Or the so-called Colorado Slasher? There was no answering panic, no racing of her heart. She didn't trust her instincts completely, but it appeared her nighttime intruder was probably harmless.

Quietly she rose to her feet, crossing the shiny wood floors and opening the door to the living room. The light from her bedroom flooded the dimly lit room, illuminating a tall, shadowy figure standing by her fireplace. He appeared to be in the middle of building a fire, and he turned at the sound of her presence with a surprising amount of self-possession.

"Can I help you?" she inquired politely, sounding more like a receptionist than a woman whose house had been invaded.

"Sorry I just barged in." His voice was deep, pleasant, with what might have been, a long, long time ago, a trace of Texas in his accent. "I'm a stranded traveler. I knocked for a long time but I guess you didn't hear me. I'm afraid I had to break a window, but I've taped it up for now. I'll replace it, I promise. I hope I didn't scare you."

"You didn't." It was too dark to see him properly, particularly without her glasses. She could make out a tall, lean figure in the shadows, with snow melting on the shoulders of his parka and in his thick dark hair.

"You're pretty brave, considering what I've been reading about in the local paper," he said. "What if I'd been a rapist and a murderer?"

"You weren't," she said with calm assurance. "Did your car go off the road?"

"About half a mile away. I should have known better than to try to make it to Steamboat tonight." His voice was rich with self-disgust. "I hope you don't mind me breaking in like this. I would have frozen my... butt off if I'd stayed in the car."

"Of course I don't mind," Elizabeth said, ignoring the sudden stirrings of uneasiness that crept across her shoulders. "I'll make you some coffee while you call the road crew."

"That would be great. But I'm afraid I've already called—they won't be out till late morning at the earliest."

She accepted that stoically enough. "Then I'd better get you some blankets. You can bed down on the couch. Would you like anything in the coffee to help you sleep?"

"Scotch would make me a very happy man," he said, dropping a match on the fire and moving back into the shadows just as the firelight would have illuminated his face. "Johnny Walker, if you have it. And you needn't bother with the coffee part."

"I have it." Still that uneasiness lingered. It wasn't a question of physical danger from the dark, shadowy stranger. More just a sense that something wasn't quite right. "My name's Elizabeth Hardy."

He moved then, crossing the room with an easy stride. As he came into the pool of light from her bedroom door she got her first good look at him. And the uneasiness increased.

He was a handsome man. His dark brown hair was cut short; his eyes seemed to be a dark blue, his face tanned and affable. But Elizabeth didn't believe that handsome affability. He held out a hand, a strong, well-shaped hand with short nails and long, artistic fingers. "Sam Oliver," he said.

She took his hand in hers, and a jolt of electricity shot through her. She dropped it, backing away in a badly disguised panic. And through that panic she recognized the expression of shock that paled his face. He must have felt the same reaction.

"Lots of static electricity," she murmured. "I'll get your drink."

Sam Oliver watched her go. His hand still tingled from the sudden, shocking connection of flesh on flesh. It wasn't that mystical, sensual reaction of two people who were sexually attracted to each other. Hell, Elizabeth Hardy was a small, quiet, almost plain woman, and those brown eyes of hers were unnerving. No, it was something else. And remembering what Phil Grayson had tried to convince him of, he stared after his reluctant hostess with narrowed, thoughtful eyes.

It had taken two hours to travel the fifteen miles from the airport to Phil Grayson's modest ranch house, where he'd lived alone for the past three years since his wife took his daughters and left him. And then another three hours over Coors and Johnny Walker and frozen pizza while Phil tried to convince Sam that he wasn't out of his mind.

"You gotta be kidding," Sam had said at first. "A psychic? You really believe all that garbage?"

"No, I don't believe all that garbage," Phil had replied. "But I don't not believe it, either. Time and time again, Elizabeth has come up with stuff that no one could know. There's no explanation for it, or at least none that I can find. All I know is that she goes into these sort of trances and something happens."

Sam leaned back. "Gimme a break, Phil. You're too old for a midlife crisis."

"Go to hell. You're too young to be so closed-minded. Elizabeth has seen things. How else would she know about the Spandau Corporation?"

"That's exactly what I intend to find out," Sam said grimly. "And she'd better have a damn good reason for knowing."

But Phil knew as well as Sam that there could be no good reason. The Spandau Corporation was one of the U.S. intelligence community's greatest debacles, a disaster ten years old and still painfully fresh, from the president through the CIA down to every minor branch of military and government intelligence. They weren't even given the option of forgetting.

It had been such a grand and glorious plan to begin with. The Spandau Corporation had been a mythical company, dreamed up by the CIA to serve as a cover for infiltrating the various splinter groups of European and Middle Eastern terrorists in the late seventies. Sam Oliver had been one of the supposed employees; so had Phil Grayson.

But somehow, somewhere along the way, everything had gone wrong. Too much bureaucratic ineptitude, too many double agents, too many chiefs, too few Indians. No one really knew for sure what had happened, but when the dust cleared, the plans for the controversial Unicorn missile, the secret accords signed between supposed enemy countries and the minute details of the U.S. contingency plans for the Middle East, Central America and Afghanistan were in the hands of the most virulent collection of international terrorists ever assembled. And just to rub salt into the wound, they called themselves the Spandau Corporation.

There hadn't been much anyone could do to salvage the situation. The plans had to be scrapped, the Unicorn missile had to be replaced with the much less efficient MX missile, and the surviving agents had crawled back to the States to lick their wounds and salvage their pride. They'd managed to keep the name of the Spandau Corporation out of the public awareness, and only a few people even recognized it.

Sam stood there in Elizabeth Hardy's darkened living room, listening to the sounds of her moving around in the kitchen. She had to know. Phil had taped his sessions with her, and Sam had spent an hour going over the tapes, listening for nuances in her speech, hesitation, guilt. That almost offhand mention of the Spandau Corporation was just too innocent, too accidental, to be believed. It had to be a deliberate taunt, a speciality of that organization over the years, tossed into the middle of something seemingly unrelated. And he was too used to distrusting everyone he met.

For one thing, she was too damn casual about a mid-night intruder. Especially with what might pass for a serial murderer loose in the area. Mary Nelson wasn't the first young woman to disappear, she was merely the latest. No woman in her right mind would accept having her house broken into with such equanimity. One more strike against her, Sam thought. She'd delicately dropped her bombshell, then sat back to wait and see what happened. But she'd shown her hand by being so trusting, he thought. She would only be that relaxed with a strange man invading her home in the middle of the night if she were convinced she con-trolled the situation.

He was totally prepared for her to come out of that kitchen with a gun in her hand. She had small hands—he'd noticed that right away. A small, pale face, and a thick shank of hair hanging down her narrow back, the flannel robe drawn tight around a body that was too thin. At least she couldn't hide a gun without great difficulty. And he was fast. His own gun was only a second out of reach—he could take her out before she could do more than aim.

He flexed his hand experimentally, every nerve alert as he stood there, waiting. He could hear the chink of ice, the slosh of whiskey in a glass, the hiss of water from the tap. And then she appeared in the doorway, the light behind her illuminating her narrow figure. She had a glass of whiskey in each hand, and there was no telltale sag in the small pockets of the worn flannel robe. Her feet were bare, her toes curled slightly against the cold, and it was those toes that decided him. There was something so small and vul-nerable about them that Sam Oliver did something com-pletely uncharacteristic. He went with his instincts and moved his hand away from the gun hidden in the pocket of his parka.

She smiled at him, a shy smile he didn't believe, and handed him a tall glass of amber liquid. He'd taken a soothing sip of it before the significance of that sank in. She'd brought him a tall glass, two ice cubes and a dollop of water. Exactly the way he made it for himself, disdaining short whiskey glasses and too much ice. And all his suspicions flared forth again. He wasn't a man who believed in coincidence.

He met her smile with a practiced one of his own. "Just the way I like it," he said evenly. "How did you know?"

Only an extremely observant man would have seen that slight shadow cross her eyes. Her smile became more automatic, and she stalled, taking a sip from her own short, paler glass. And then she shrugged. "Just a lucky guess," she said, moving away from him. "You must be exhausted. Let me get you some quilts, and then you can get some sleep. If I know the road crew, we're pretty low priority out here—not enough people around to make it worthwhile. I'd be surprised if we saw them before noon. These winter storms can be pretty overwhelming...."

She was babbling, Sam thought distantly, and she struck him as a woman who seldom babbled. She was nervous, edging away from him.

"I'm sure they can be." He kept his voice low and soothing. "You sure you don't mind my taking advantage of your hospitality?"

She shook her head, and that heavy mane of dark brown hair swung around her narrow back. "Of course not. I couldn't turn you out into a night like this. Take off your parka, and I'll be right back."

He watched her go. If she were an operative she'd know he had a gun in the parka, and her suggestion would hold a wealth of meaning. But she'd also know that he had at least one other weapon on him.

As a matter of fact, he had two. A very small, very efficient snub-nosed gun in an ankle holster, and a knife tucked inside his left sleeve. Between the two of them he could take care of someone Elizabeth Hardy's size. Even if that sleepy, slightly shy demeanor hid the nature and talents of a harpy, he could still manage to control her. Unless, of course, she'd poisoned the whiskey. He stared down at his glass.

But she'd have no reason to kill him, he thought. Not yet. He took another meditative sip and once again noted the perfect mixture she'd accomplished seemingly by accident. What else did she know about him?

He'd come to Colorado to check out Elizabeth Hardy. Despite Phil's defense, Sam was certain she had to be involved with the Spandau Corporation in some way, and he had every intention of playing along until he found out how. At best, she might be an innocent pawn. He hated to think of the worst possible scenario.

She was back, carrying an armload of quilts. She dropped them on the sofa, looking pleased. "These should keep you warm. I'm sorry I can't offer you more comfortable accommodations, but I don't have any furniture in the guest room. Besides, it's warmer in here."

There was no pillow, Sam noticed. Of course, if she had no second bed, she probably had no extra pillows, but he couldn't stop wondering just how much her bosses knew, how many intimate details the Spandau Corporation had discovered about his personal life.

"Got a pillow?" he inquired pleasantly. Once again the shadow darkened her eyes.

"A pillow?" she echoed stupidly. "Of course. I'm sorry, I must have forgotten." She turned to go, glad to be out of the range of those unnerving eyes. Her hands shook slightly as she headed back toward the linen closet, which was surprisingly well stocked, a legacy from her Appalachian grandmother. Why in God's name had she thought he wouldn't want a pillow? And how had she known about the damn drink?

Stupid question to ask herself, she thought, curling her lip in disgust. She should have gotten used to knowing these things, to having unexpected, subconscious bits of knowledge crop up like that. If she were more alert, more careful, she wouldn't be caught out the way she had been, twice in the past ten minutes. Explanations were embarrassing and unbelievable, and she'd let herself slip.

It was odd, though, she thought, pulling out the thick feather pillow and grabbing one of the embroidered cases with Granny Mellon's handmade lace. She didn't usually come up with so much about one person. Maybe it was just an aftereffect of today's session. She hadn't had the chance to sleep it off, and maybe some of whatever came over her was still lingering.

He was watching her when she came back into the room, taking the pillow in those large, strong-looking hands of his, the skin tanned and dark against the snowy-white pillowcase. He'd taken off that enveloping parka, and he was leaner than she'd thought. In the bulky down he'd looked overwhelming; in the thick wool sweater he was pared down, whipcord lean and dangerous looking. She might almost have preferred the bulk.

She knew that danger wasn't directed at her. Of that she was certain. But Sam Oliver wasn't a skier heading for Steamboat Springs on a snowy night. And he hadn't found her house by accident. That knowledge was immediate and inescapable. The only way she was going to know for sure that she was safe from him in every way, the only way she was going to recapture some of her desperately needed sleep, was to touch him.

She didn't want to. That first, accidental touching had been powerful enough, setting off mental and emotional and psychic sparks that still had her reeling. But she hadn't been questioning at the time. And the only way she could find out if she could trust her voices was to touch him.

It was going to be difficult, she thought. He was standing there, looking down at her, his arms wrapped around the white pillow and hugging it against his tall body. She wasn't the sort to touch casually; it wasn't in her nature to reach out and place a hand on his arm as she wished him a good night's sleep.

He didn't seem inclined to help her. ''Thanks for everything,'' he said with that faint hint of a drawl, clearly waiting for her to leave him. She could feel his eyes on her, those clear, dark blue eyes, but she couldn't even begin to tell what he was thinking.

"Well, good night," Elizabeth said. "I'll just get the kitchen light...." She started to move past him.

"I can do it," he said, moving at the same time.

They collided. His hands reached out to catch her arms, to steady her as she stumbled against him, and for a moment she was pressed against his chest. It was a warm, hard chest, with a steady heartbeat, and the wool was scratchy beneath her face. The long fingers on her upper arms were strong, flexing, and he smelled like Scotch and pizza. For a moment she shut her eyes, trying to read him.

But clearly he misread her hesitation. "I'm game if you are, lady," he muttered under his breath, and before she knew what was happening, he'd tipped her face up to his, and his mouth came down on hers.

It was a raw, rough insult of a kiss. Elizabeth knew that immediately, recognized the deliberate, almost studied sensuality of his openmouthed kiss, his tongue rudely catching hers and forcing it back in her mouth. His hands had slid down her arms to catch her bottom and pull her up against him. Her hands were on his shoulders, on the scratchy wool sweater, pushing him away, but all the while her mind was telling her that even a rude insult of a kiss was better than no kiss at all, a situation she'd lived with for far too long.

And then it left her. The hands on her body, the mouth on hers, the smell and feel of him vanished, and there was blood everywhere. Blood on the red shoe, blood on her hands, blood on Sam Oliver's hands. And blood in a pool around Phil Grayson.

She shivered, trying to break away, but the warmth, the human touch, was having its usual, devastating effect, increasing her visions, bringing them horrifyingly close, surrounding her. And she saw Sam watching Phil, watching the lifeblood drain away, and his face was a mask of murderous rage.

She felt the scream form in the back of her throat, and her hands curled into fists as she fought to break free of him, to break free of the vision that she couldn't face. A moment later she found herself backed against the wall, staring at her uninvited visitor.

Sam shrugged. "Sorry. I must have misread the situation. I never offer my attentions where they aren't wanted."

It was a good act, Elizabeth had to concede him that. He sounded like a wounded ski bum on the make, a little insulted, but more than willing to move on to the next available female.

But Elizabeth didn't believe him. That touch, that kiss, that quick, hideous vision, had cleared away the mask that stood between them. Who are you? she asked him without words. But she knew he wouldn't tell her.

"Yes," she said evenly. "You misread the situation." And she moved to the telephone, wondering whether he'd try to stop her.

He didn't move. Instead he sat down on the sofa by the fire, watching her as she dialed, his face still set in that faintly offended expression.

"If you're calling the road crew you don't need to worry," he said. "I told you, I won't bother you."

"I'm calling the police," she said.

"Lady," he whined, his eyes sharp and clear. "For pity's sake . . ."

Phil Grayson's sleepy voice answered on the fourth ring. "It's Elizabeth, Phil," she said in a clear, calm tone.

The voice on the other end was immediately alert. So was the man in the room with her. "What's wrong? Are you okay, Elizabeth?"

"I'm fine. I just want to know if you sent him."

There was a long pause at the other end, and Elizabeth had her answer. "Elizabeth," he began, but she carefully replaced the telephone, turning back to Sam.

He was watching her, and he no longer bothered to disguise his watchfulness. "Give me the pillow," she said.

"You mean you aren't going to let me stay after all?"

"You can stay. I trust Phil, even if he doesn't happen to trust me," she said, her voice icy.

"So why do you want the pillow?"

"Because you and I both know that you never use one," she said, holding out her hand.

He handed it back to her, probably for lack of anything better to do, Elizabeth thought. "You don't want to ask any questions?"

She shook her head. "Tomorrow will be soon enough. I hope you don't snore." Her voice was polite.

The skepticism had been waiting; she'd known it was there, and now it blossomed forth, twisting his handsome face. "You tell me," he countered.

She felt the hot bile of temper rise in her stomach, and it took the last of her energy to push it back. "Good night," she said instead, and turned toward her bedroom.

He had the last word after all. "Pleasant dreams, Elizabeth."

Chapter 3

Phil Grayson arrived at Elizabeth's house sometime after nine the next morning. The road crew had been more efficient than usual, encouraged, no doubt, by the combined pressure of the Denver police department and the United States government, and for the first time Elizabeth's driveway suddenly became top priority.

She lay in the center of her double bed, a narrow, huddled figure, the electric blanket pulled over her head. She woke up long enough to hear the voices in the living room, to recognize Phil's midwestern twang, and to smell the coffee. And then she sank back into the deep, comforting fog of sleep. Maybe by the time she was ready to face the world they'd both be gone.

"So what do you think?" Phil took the mug of coffee Sam handed him and sat down on the living room couch.

Sam waited for a moment, letting the much-needed caffeine take effect. He'd had no more than four hours of sleep in the past forty-eight, and though he'd long ago trained his body to ignore things like deprivation, the coffee helped. He drained half the mug of strong, black brew, and leaned his shoulders against the mantel. "I think she's a phony," he said flatly. "An operative, part of the Spandau Corporation, and not to be trusted."

"Sam, I've worked with her for almost two years—" Phil began, but Sam cut him off.

"You know as well as I do that a sleeper agent can live for decades like any normal citizen, until they're needed."

"But we're not talking KGB, Sam. We're talking about a bunch of loonies. Terrorists are notoriously unstable. They can't support something of this complexity. Not to mention the patience involved in a long-term plan."

"The Spandau Corporation...damn, I hate calling them that," he said bitterly, draining his coffee. "The Spandau Corporation doesn't consist of your run-of-the-mill terrorists. They're the cream of the crop, the smartest, fastest, deadliest bunch of fanatics you'd ever want to meet."

"And you think that exhausted little girl asleep in there is one of them."

"Exhausted little girl?" Sam echoed. "What the hell happened to your brain, Grayson? That little girl could very well be a dragon lady, and you have nothing but your instincts and a sentimental streak to tell you otherwise. You know what that kind of trust can do to you—you've seen it as often as I have."

Grayson shook his head. "I think you've been in the business too long, Sam."

"And I think you've been *out* of the business too long," he shot back, setting the empty mug on the mantel with a decisive snap. "I want more on her. Your police files had diddly-squat about her past."

"Sam, we weren't investigating her."

"Well, I am. Did anything come through on the computer this morning?"

"Not when I left. There's a time difference—"

"Which should work in my favor," he interrupted. "Phil, if you didn't want to help, why the hell did you call me?"

"I do want to help. I just don't want Elizabeth Hardy crucified like..." His voice trailed off.

"Like Amy Lee," Sam supplied in a flat voice.

"Sam, I didn't mean to bring her up."

"No, of course not. And we're not going to get anywhere if we hide behind polite phrases. We both know that Amy Lee died, and the two of us could have saved her. I learned to live with it, and I thought you had, too."

"Why do you think I retired?" Phil demanded. "Hell, Sam, you may be able to forget that your wife was killed, but I have a harder time dealing with it."

"Do you really?" Sam said evenly.

A long, uncomfortable silence reigned in the rustic living room, broken only by the hiss and crackle of the fire and the drip of melting snow outside the front window. Sam looked at his old friend in the merciless light of day, and his cold, bleak rage vanished as abruptly as it had appeared. Phil had aged—he looked ten years older than his fifty-one. Damn Marge anyway, he thought savagely. And damn Phil, for marrying a woman who couldn't take the rigors of being married to someone with their kind of dangerous life-style, and then letting her tear his heart out.

He reached out a hand and clasped Phil's sagging shoulder. It was a brief touch, reaffirming their friendship, and Phil managed a weary smile. "Got any more of this coffee?"

"Enough to float half of Denver. I'll get us both some while we go over what we know about Elizabeth Hardy."

"It's not much." Phil trailed after him, out to the spotless galley kitchen that clearly didn't see much cooking. The whole place reminded Sam of a convent, a place not much given to the physical pleasures of life.

"She's what...twenty-nine?" Sam said, pouring the coffee. "Never married, born in North Carolina, raised by her grandmother. Moved to Denver a little over two years ago. Right?"

"Right," Phil agreed.

"How long has she been in this house?"

"Two years."

Sam looked up, startled, and took another curious glance around the bare confines of the kitchen. "Really? It's not what I'd call a homey place. What does she do for a living? How'd she pay for this place? It's small, but I have a pretty good idea what even a tiny house outside of Denver would cost."

"I don't know. She doesn't have a regular job. She helps me out, but she doesn't take any money for it. Every time I've called her, she's always been home. As far as I know she doesn't have any friends, apart from me."

"Apart from you," Sam echoed flatly, wishing he could trust his old friend's instincts. "What about lovers?"

There was no change of expression on Phil's lined face. "None, as far as I know. But then, I'm not nosy."

"Well, I sure the hell am. I want to know everything about her. What happened to her parents, where she got the money for this place, how she supports herself, what she does all day long. I want her life history tattooed on my brain. I don't want a day unaccounted for."

"And how do you plan to do that?"

Sam smiled briefly. "I have friends in high places. You've forgotten how efficient they can be when they have the right motivation. And the Spandau Corporation is a high priority. Not to mention . . ." He considered for a moment.

"Not to mention?" Phil echoed. "What else is going on, Sam? Is there something happening out there with Spandau right now? Something that made you come hotfooting out here?"

"You might say so. I don't know if there's a connection between your helpless little flower and the current situation—I decided not to say anything about my suspicions until I checked things out here."

"Are you going to tell me?"

"It's a need-to-know situation. . . ."

"Don't give me that, Sam!" Grayson snapped. "I'm not in the service anymore. If you want my help you're going to have to be open with me. What the hell is going on?"

Sam just stood there in the barren, sunlit kitchen. "Why don't we ask your little friend?"

"Cut it out, Sam. She doesn't need tests to prove herself. Besides, she'll probably be sleeping for another..." The distant sound of the shower drifted to the kitchen, and Phil shook his head. "You always had the damnedest hearing. Okay, we'll ask her. But give her time to have a cup of coffee first."

Sam smiled faintly. "She can have a cup of coffee," he agreed, and headed back into the living room.

The shower felt absolutely wonderful, so wonderful, in fact, that Elizabeth considered just staying there until her unwanted visitors left. Considered, then rejected the idea. For one thing, her hot water supply wasn't inexhaustible. For another, Sam Oliver wasn't the type of man who'd take a hint.

What in heaven's name did he want from her? It was more than clear that he didn't believe her, didn't believe in her dubious gifts. That was fine with her; she was used to skepticism, and even preferred it to certain people's macabre fascination. But what had caused Phil Grayson, a man whose trust she counted on, to summon assistance in the form of that tall, forbidding stranger?

For that was what he was. Despite the easy smile, the handsome face, the phony charm that she'd wanted to believe, Sam Oliver was a very dangerous, distant man. Someone whose defenses and masks would be impossible even for her to penetrate. He frightened her a little, she thought, turning off the streaming jets of water. And whether she liked it or not, he attracted her.

It was probably just proximity, she thought, wrapping a towel around her wet tangle of hair. She'd been so careful not to let any man close, any man near enough to breach her defenses, not since Alan died. Sam Oliver had slipped through when she wasn't looking. Hell, she'd probably respond to a kiss from King Kong at this point. She'd never tried to deny the fact that she had normal, healthy desires like anyone else. She just didn't dare fulfill them.

Why was he here? Why had Phil sent him? And, more important, how soon would he leave?

They'd certainly made themselves at home, she thought with a trace of irritation when she finally unlocked her door and stepped out of her bedroom. Her feet were bare on the chilly floors; the cotton sweater was oversize and enveloping on her slender body, and her jeans were baggy and faded. She'd wound her wet hair in a coil at the back of her neck, and it sat there, chilly and damp, ready to bring on a cold, she thought gloomily.

The two conspirators looked up. They were sitting across from each other, each having taken possession of one of the living room couches, and she could smell the coffee. "Don't let me disturb you," she said politely, moving straight past them toward the kitchen.

Sam was ahead of her. He didn't touch her, and for that she could be profoundly grateful, but his sheer size stopped her cold. In the daylight he might look less menacing to a normal person. But not to her. She looked up, way up, into his dark blue eyes, and knew they had looked into hell without flinching. And would do so again. His mouth was wide, a little grim, his cheekbones high, and his dark hair was cut too short. Army short, she thought.

She just stood there, waiting. Patience had always been her strong suit, patience and self-control. She could stand there forever.

"Come off it, you two," Phil said from his spot on the sofa. "Bring Elizabeth some coffee and then we can talk. Come back here, sweetheart. I'm sorry I sprang Sam on you without warning."

She turned back to him, turning away from the tall man in front of her. She was genuinely fond of Phil Grayson, and forgiving him was simple enough. Forgiving the rock-hard man who'd just walked into her kitchen as if he owned it might be a different matter entirely.

She sat down on the couch opposite Phil, curling her feet under her. "You want to tell me what's going on, Phil?" she asked quietly. "Has Mary Nelson been found?"

"Still no word on her," he admitted, and she recognized the usual softening in his eyes as they rested on her. "As for what's going on, I'm not quite sure. Sam wanted to wait until you were up before he explained it to me."

"But why did you call him?" she persisted. She could feel the man return from the kitchen, could feel the cold, wet bun of hair at the back of her neck warm with the uncomfortable heat of his gaze, but she refused to turn and look at him. Refused to ask him any questions.

"Here's your coffee," Sam said, moving around the couch and holding out her mug.

She looked at the coffee. His hands were large, in keeping with the rest of him, and his fingers were long and narrow. The mug was barely visible beneath those large hands, and she nodded toward the coffee table, unwilling to risk touching him again. "You can put it down there."

Sam just stood there, holding out the coffee, not moving. His dark blue eyes were opaque as they looked down at her, only a faint hint of challenge filtering through, and Elizabeth knew with sudden clarity that here was a match for her own patience and stubbornness. And damn it, she needed her coffee.

She sighed. "Aren't you a little old for games, Mr. Oliver?"

"Colonel Oliver. Army Intelligence," he corrected. "But you may as well call me Sam. You want your coffee, Elizabeth?"

"Sam..." Grayson said, but they both ignored him, brown eyes staring up into blue ones, anger and distrust and something else flaring between them.

"Yes, I want my coffee."

"Then take it from me," he said, still holding the mug out for her.

She could do it without touching him. She'd had plenty of experience avoiding human contact, never knowing what it might set off, and when someone was as dangerous as Colonel Oliver, she knew she had to be doubly careful. She reached up for the coffee mug, for the proffered handle.

Her hand was shaking. She noticed it as she reached, and in what seemed almost like slow motion, her hand reached for the coffee mug and instead touched him. His flesh was warm, smooth, alive, against her fingers, and she jerked away. The coffee went flying, over the couch, over Sam Oliver's legs and over Elizabeth's hands, scalding her.

She didn't move, didn't jump away. She sat back, wrapping her arms around her body and tucking her hands away. "I drink too much coffee anyway," she said in a tranquil voice.

Sam ducked down to retrieve the fallen mug, set it on the table where he should have put it in the first place and moved back to his spot by the mantel. "We'll go by the assumption that you really don't have anything to do with what's going on," he said, ignoring the coffee incident completely. "Since you're unlikely to admit you're a member of the Spandau Corporation..."

"The Spandau Corporation?" Elizabeth echoed. "Is that what started all this?"

"What do you know about the Spandau Corporation?" Sam demanded, sounding less and less like the charming ski bum he'd pretended to be and more like a drill sergeant.

Elizabeth glared up at him. Somehow his handsome face made his icy manner even worse, she thought. If he were old and ugly she wouldn't be tempted to go find another cup of coffee and douse him more thoroughly. "Their name was printed on the side of a panel truck," she said. "Actually, it had been painted over. That's the only time I've seen it or heard of it."

"Where?"

"I beg your pardon?"

"Where did you see the panel truck?"

That stopped her for a moment. She turned to look at Grayson, and the older man nodded slightly. Sam Oliver knew exactly where she'd seen it. He was just trying to make her uncomfortable by having to explain it to him.

Well, that was one game she wasn't going to play. "Don't bait me, Colonel Oliver. You know as well as I do that I saw the panel truck in a vision. A psychic dream, if you will. Now, why don't you go ahead and laugh?"

Sam controlled his irritation. "I'm not in the mood."

"Good. Because neither am I. I help out the Denver police and Phil because I want to. I don't owe them anything, and I certainly don't owe you anything. I want you out of here, and I want you out now."

He didn't move, visibly unimpressed by her sudden show of anger. "If you *are* telling the truth," he said, "then you do owe me something. You owe your country something. You owe us your help."

There was one thing Elizabeth couldn't fight. And that was when someone asked, even demanded, her help. The only thing that made living with her gift bearable was using it to help people. There was no way she could say no, even though she despised Sam Oliver for his contempt and distrust, even though she saw right through his sudden flag-waving. She opened her mouth to tell him to leave, then shut it again. She couldn't.

Phil leaned across the table and patted her knee. He knew her well enough to know she had no defenses against what Sam Oliver had just done to her. She wondered if he felt any guilt at standing by and allowing it to happen. Looking into his weary eyes, she knew that he did. And for his sake she lifted her head and managed a smile she was far from feeling.

"Okay, Colonel Oliver," she said. "You painted me into a corner. It's damned if I do and damned if I don't, right? If I come up with answers they're suspect. If I don't come up with answers I'm a cowardly traitor. What is it you want from me?''

Bad way to put it, she chastised herself. The sudden narrowing of his eyes sent a brief, unbelievable message, one that came and went so quickly that she refused to accept it. Men like Sam Oliver didn't want women like Elizabeth Hardy.

"I want to find the place where you saw the panel truck," he said without a moment's pause, and she knew she must have imagined that sudden moment of heat. "I want you to show us where the blood and the shoe were." He listed the details of her hard-won vision with callous unconcern, and she clenched her hands, ignoring the sting from the coffee burns.

"I don't know..." she began.

"But you can find it, can't you, Elizabeth?" He pushed her, his voice a silky menace. "Someone with your...talents should have no trouble pinpointing the place. We already figured it had to be somewhere in the mountains, and not too far away. Now it's up to you to lead us to the spot."

"Aren't you afraid I'll have some of my fellow terrorists waiting to ambush you?" she shot back.

"How did you know we were talking about terrorists, Elizabeth?" Sam said gently. "No one said anything about terrorists."

"Sam," Grayson interrupted. "Stop badgering her. No one can make you believe her or not, but you don't have to use her for target practice."

"She doesn't look wounded," Sam pointed out.

"Don't worry about it, Phil," Elizabeth said, uncurling her body and stretching her legs and arms in a completely false display of ease. "It would take more than a tin soldier to demoralize me." She knew she wouldn't fool Grayson, who knew her far too well, but maybe she might fool his wretched friend. If she were really lucky, she might even fool herself. "If he wants to play guessing games we can keep it up for hours. I have nothing else planned for today."

"I do," Sam said.

"I know." Elizabeth kept herself from sounding smug as she waited.

Sam looked down at her, at the small, white hands and feet, the wire-rimmed glasses that sat so daintily on her small, pale nose. "The Spandau Corporation is a group of terrorists," he said, and Elizabeth didn't have time to be surprised by his sudden loquacity. "They're suspected of having kidnapped Shari Derringer."

"The daughter of the secretary of state?" Grayson gasped. "I didn't even know she'd been kidnapped."

"No one does," Sam replied. "For now it's being kept completely quiet. We're waiting to see what sort of demands are being made. We're waiting to see if it really was a kidnapping, or if she went willingly."

"That pretty girl? You've got to be kidding," Grayson protested.

A savage smile slashed Sam's face. "You've got a blind spot for pretty little girls, Phil," he said, and Elizabeth wondered why she was stupid enough to be pleased by that obvious referral to herself. "Shari Derringer isn't the sweet little debutante the media think she is."

"They never are," Grayson said sadly. "So what's the connection?"

Sam turned to look down at Elizabeth. "You want to tell him?" he drawled, his voice a challenge.

She glared up at him. "All I can do is make an educated guess, Colonel Oliver."

"And what's that?"

"I know that Shari Derringer and Mary Nelson are the same age and same general physical type. If I remember correctly, their resemblance may be even stronger than that. So I would suspect that one of them is going to substitute for the other."

Sam nodded. "Give the lady a cigar. And we're going to find them before they do. We're probably too late to help Mary Nelson, but we can stop them from fulfilling the rest of whatever they've got planned. And you're going to find them for us, aren't you?''

Elizabeth looked at him. A thousand things flew into her mind, not the least of which was the thought that she didn't want to be around him for one second longer than she had to. Far more dangerous to her than his hostility and distrust was the perverse, undeniable attraction he held for her. But she had no choice, and she knew it.

''Yes,'' she said, shutting her mind to the horror and death that would follow. ''I'll find them for you.'' And she closed her eyes.

Chapter 4

Elizabeth wasn't used to feeling hatred for any living soul. She wasn't used to feeling much of anything, at least not directly. She could feel anger, fear, passion, even happiness, through her visions, through other people's emotions. But her own reactions had been tucked away in a dreamlike limbo. She cared about Phil. She could trust his safe, older brother kind of concern, and she knew he wanted nothing from her. She used to have friends, family, people she liked. But for the past two years she'd lived alone, shut off from everyone and everything.

Until Sam Oliver forced his way into her life. She sat beside him in Phil's late-model Chrysler, her eyes shut as they drove higher and higher into the mountains, and she hated.

Even Phil's calm presence in the back seat didn't penetrate the fog of anger that enveloped her. It didn't matter that he clearly liked, trusted and respected Sam Oliver. It didn't matter that she'd always believed in Phil's judgment. She hated Sam Oliver with a strong, life-affirming rage, and nothing she could do could bring back her safe cocoon of apathy. She'd been dragged out of it, by Oliver's strong, electric hands, and she was mortally afraid she wasn't going to be able to return.

"This place look familiar?" Sam's deep voice rumbled beside her, the faint curl of mockery twisting the edges.

She turned to look at him, at the too-handsome profile, the too-short hair, the too-cold eyes. "I've never been here before."

"Not even in a trance?"

"They aren't trances," she snapped, feeling the rage crackle around inside her. "I just . . . see things."

"You just see things," he mimicked. "All right, swami. Have you ever *seen* this place before?"

She found she was clenching her fists, and she slowly, deliberately relaxed them. "I don't think so," she said, her voice neutral once more. "Keep driving."

She could feel movement in the back seat, and it didn't take exceptional powers of observation to know that Phil was uncomfortable with Sam's treatment of her. But he said nothing, and Elizabeth could feel her anger grow to encompass everyone in the big American car. Including herself.

She reached down for the thermos of coffee that rested at her feet and took a deep swallow of the rich, sweet stuff. She couldn't seem to get warm, despite the heat blasting from the car heater, despite the relative warmth of the day. The heavy snowfall was melting in the bright sunshine, and Elizabeth sat there in her down coat, her arms wrapped around her narrow body, and shivered.

She could feel Sam's eyes on her, and she met his gaze defiantly. "Got any coffee left?" he asked.

"This has cream and sugar in it. You drink yours black."

"Forget the parlor tricks, Elizabeth. I'm not impressed. Give me the coffee."

She passed if over to him, watching in dismay as he tipped it back and swallowed. He handed it back, and there was a challenge in his dark blue eyes, one she knew she should ignore.

She put her mouth where his had been, draining the coffee, shuddering slightly at the sweet sludge at the bottom of the Thermos. "Next time bring your own," she said.

"Next time? What makes you think there's going to be a next time?" He sounded genuinely horrified at the notion, and Elizabeth found herself smiling.

"I hate to tell you this, Colonel Oliver, but life is not that simple. I can't just tell you how to get to the place I saw in my 'trance.'" She used his word mockingly. "I don't know where it is. All we can do is drive around until I start feeling something."

"I'm feeling something right now," Sam snarled. "Irritation, bordering on exasperation."

"That's nothing to what you'll be feeling in a few days," Elizabeth said, her voice a soft purr of malice.

Phil leaned over the seat, suddenly the peacemaker. "This doesn't feel familiar, Elizabeth?"

"Not at all." She pulled her coat tighter around her. "And it's getting dark."

"Can't see in the dark?" Sam chided. "What the hell kind of psychic are you?"

"A very, very good one," she murmured. "But it doesn't take special gifts to know that you're a—"

"Children, children," Phil said, putting a restraining hand on Elizabeth's tense shoulder. "Let's not fight. We're all working for the same thing. Let's go home, get a good night's sleep and get an early start the next morning."

Elizabeth leaned back against the cushioned seat, willing herself to relax. She hadn't had time to fully recover from her last session with Phil before this large, disturbing creature forced his way into her home, into her life. If she was going to find that deserted spot in the Rocky Mountain foothills, she was going to need all the rest she could get. And she wanted to find that location with a need that bordered on desperation.

Because that was the only way she was going to get rid of Sam Oliver. He was as tenacious as a bulldog—it didn't take special gifts to see that. He wouldn't let go of her until he found out everything he wanted to know, and she needed him gone, quite desperately. She needed to crawl back into her safe, quiet world, where anger and frustration had no place, except as the vicarious leavings of other people's emotions. Her own feelings were dead, and they were going to stay that way.

Sam cursed, a short, sibilant obscenity, as the big car slid on the iced-up road, and he started back down into the twilight, toward the sprawling environs of the Mile High City. Outside the Chrysler the temperature dropped as the sun went down, and a thin layer of ice formed on the road, which was wet with melted snow. Elizabeth felt the car's heat finally penetrate her bones as they drove farther and farther down toward the tiny suburb. And she knew with depressing certainty that they'd been close, too close, to the place where Mary Nelson had met her end.

"Feeling better?" Phil asked, leaning over the front seat again.

"Yes." She kept her voice noncommittal, but she could still feel Sam's intent gaze washing over her.

"What was wrong?" Sam demanded.

"We were getting close. It can . . . affect me."

"Hell and damnation!" Sam stomped on the brakes, and the car began to fishtail on the icy road, swinging back and forth until it finally landed in a snowbank on the side of the road.

"You can't jump on the brakes on roads like these," Phil said mildly enough. "Want me to drive?"

Sam told Phil what he wanted him to do in short, succinct terms that paid no attention to Elizabeth's genteel ears as he shoved the car in Reverse, spun the wheels for a few moments and then gradually edged back on the road.

"I take it you were in the Army together," Elizabeth murmured. "You couldn't have learned language like that in civilian life."

"You wanna bet? You should see some of the scum I have to deal with on a day-to-day basis," Phil said. "They'd make Oliver up there sound like a gentleman."

"That's impossible," Elizabeth said sweetly, and was rewarded with Sam's glare.

"Why the hell didn't you say something sooner? You told me that nothing looked familiar," he snarled.

"Nothing did. But we had to be close. It was too cold."

"Oh, hell," Sam said. "Are we going to be spending the next few days in a Stephen King novel?"

"You can spend the next few days back in Washington with my blessing," she said. "I'm sure Phil is more than capable of handling things around here."

"The problem is, I think you're more than capable of handling Phil," Sam said. "I don't trust you, and I don't trust Phil's blind faith in you."

"Go to hell, Sam," Phil growled.

"I've been there. You know that as well as I do," Sam said bleakly.

"I was there with you," Phil said.

"So you were."

Elizabeth leaned back against the seat, shutting her eyes. For a moment the men, locked in their own dark memories of something they'd rather forget, had forgotten she was there. She could feel it, feel the searing pain that swept between them like a satin ribbon of blood, and she pulled her coat tighter around her once more. A name came into her mind, one that was little more than a shriek of agony, and then it vanished, swirled away on billows of smoke.

She opened her eyes when the car stopped, realizing with surprise that they were back at her house. It was a dark shape, alone in the tall woods, and the whiteness of the fresh snow glistened in the moonlight.

"Didn't you think to leave a light on?" Sam demanded, slamming out of the door and heading toward the house, his tall, strong body radiating irritation. Elizabeth watched him go, not moving for a moment, and then she turned to Phil.

"Who was Amy Lee?"

"God, don't ask Sam about her!" Phil said with a shudder. "Where the hell did you come up with that name?"

Elizabeth shrugged, both of them knowing how unanswerable that question was. "Is she the reason he's such a bastard?"

"He isn't. He's a good man, Elizabeth. I'd trust him with my life. Even more, I'd trust him with yours. I don't really know what's gotten under his skin right now, but when the chips are down you can count on him. I promise you that."

"I just wish he'd go away."

She could feel Phil watching her, sense his concern. "Be patient," he said finally.

"I don't seem to have any choice in the matter," she said wryly, stepping out onto the snowy driveway. "Do I?"

Phil got out beside her, and together they watched her house flood with light as Sam went through and turned everything on. "No," he said quietly. "I don't think you do."

Muhammed Ali Reza knew it was getting colder. He'd trained himself long ago not to give in to physical discomforts. Not to give in to days of sleeplessness, hunger, cold or heat. Not to give in when he'd been without water and was on the brink of dehydration, not to give in to headaches, or electric cattle prods and other, more refined forms of torture. He would recognize and accept these things, but he never let them reach his inner core, where a fire of determination burned so brightly that nothing could quench it.

Standing in the dark, silent forest outside Elizabeth Hardy's house, he could see his breath form ice crystals in front of him. His fingers were getting numb, and he flexed them in the pockets of his down parka, making sure they could still function. He had no intention of making his move, not yet, but he was a man who knew to expect the unexpected, and that move might be thrust upon him by the man he'd been following, by the man who'd joined him, maybe even by the woman.

Any other man would have been long gone by now. He'd done his part; there was no need for any more random victims to cover his intent. It was the one weakness in a man thought not to have any. He was a little too thorough.

The Americans were very stupid, particularly the police. He should leave the country and count on the man in the house, the police detective he'd been keeping tabs on, to botch the job and accept Ali Reza's setup at face value. Mary Nelson was simply one more in a line of victims, one whose body would never be found. At least, not found as Mary Nelson.

But his instincts were telling him that it wasn't going to be that simple. And the man who'd arrived yesterday wasn't someone to be lightly dismissed. Ali Reza didn't know him, but he recognized the way he held himself, the lack of expression in his face, the wariness that radiated from the tall, military body. The man who'd joined Grayson was a man like himself, a wolf, and therefore a danger.

But the one who worried him most of all was the woman. He had one other weakness, and that was a streak of superstition that ran down his backbone. He couldn't see Elizabeth Hardy without making the sign of the devil, and at night he didn't dream of Mary Nelson's terrified blue eyes, or the eyes of any of the other women he'd killed. He dreamed of Elizabeth Hardy's eyes, following him, watching him, no matter where he went.

He was going to close those eyes. She'd be the final victim of the Colorado Slasher, and if that seemed just a bit too convenient for the Denver police, he'd be long gone. But maybe, just to be certain, he'd finish Police Detective Phillip Grayson. It had been a long time since he'd had a man.

The small house was ablaze with lights; the big American car was still in the snowpacked drive. Ali Reza rubbed his hands together, blowing on them to loosen the frozen muscles. Not tonight. Not yet. He still wasn't sure how much they knew, how close they were going to get. He had to make sure that it was just that woman's witching eyes, not a loose tongue somewhere back in Italy. A few days of watching, of anticipating. It would only make the deed sweeter.

Sam was standing in Elizabeth Hardy's almost empty kitchen, pouring himself a stiff glass of whiskey. The snow had started again, swirling down lightly outside her window, and he stared into the woods surrounding the place, his eyes narrowing slightly as he tried to pierce the gloom. He could hear Elizabeth's soft, quiet voice as she spoke to Phil, a far different tone from the terrier snappishness she reserved for him. Hell, he did his best to encourage it. He didn't want any of that soft, melting charm oozing over him. He didn't trust it. He didn't want it. Or maybe he wanted it too much, and that was what he didn't trust.

Either way, it didn't make any difference. He hadn't been tricked by a woman since he'd been eighteen and fallen in love with a hooker in Da Nang. And he hadn't gotten close to a woman, emotionally close, since Amy Lee. He wasn't about to start with someone like Elizabeth Hardy.

He wondered how long it would take her to get up enough nerve to join him in the kitchen. She'd try to send Phil, but Phil would make an excuse. He knew Phil well enough, and he already knew Elizabeth. She was scared of him. He found that odd. He wasn't used to scaring people he didn't mean to hurt. Maybe she knew they were on opposite sides. No, he didn't really believe that. But there was something about him that made her angry, uneasy, frightened. And he couldn't help wondering if it was the same thing that was bothering him.

"You're going to need more Scotch," he said without turning when he felt her presence.

"I don't usually drink it."

"I do."

"You think you're going to be spending more time here?" Her voice was cool, neutral, but Sam wasn't fooled. He turned to look at her, leaning back against the counter.

"What do you think?"

"I think you can buy your own whiskey. I can't get rid of you, but I don't have to welcome you."

He moved then, crossing the kitchen with the fluid, stalking movement he'd long ago perfected in jungles that he'd never see again. She stood her ground, staring up at him unflinchingly, and once more he had to admire her courage, even as he cursed her stubbornness. "No," he said softly. "I wouldn't say you've welcomed me. Just be patient, Elizabeth. In a few days I'll be gone. In the meantime, loosen up. Have a drink."

He took her hand in his and wrapped it around his warm glass of whiskey. He could feel the electricity prickling through her skin, but she didn't fight his touch. His long fingers covered hers, covered the glass, and she looked up at him, startled, something flaring in her brown eyes, something dark and stormy, something he couldn't fathom.

"I wish I knew what was going on in that convoluted mind of yours," he murmured.

"No, you don't." Her voice was only a thread of sound, barely audible above the beating of her heart, the pounding of her pulse. "You wouldn't want to know anything that's in my brain."

"Maybe not," he said. "Maybe I like surprises." He was crazy, he knew it, but he couldn't help himself. He wanted to kiss her again, to see if that anger went any deeper. He leaned forward, brushing his mouth over hers. She didn't flinch, didn't jerk away. She just stood there, staring at him, and her lips parted in unconscious invitation.

He was about to kiss her again when Phil strode into the kitchen, oblivious to the tension between the two of them. "What's going on here?" he demanded. "A tug of war? I'll get you a drink if you want one, Elizabeth."

The glass of whiskey smashed to the floor at their feet as both of them jumped back, suddenly guilty. "Damn," Sam said, looking around for something to wipe up the mess.

"Don't worry about it," Elizabeth said from her safe position on the far side of the kitchen, well out of his reach. "I'll clean it up after you've gone."

"I'm not going," Sam said, surprising even himself.

Elizabeth turned a stricken face toward Phil, but for once he was oblivious to her desperate need. He was nodding. "That's probably a good idea. I don't like the idea of her being out here all alone, not with a maniac on the loose."

"If it is a maniac," Sam muttered.

"Besides, I trust your judgment. You always had a sixth sense about these things. I'd go with your instincts faster than I would with hard facts anytime. Hell, I wouldn't be surprised if *you* were a psychic." He laughed at his own joke.

Sam could feel the curiosity in Elizabeth's eyes, and he cursed Phil's voluble tongue. "Sure, Phil," he drawled. "I do tarot readings on the side, too."

"There's really no need for you to stay," Elizabeth said hurriedly. "I'm going straight to bed. I'll lock all the doors and windows."

"Locked doors didn't keep Mary Nelson safe," Phil reminded her. "They didn't keep Sam out last night."

"I'm not in any danger. Believe me, I'd know."

"Would you?" Sam countered.

She leaned back against the wall and shut her eyes, and he could see pale mauve shadows surrounding them. She looked white and thin and frail, and he had the sudden, completely irrational urge to take her in his arms. That wasn't what he wanted in life. A woman to take care of. He didn't want any sort of woman at all, at least not on any permanent basis. And Elizabeth Hardy was a permanent sort of person.

"I don't know," she said after a moment, her voice weak. "At this point I'm so tired I don't know anything."

"Then go to bed," Phil said, putting one burly arm around her and pushing her toward the living room, herding her past Sam's tense body. "I'll go out for pizza, we'll finish your Scotch and Sam can bed down on the sofa again. I'll be back tomorrow before you even wake up."

"I don't . . ." she began to protest, but Sam cut her off, coolly, efficiently.

"You needn't worry I'm going to jump your bones, Elizabeth," he said. "I can control my raging animal lusts if you can control yours."

She ignored him, as he deserved to be ignored, he thought, and headed toward her bedroom.

"What the hell's your problem, man?" Phil demanded. "Can't you get off her case for a few hours? She's just trying to help, and you're treating her like a criminal. This isn't like you, Sam. You never used to be so vindictive. So downright cruel."

"You're really that certain she's bona fide? That she's not a mole planted here two years ago, waiting for her mission to go into effect?"

"I learned long ago never to be certain of anything," Phil said flatly. "But I trust her. As much as I can trust anyone."

"That's not good enough for me, and you know it. Trust the wrong person and you'll end up with a knife in your throat."

"Like Amy Lee."

"Like Amy Lee," he agreed, his voice brutal.

"Just lay off Elizabeth, will you? You don't have to believe her, but for God's sake stop baiting her. It's giving me an ulcer."

Sam laughed. "In deference to your stomach, then," he agreed. "Maybe you'd better give up pizza and Scotch."

"I'd rather give up listening to you two bicker. Behave yourself, Oliver. Or I might have to teach you some manners."

"You and who else? No anchovies on the pizza."

"Yes, sir, Colonel Oliver. Anything else?"

"Don't buy any more Scotch. I think I'd better not let my brain get fuzzy."

Phil's round face grew deadly serious. "You really think there's a problem here? Danger? Why?"

Sam hesitated for a moment, then gave the easiest answer. "Instinct Phil. I can feel it in my bones, and my bones don't let me down."

"And you call Elizabeth ridiculous," Phil tried to scoff, but the humor had gone from his eyes. "Do you want me to call in some help?"

"You think I can't handle anything that comes up?"

"Pardon me. I forgot you were superagent," Phil drawled. "I'll be back in an hour. Keep away from Elizabeth, willya? She needs a break."

"Sure thing. No anchovies."

"On your half," Phil agreed.

Elizabeth snuggled down under the electric blanket, closing her eyes in exhaustion. She could hear him moving around in her living room, hear the quiet sound of the telephone as he dialed countless numbers, the unintelligible murmur of his voice. Probably checking up on her again, she thought muzzily. He wouldn't find out anything interesting. To all observers she'd lived an ordinary enough life, with family, friends, even a fiancé.

She shivered, huddling down further in the bed. Her family was dead now, starting with her parents when she was only seven, her rigid aunt and uncle a few years later, and dear old Granny Mellon, the oldest, and the last to go. Her friends had scattered, and no one even knew where she'd gone after Alan died. She'd disappeared, unable to accept their sympathy, their offers of help, their curiosity. Unable to accept the fact that Alan had died, and she could have stopped it from happening.

It wouldn't happen again. She wouldn't care for someone so much that it clouded her visions, made her distrust the twisted talent that had been thrust upon her, unasked. As soon as this current mess was cleared up, as soon as Sam Oliver left and went back to Washington, she'd pull her defenses back around her and not let anyone near again. In the meantime she'd survive the newly awakened awareness by ignoring it. And she would hope they found Mary Nelson, or the answer to her disappearance, soon.

Before Sam Oliver kissed her again. Before she made the mistake of kissing him back.

Chapter 5

Elizabeth Hardy's house was too damn small, Sam decided at three forty-five in the morning. Her couch was too short for anyone of reasonable height, which included his own six feet three inches; her walls were too thin, making him uncomfortably aware of her soft, even breathing, of the nightmares that came and went, leaving her still sound asleep. And she only had one bathroom.

He'd rather share a bed with a woman than a bathroom, he decided, for want of something better to think about at that hour of the morning. Beds were to be expected. But sharing the same sink, the same bathtub, hell, even the same soap, made him feel uneasy. Intimate. And he wasn't about to get intimate with anyone. Particularly a lost soul like Elizabeth Hardy.

He was crazy to be here. Phil had a very comfortable guest room, now that his family had left him, complete with queen-size bed, flannel sheets and all the Johnny Walker he could allow himself. He would even have his own bathroom, although it had been decorated in shades of pink by

Phil's teenage daughters. There was absolutely no reason to think Elizabeth would be in any danger. If she disappeared, if her body turned up, slashed and brutalized the way every body but Mary Nelson's had, it would be a coincidence that would send alarm bells ringing in every self-respecting cop's head in the Rockies. It would be a stupid blunder, and the people he suspected he was up against were neither stupid nor prone to making mistakes.

Therefore Elizabeth was safe. Therefore, there was no need for him to be thrashing about on a short sofa, thinking about someone he couldn't have and didn't want. He shouldn't be worried that she had gone to bed without eating when she was far too skinny already. Tomorrow morning he'd force-feed her if he had to. If he was going to believe in her gifts, and he supposed that right now he was, then she'd need to take better care of herself. She wouldn't be able to find a murder scene if she fainted from hunger.

Phil was right. The bickering was getting them nowhere. The problem was, if he didn't fight with her he might soften. And that was something he didn't dare do. He was a tough man, a hard man, without a sentimental bone in his body. He wasn't about to get suckered by a pair of lost brown eyes and a vulnerable, enticing mouth.

An early start the next morning, and the hell with whether he'd slept or not. He'd feed Ms. Hardy, get her out on the road, and they wouldn't stop until they found that mysterious cabin with the bloody shoe. He'd almost memorized the sound of her soft, eerie voice on the tape as she went through her hocus-pocus. If anything could convince him, it was that tape.

Sleep, he ordered himself. You won't get anything accomplished if you don't get at least a couple of hours' sleep. And, like a good career soldier, he promptly obeyed his own order, shutting out the thought of Elizabeth Hardy sound asleep in the other room.

By three-thirty the next day Elizabeth Hardy was ready to cry. She knew she wouldn't actually do it—she hadn't cried in more than two years. Not since she'd stood on the banks of the rain-swollen Potomac and watched them bring Alan's body to the shore. She'd seen him drown. Seen him struggle in the chilly, bone-numbing depths, calling out for help. She'd seen it days before it had happened, and she'd shut it away, refusing to face it, just as she'd been refusing to face any of her nightmare visions for the past two years. She'd learned that day that hiding from something didn't keep you safe. And she would go to her grave knowing that if she'd been brave enough to face it, to tell the man she loved, the man she was going to marry, that she'd seen his death, then maybe he wouldn't have kept jogging along the river path, maybe he wouldn't even have noticed the dog being swept downstream in the heavy current. Maybe he would have had enough sense to go for help, instead of trying to do it himself.

But Alan had been like that. Never thinking of himself, always thinking of others. From a drowning puppy to a lost waif of a female like herself, he'd taken them all under his wing, protecting, encouraging, loving. And he'd died for it.

She shook her head, trying to shake loose the memory, trying to shake free some of her damnable talents, but they seemed firmly entrenched and unwilling to cooperate. She usually kept thoughts of Alan to the quiet hours of the early morning, when the nightmares woke her up. How many times had she relived those awful moments, the moments she'd seen only in her dreams? And how many times had she watched her parents burn to death in their old farmhouse, screaming for help, with no one to save them, and no one to believe their five-year-old daughter on a visit to her grandmother's house in Raleigh?

Phil and Sam Oliver were over by the edge of the road, talking in quiet voices. She looked at them through the hovering darkness, wishing, just wishing, this was over. But after a day of driving, wandering around the foothills of the majestic Rockies, they hadn't gotten any closer than they had the evening before, and Mary Nelson's murder site seemed impossibly out of reach. Sam Oliver seemed planted in Colorado forever.

A wind had come up, riffling through Elizabeth's tightly coiled hair, whispering down the collar of her coat. She stood apart from the men, hands in her pockets, listening, waiting, for something, anything. Where are you, Mary Nelson? her mind called. There was no answer but the cold north wind.

She didn't notice Phil climbing into the driver's seat of the big Chrysler. She didn't notice Sam's approach, until he blocked her vision, shutting out the dark threat of the mountains behind him. "We may as well go back now," he said, his voice flat. "Another day wasted."

She didn't move. "Maybe your entire time here is wasted. Maybe I'm just a neurotic spinster with hysterical dreams. Maybe the Colorado Slasher is just an ordinary serial killer, with no connection to terrorists and state secrets. Maybe you should fly back to Washington."

"I live in Virginia. Didn't your hookie-pookie elves tell you that much?" His voice was a mocking drawl, but for once the hard edge was missing. He reached up, and before she could move away he pulled her collar close about her face, buttoning the top button. He wasn't wearing gloves, and his fingers were cool against her chilly skin. It made no sense that she felt burned.

It made no sense that she didn't pull away from his touch, or that he didn't release her. They stood there for a moment, both bemused, and the visions she'd been calling came now, unbidden. But they had nothing to do with Mary Nelson.

They were on a bed. She, Elizabeth Hardy, probably the only twenty-nine-year-old virgin in the United States, was lying on a bed with Sam Oliver. She was wearing a red dress; he was wearing a pair of jeans and nothing more, and his hands were strong and tanned against the bright crimson that spilled around them. The emotions came, hot and immediate, burning in the pit of her stomach, burning between her legs, and she jerked her eyes up to stare, astonished, into his hot, intense gaze. And then she pulled away, just as he released her, and stumbled toward the car, scrambling into the back seat and pulling the door shut behind her.

"You okay?" Phil questioned from the driver's seat.

"Of course." Her voice was low and hurried as she contemplated the impossible. It was almost as if he'd read her mind, shared her vision, the blinding, unfamiliar surge of passion that had swamped her. But he couldn't have.

The door beside her opened, and Sam climbed in. Mistake number five hundred and twenty-seven, she thought. She should have gotten in the passenger seat beside Phil and locked the door. She hadn't, because she didn't like the idea of Sam's eyes boring into the vulnerable nape of her neck. But the weight of his big, strong body beside her, the sound of his breathing, the warmth of his flesh, was much, much worse.

"So I get to be the chauffeur?" Phil demanded lightly. "I want some company."

"Drive," Sam said, his eyes not moving from Elizabeth's face. "We have work to do."

She could see Phil's worried expression in the rearview mirror, but there was nothing she could do. Nothing *he* could do. Sam Oliver wasn't going to hurt her, and the more fuss anyone made, the worse it would be.

"Okay," Phil said, starting the car and pulling onto the road. "But no necking."

She'd already tucked her hands back in her pockets, huddling into the corner of the car. Sam reached out and hauled her hand free, wrapping it in his own large grasp. "Just a little hand-holding, Phil. Our lady's psychic meter jumps every time someone touches her. I'm going to see if I can amplify her powers."

"Let go of me," she said, yanking fruitlessly against his imprisoning grip.

"You could always try sitting on my lap," he countered. "That might work even better."

"Why don't we just take off our clothes and…and do it? Maybe then I'll be able to tell you where Mary Nelson is," she said bitterly.

"Sorry, not interested."

She could feel the color flame into her face, and she cursed her fair complexion, cursed the totally irrational fact that she would even care. His hand tightened around hers, his long fingers curiously caressing, even as his expression was cold and distant.

"What makes you think I am?" she countered rashly, then bit her lip as his wintry eyes took on that damnable light of amusement.

It even reached his mouth in the faintest of smiles. "Certainly nothing you've said or done," he said, his hand still holding hers.

She tugged, uselessly, then leaned back against the seat, defeated. Phil had the radio on by then, and he was whistling tunelessly along with it. "Listen," she said, her voice pitched low so it wouldn't carry to the front seat. "We're agreed that you hate me and I hate you. Why don't you just give up and go away? It doesn't matter whether you trust me—you trust Phil. He'll let you know if I come up with anything."

"Who says I hate you?"

"What has that got to do with anything?" She was getting desperate by this point, her defenses shattering around her.

"Maybe nothing. Maybe a lot." He turned her hand over, running his thumb against the softness of her palm, and with a blinding clarity she could see his hand run up her red-covered thigh.

This time when she pulled he released her, and she scuttled back into the corner of the big car like a wounded animal. He watched her without moving, making no effort to recapture her hand. "I don't hate you," he said finally. "Any more than you hate me."

"Yes, I . . ."

"No," he said flatly. "You don't. And we'll work on that after we find Mary Nelson." With that he leaned back and closed his eyes, shutting her out.

He was still too close. There was something warm and cocoonlike about the back seat, enclosing them in an intimacy that she refused to accept. Shut him out, she ordered herself. Shut your eyes, think of warmth, think of summer, and forget about everything else.

She wasn't sure when his hand reached over to recapture hers. She kept her eyes closed, ignoring him, ignoring the pulsing heat that spread like fire from his hand up her arm, through her body. She relaxed her tight muscles, letting the sensations flow over her, and waited with resignation for the erotic images to continue.

They didn't. She was back in that barren, mountainside clearing, the wind whistling around her, and she was cold, terribly, terribly cold. The truck was gone, with its bloody burden intact; the small cabin was deserted, its broken-hinged door swinging in the breeze. The snow had been blasted away by the briskness of the wind, and the hard, frozen ground was empty. No red shoe, no blood. No sign that Mary Nelson had met a horrible death on that spot.

Elizabeth was shivering, shaking with the cold, but the car with its powerful heater had ceased to exist. The man whose hand clutched hers had ceased to exist. "Take the next left," she said out loud, not opening her eyes.

Phil knew better than to argue. The dull irritation of the car radio was switched off, and the only sounds were the blast of the heater fan, the murmur of the engine as the car climbed into the mountains, the even breathing of the three occupants. And Elizabeth's instructions.

She didn't move when the car pulled to a stop. "We can't go any farther, Elizabeth," Phil said. "What do you want me to do?"

Slowly she opened her eyes. It was getting dark now, twilight closing in around the car, but it wasn't a friendly twilight. It wasn't a friendly spot. The narrow, snowpacked dirt road Phil had been following had ended, the narrow track blocked with recently felled trees.

She was drenched with a cold sweat, something the heater couldn't even begin to penetrate. "Now we walk," she said wearily. She looked down, noting with amazement that her hand was tightly clutching Sam's. It took her a moment to release him. The muscles in her fingers had cramped from clinging too hard.

"Are you sure?" Phil said, peering at her from the front seat. "It's getting dark, and you look frozen. We can come back tomorrow."

"Tomorrow she may not be able to find it again," Sam said, overriding Phil's concern.

"Sam, she's miserable."

"Can you retrace your route? Find your way back here in the morning?"

Phil frowned. "I'm a professional—of course I can."

"You've also gotten soft. I've waited long enough. We walk." Sam's voice allowed for no further argument, but Elizabeth was already ahead of him, opening the door and climbing out into the chilly afternoon air. She could see her breath form an icy vapor, and the sight somehow comforted her. She started off, neither noticing nor caring if the two men followed her, moving with surefooted determination over the rocky ground.

She was closer than she'd realized. A hundred yards beyond the scrubby brush stood a clearing. The tire tracks were frozen in the mud, the cabin was deserted. The sun was going down in a flaming blaze of orange and crimson, and the world was coated with ice. She stood in the center of the clearing, unmoving, as the men reached her.

"Is this it?" Phil demanded, puffing slightly from the cold and the unexpected exertion.

Elizabeth nodded, not looking at either of them, her vision turned inward, closed up, unwilling to face the horror and pain that were thick in the air around her.

She was vaguely aware of Sam advancing toward the gaping door of the cabin. In his hand, the hand that had held hers so warmly, was a serviceable-looking gun. He was beginning to believe her, she thought. Or else he thought she'd led them into a trap.

For fifteen minutes the two men scoured the site as the sun sank lower behind the towering mountains. When they finally returned she had gone beyond cold to frozen, the blood congealed in her veins, the tears frozen in her eyes and on her pale cheeks. They were empty-handed, and she looked first at Phil, at the disappointment and concern on his broad face. She didn't need to turn to Sam to recognize the frustration and contempt that would be riding him hard.

"Got any proof, lady?" he drawled. "There are probably a hundred clearings like this in the foothills around Denver. Where's your mysterious panel truck? Where's the body? Habeas corpus and all that? Where's a single stinking clue?"

"Under the porch." Her voice was frosty in the night air.

"I looked under the porch," Sam snapped.

"Look again."

This time she watched as he stalked over to the sagging porch, kneeling on the frozen ground with a blatant disregard for his clothes and the bone-chilling temperature. "Bring me your flashlight," he said, his voice changing, and he finally put his gun away.

Phil moved swiftly, handing him the pencil light he carried with him. "And a handkerchief," Sam added. "There might be fingerprints."

Elizabeth shut her eyes again. She couldn't shut out the sounds. The wind in the trees. The distant call of a hawk, wheeling and turning through the Colorado sky. And the rustle of men pulling evidence from beneath the porch.

"Let's go." Sam's voice was gruff in her ear, his hand under her arm strong and rough.

She looked up at him, a question in her eyes. "What did you find?"

"You know damn well what we found. Mary Nelson's red high-heeled shoe, splattered with dried blood. One cigarette butt, from a British brand. Got any other messages from beyond, swami?"

"Yes," she said, her voice shaking with cold. "Why don't you go—"

His hand covered her mouth, stopping her. "Ladies don't say things like that," he chided.

"Who says I'm a lady? And how do you know what I was going to say?"

He shook his head. "I don't need to be a psychic to guess what your suggestion was going to be. And whether you like it or not, you're a lady. Unless, of course, you're a lying murderer trying to fool us all."

"Are you fooled?"

"I believe you. God knows why. Common sense and experience tell me you've got to be behind this. There's no other sensible reason for you to know what you know."

"So why don't you arrest me?"

"I'm in Army Intelligence. I can't arrest civilians."

"Than have Phil arrest me."

"Phil believes you."

"Then what choice do you have?"

"I could kill you."

For a moment she couldn't believe she'd heard him. "What?"

"I said I could kill you. I've done it before. If I thought it was a matter of national security, the safety of millions, and there was no other way I could ensure that safety, I could kill you."

"You've done it before?" She stared at him in horror, half expecting to see blood on his hands. How could she not have known? How could she have missed it? Were her hor-

mones in such an uncustomary uproar that she didn't realize she was attracted to a man without a conscience?

"When necessary." His face was still distant, removed,
but his dark blue eyes were watchful. "What do you think
of that?"

She tried to summon forth outrage, disgust, contempt.
Tried and failed. Despite what he'd told her, despite what
her own common sense told her, she already knew him on a
deeper level than he might even know himself.

"I think you must have had a good reason," she whispered, her voice carrying to his ears and no farther. "And I
think you must have suffered for it anyway."

For a long moment he didn't move. His expression didn't
change; his bleak, watchful eyes didn't lighten. "Let's get
back to the car," he said finally. "In another few moments
you'll be frozen."

"I already am." She stared down the pathway, knowing
he'd be behind her, knowing that if she stumbled he'd catch
her. Knowing that if he caught her he'd hold her, and if he
held her he'd kiss her. And if he kissed her, she'd kiss him
back. She walked very, very carefully.

She didn't get into the front seat of the Chrysler. Phil had
the red shoe on the front seat, and she couldn't bring herself to look at it, to touch it. She climbed in the back, waiting for Sam to join her. Wondering if he was going to take
her hand again.

With surprise and resignation she watched him climb into
the front seat beside Phil, ignoring her presence behind him.
"We have to remember how to get back here," he said.
"You keep track of landmarks on the right, I'll watch on the
left. When you get back to town, drop me at a motel."

Phil looked up in surprise. "You don't think Elizabeth's
in any more danger?"

She waited for his answer, holding her breath. "I don't
know. If you think it's warranted, assign someone to her.
I've got to get back to Washington."

"You aren't taking that shoe with you. That's part of an ongoing local investigation. You can't just run off with evidence," Phil protested.

"Watch me," Sam said, his voice dry. He held up the shoe for a moment, and Elizabeth had no choice but to look at it, the elegant vamp, the narrow instep, the high heel. And the dried blood. "Who'd have thought a Colorado housewife would wear shoes like these?"

She shouldn't have told him. He didn't deserve any more help, but for some reason she couldn't stop herself, and the words just tumbled out. "That's not Mary Nelson's shoe," she said. "That belongs to Shari Derringer."

It was a simple enough matter to follow them, even in the darkness. They had no suspicion that anyone would be watching them, and they went about their search with an innocent openness that made him laugh with contempt. Until they found the cabin. And the shoe.

Muhammed Ali Reza felt the anger and shame sweep over him. He never made mistakes. He'd enjoyed that little bit of cleverness, making the frightened woman put on those shoes before he killed her. He'd never noticed that one had fallen off when he'd dumped her body in the refrigerated truck. Now she was lying wrapped in a tarp, thousands of miles away, one foot bare, one foot encased in a too-small, bloodstained shoe.

He had to get the other shoe. He had to silence those three people. A sharp turn on an icy road, a steep drop-off, and it would be nothing more than a tragic coincidence. They were halfway down to the city now, halfway down to civilization and witnesses. Clenching the steering wheel of his Toyota, he pressed the accelerator to the floor.

Chapter 6

Someone's following us." Sam kept his voice casual as he glanced in the rearview mirror. The lights had been behind them for five minutes now. On the narrow, winding mountain road a driver would have no choice but to tail the car ahead of him, but Sam knew this wasn't a simple matter of an innocent Denver resident heading in the same direction. The car behind them spelled trouble, big trouble, and he hoped to hell that Phil Grayson had kept some of his inestimable talents sharpened. Ten years ago he'd been the most formidable driver in Sam's small, elite unit. If Phil was at the wheel no one could even come close.

But ten years of local police work, of chasing armed robbers and jaywalkers and hobnobbing with psychics, could have worn away his gifts. They had no choice but to find out. Phil knew these roads better than he did, and they couldn't afford to waste time in changing drivers.

"What makes you think they're after us?" Grayson's voice was just as easygoing, but Sam breathed a small, partial sigh of relief.

"I know," he said simply.

"You always did."

Sam glanced over his shoulder. Elizabeth Hardy was sitting in the corner of the Chrysler, huddled against the cold, her face pale and pinched. "If you don't have your seat belt on," he told her gruffly, "you'd better fasten it. We're going to be in for a rough ride."

"Hey, I resent that," Phil said, the crazy edge of excitement, an excitement they'd all known and craved too much, dancing around in his voice. "I could have outrun that Toyota without Elizabeth even noticing."

"I don't think so," Sam said dryly as the Toyota loomed up behind them, bright headlights spearing the interior of the Chrysler. "I think whoever's behind us is out for blood."

The impact was slight, just a kiss of the bumpers, but the message was clear. "Damn," Phil said genially. "The bastard means business." The American car shot ahead smoothly, out of reach of the menacing Toyota, at least for the moment, as the road turned sharply to the right, heading down toward the lights of the city.

Sam looked at Elizabeth again, wondering how she'd react in the face of possible death. If anything, she looked even calmer, her hands lying loosely in her lap. "Have any idea who's chasing us, swami?" he muttered.

"You still don't trust me? If that was an accomplice of mine he wouldn't be trying to kill me, would he?"

"Not necessarily true. If we *are* dealing with the Spandau Corporation, they'd slit their own mothers' throats without a second thought. All for the bloody glorious cause, whatever the hell that happens to be." Phil swerved deliberately, and Sam banged against the side of the car, hitting his head. He swore, glaring at his friend, before turning back to Elizabeth.

She had the faintest hint of a smile on her face, and he just knew it was caused by his own discomfort. "Besides," he growled, "I wasn't asking if you personally knew the person who's so intent on running us off the road. I was asking if you could look into your crystal ball and tell me who's trying to kill us. You included.''

"I haven't the faintest idea."

"Don't you care that you might be about to die?"

That startled a reaction out of her. She took off her wire-rimmed glasses, cleaning them on her coat, stalling for time. "I don't think so," she said finally, looking up at him without the protection of her glasses, her brown eyes vulnerable and defenseless and full of such a deep sorrow that it pained him to look.

He turned away from her, facing the narrow roadway, glancing at the headlights in the rearview mirror. He could think of a dozen things to say to her, starting with, "Well, you should," but somehow everything seemed prosaic. If the fool woman didn't care whether she lived or died that wasn't his problem. Assuming they survived Phil's plummeting descent down the mountain, he'd take Mary Nelson's, or Shari Derringer's, shoe back to Washington and never again have to deal with the crackpot in the back seat. If they wanted more information from Elizabeth they could send someone directly involved in the investigation. He didn't want to have anything more to do with her.

He glanced in the rearview mirror, looking for the Toyota, but found himself watching Elizabeth, her calm, fatalistic expression, the darkness in her eyes. He swore then, a short, sibilant word muttered under his breath.

"What's the problem?" Phil demanded as the huge Chrysler slid around a steep corner at close to seventy miles an hour. The Toyota was falling behind, unable to keep up the pace. "I've got him licked. Were you maybe looking for a little more excitement?"

"I'm looking for a good night's sleep and a flight back to Washington," Sam snapped. "Do you know of a spot where we can pull off and see who's so eager to catch us?"

"I don't know if we can get far enough ahead. He hasn't given up on us yet, but I know damn well that car doesn't have the power to keep up, particularly if he's put it in four-wheel drive.''

"What if he puts it in two-wheel drive?''

"He'd slide off the mountain. I can drive these roads at these speeds, but not very many other people can. And I don't think our Toyota-driving friend is used to snow.''

"What do you think he's used to?''

"Deserts. Sand. Maybe airports,'' Phil said.

"He might be used to Northern Ireland. Doesn't it snow there?''

"Not like it does in Colorado.'' Suddenly the headlights loomed up behind them, and this time the impact wasn't a kiss, it was an outright assault. The Chrysler went spinning dizzily out of control, sliding sideways across the narrow road, heading for the side of the mountain.

The state of Colorado clearly didn't believe in guardrails on steep mountain roads. The only things that stood between oblivion and safety were Phil Grayson's rusty driving skills. Sam glanced at him, at the grin plastered across his friend's face as he wrestled with the big car. He looked in the rearview mirror, at the headlights receding, turning off, convinced the job was done. You don't know Phil Grayson, Sam thought. He looked at Elizabeth, though he didn't want to, and noticed that one of her slender hands was clutching the door handle very tightly. He found himself grinning. Whether she knew it or not, she cared whether she lived or died.

And, damn it, so did he. He hadn't thought it mattered, not since Amy Lee had died, not since life had taken such a nasty, hopeless turn. But somehow, sometime, he'd changed his mind, just as Elizabeth Hardy had changed hers. He wanted to live.

"Can't you control this damn car?'' he demanded of Phil as they skidded, sliding toward the edge of the cliff. "Stop fooling around.''

"But I'm enjoying myself,'' Phil protested, wrestling with the wheel. Beads of sweat were standing out on his forehead; strain etched rigid lines on his face, and his eyes were lit with amusement.

"For God's sake, how can you joke about it?" Elizabeth finally demanded from the back seat.

"Easy," Phil said, stomping on the accelerator and yanking the steering wheel in the direction of the cliff.

Elizabeth shrieked and covered her eyes, clearly unable to face her upcoming demise. Sam watched, with both admiration and complete assurance, as the oversize tires of the Chrysler caught just on the edge of the cliff, and Phil pulled smoothly onto the road, with all the aplomb of a father out for a Sunday drive. They drove for almost a mile, at an absurdly sedate pace, before Elizabeth recovered enough to look up.

"You knew he'd make it," she said, her accusation directed at Sam.

"He's the best driver I know. If he couldn't do it no one could. I think, swami, that you'll know when your number is up. And you'll probably let your fellow passengers know, too. As long as you didn't seem ready to meet your demise and Phil was at the wheel, I figured I was in good hands."

By the time they reached the highway the Toyota was long gone. "I hope that bastard didn't dent the car," Phil grumbled cheerfully as they pulled into the sparse traffic. "I've only had it three months." He glanced over at Sam. "You didn't happen to get the bugger's license plate number, did you?"

"You're the cop. Why didn't you?"

"In case you hadn't noticed, I was busy driving."

"No license plate," Sam said. "At least, not on the front of the car."

"Definitely a no-no," Phil said. "When I meet that gentleman again I'm going to be forced to give him a ticket."

"Sounds well deserved. You think you're going to meet him again?"

"I expect so. The Corporation tends to be thorough. Mistakes aren't common. I expect our friend will do everything he can to right his error."

"I expect so."

"What are we going to do about Elizabeth?"

Sam felt himself stiffen, but he refused to turn around and look at her, refused to meet her gaze in the rearview mirror. "What do you mean?"

"Do you still think it's safe to leave her alone? That she's not in any danger?"

"I think she's safe," he said stubbornly. "If it makes you feel any better you can get a policewoman to stay with her."

"Tomorrow. You won't be flying out tonight anyway. Not in this weather." Snow had started to fall, the sky going from empty to blizzardlike conditions in a matter of moments. "You can stay there tonight."

"There's no need...." Elizabeth said.

"I told you, I have things to do..." Sam said at the same time.

Phil was having none of it. "What are you afraid of, Colonel? Think you can't handle it?"

Sam's reply was short and succinct, knowing he was beaten. He, a man who didn't know the meaning of the word coward, was scared spitless at the thought of spending one more night in close proximity with Elizabeth Hardy. She was skinny, neurotic, plain and unfriendly, and he couldn't look at her without wanting to get her into bed. It made no sense, and the sooner he got away from her the sooner he'd be sane once more. He didn't want to spend one more night snowed in with her, but the more he protested, the deeper the pit he dug himself into.

"I can handle a dozen psychics with my eyes closed," he drawled. "I'm just tired of baby-sitting. But I can do it for one more night. As long as she doesn't decide to hold a séance in the living room."

"Go to hell," Elizabeth said.

"First thing tomorrow morning, swami," he replied, flashing her his sweetest, most irritating smile.

"It won't be soon enough," she said between her teeth.

She was lying, and he knew it. "Same goes for me," he said, echoing her lie.

And Phil Grayson just shook his head in mocking disbelief.

They didn't speak to each other when Phil dropped them off at Elizabeth's house. The temperature inside was frigid, and Sam swore under his breath as he jacked the thermostat up and then set to work on making a fire in the fireplace.

"Electricity costs money," Elizabeth said pointedly, ignoring the bloodstained shoe Sam had brought with him. "I keep the thermostat at fifty-five on purpose."

"I don't see you hurting for money," he muttered, not bothering to look at her. "Where does it come from, anyway? The Denver police don't pay you anything for your services, and as far as I can tell you don't do anything besides go into trances. So how do you support yourself?"

"What makes you think the police don't pay me? Don't you think I offer them anything worthwhile?" She was rubbing her hands along her upper arms. It was cold, too cold, in the house, but she'd be damned before she'd admit it to the obnoxious, too-handsome man making a botch of a simple wood fire.

"I did the obvious thing," Sam said, blowing on the tiny flame. Blowing it out. "I asked. But it only made sense—any taxpayer worth his salt would scream holy murder if there was a budget listing for psychics." He turned his head, and his dark blue eyes speared into hers. "And no, I don't think you offer them anything but paranoid fantasies and half-baked new-age garbage."

"What about the shoe?"

"A coincidence. Or maybe a plant. Maybe you're just a sick, lonely woman desperate for attention."

"I'd like to be a lot lonelier," she said pointedly. "And if you think that about me, then why are you here?" Her voice was low and taunting, furious.

He rose, towering over her, and the stubborn fire caught. "Damned if I know," he said. "Maybe, despite my better judgment, I'm open-minded enough to consider that I could be wrong."

Elizabeth couldn't help it, she laughed. "I wouldn't worry about it if I were you. No one's ever going to mistake you for someone with a sense of fair play." She turned away from him, but he caught her arm, jerking her around to face him again, and he was too close.

"You're lucky you underestimate me," he said after a long, tension-filled moment.

"Am I?" His hand felt like a vise on her arm, and yet she knew he wasn't holding her that tightly. It burned her, yet she knew his skin was as cold as hers in the chilly house. For a moment she considered the unexpected erotic appeal of him, of his strength, his implacability, his damn narrow-minded sureness in a world that was far from certain. And then something else came through, a vision, slicing through her semiconsciousness.

He blinked, his dark blue eyes suddenly dazed, and released her abruptly. "I'm going out," he said, spinning around and leaving her alone in the center of the room. "Lock the door."

She wrapped her arms around her narrow body, no longer worried about hiding the shivers that were racking her, at odds with the rising temperature of the room. She was only vaguely aware of the slamming of the door, the distant sound of an engine starting. Her mind was no longer on her unwelcome guest. It was on that brief, transient vision. A vision of blood and death.

Muhammed Ali Reza didn't often make mistakes. He'd made too many on this last project, and he knew the best way to wash away mistakes was with blood. It had been a simple matter to follow the man who'd outdriven him. He'd dropped the other man and the woman with the devil eyes at the cold house, and then driven away. Ali Reza followed him, always keeping a few cars between them. There were plenty of Toyotas around Denver, but any man who could drive like that couldn't be underestimated.

He'd take his time with him, he thought. He'd find out just how much they knew, how much they suspected. He was very good at finding out information from even the toughest sources, men and women who had thought they could endure the torments of hell before they told him what he wanted to know. It didn't take long before they learned that he was adept at offering just that, the torments of hell. And that he enjoyed his work.

This whole mess had dragged on too long. He'd finish it tonight and get back to warmer climates, to something new. This had been in the works for too long; he was getting impatient for the culmination.

A bad sign, he warned himself. Emotions clouded judgment. Patience. Patience was the watchword. He'd be patient when he killed Phil Grayson. Slow, deliberate and very patient.

Sam drove fast. Too fast. His palms were sweating, his heart racing, and his sense of horror and dread kept building. It was crazy. He'd been around Elizabeth Hardy too long, and he was having a walking nightmare because of it. This was all a paranoid fantasy, brought on by listening to that damn woman's craziness, and he was nuts to go racing out into a snowy night on a fool's errand.

He couldn't help it. That sudden sense of panic had been smothering. He couldn't even look at Elizabeth, touch her, breathe the same air she was breathing. He had to get out, to get to Phil, to make sure he was all right.

He'd been feeling restless, uneasy, all day, but he'd ignored the symptoms, telling himself he was sick of wasting his time in the mountains of Colorado when all the action was in Washington right now. Even finding that bloody shoe hadn't helped; it had only increased his sense of restlessness.

Hell, he had to be going nuts. He wasn't going to spend one more night in this damn state, blizzard or not. He'd have no trouble finding someone to fly him—there were enough crazies still in the service who had something to prove. Thank God he wasn't one of them.

It didn't matter that escaping from Colorado was getting too close to cowardice. It wasn't his life or safety that worried him. It was his mental health, and that was something a little more ephemeral. He wanted to forget about Elizabeth Hardy and everything she stood for. He wanted to be back in his apartment, away from snow and psychics.

He'd just make sure Phil was okay. Not that he really had any doubts. No one had any reason to kill Phil Grayson, and that sudden panic had been crazy. No, he'd drive to Phil's, share a final pizza and beer, and head off for the airport, leaving Elizabeth to Phil's tender mercies. Phil clearly thought the girl was another daughter, and that was fine with Sam. Phil missed his own girls too much—he could mother Elizabeth. She needed mothering.

But that wasn't his worry. He just needed to prove to himself that he'd been getting too little sleep and that his sudden, irrational fear was for once completely off the wall. By dawn he'd be back on the East Coast, away from loonies and psychics and gullible cops.

The roads were slick, icy, as the new falling snow hit the warmer pavement, melted and iced up again. He wasn't used to driving in snow, and his mind was too caught up with other things. He took the next corner fast, too fast, and the car began to slide. He tried to steer in the direction of the skid, but it was too late. He felt himself slip, with a sickening certainty, until the big rental car finally came to a stop in a ditch with a crunching of metal. He sat there and cursed, knowing that he didn't need to worry about rush-

ing anymore. He knew he wasn't going to be going anywhere for a long time.

At least he didn't have to worry about Phil. That sudden, mindless panic had been both overwhelming and absurd. While Phil sat in front of the TV and ate a frozen
pizza, Sam would be out in the snow freezing his butt off.
He'd even left his gloves behind in his hurry. It wasn't fair,
and it served him right. He climbed out of the car, noting
with grim satisfaction the bent frame, the flat tire, the
hopelessly crumpled fender. At least Phil was safe. For the
next few hours he could concentrate on getting himself the
hell out of there. Then he could worry about what had sent
him on such a wild-goose chase.

It wouldn't come into focus. Elizabeth stoked the fire,
turning it into a roaring blaze that threatened to turn her tiny
house into a sauna, but her body was still racked by shivers. She kept the electric heat up high, piled on sweaters, but
the chill wouldn't leave. And the vision, that brief, bloody
flash, wouldn't come back.

Phil didn't answer the phone. She tried not to let that
worry her. He hadn't actually said he was going home, had
he? Maybe he'd thought of something and gone in to the
station. Maybe he had to report that they'd found the shoe.
But not if Sam Oliver had his way, and Sam had a habit of
getting his own way, she thought.

Where had he gone, anyway? Maybe the two men were
out in some bar, watching football and drinking beer, as the
snow piled up outside and she sat alone, struggling to recall
something she didn't really want to see. Damn them. Damn
all men anyway, she thought, shivering.

Sam had left his gloves on the floor by the fireplace. He'd
been so eager to leave he hadn't taken them. Mistake number one, she thought smugly. You didn't go out in a blizzard without gloves.

She picked them up. They were leather, with a fur lining,
and they were very old and soft. They were warm, prob-

ably from their proximity to the fire, but she couldn't dismiss the notion that they still held his body heat.

Her own hands were cold, icy. Without thinking she slipped his gloves on, her small hands disappearing in their soft warmth. For a moment a sense of comfort swept through her, heat and safety and peace. Followed, a split second later, by the clearest, most horrifying vision of all. Phil Grayson, lying in a pool of blood. And Sam Oliver kneeling over him, the large hands that should have been safe inside these gloves now red with Phil's blood. A quiet moan of horror broke the silence of the room, and she threw the gloves into the fire.

It took her less than half an hour to drive to Phil's modest ranch house. She paid no attention to the icy roads that usually would have terrified her. She ignored traffic, visibility, her own racing heart. Over and over she whispered beneath her breath, a combination of prayer and despair.

"No," she whispered as she drove. "No, no, no."

The lights were on at Phil's house. There was only one car parked in the snowy driveway, Phil's Chrysler. No sign of Sam's rental car. No sign of anyone else.

She was past hope. This had happened too many times for her to think she might be mistaken. Too many times she had dreamed of horror, then found it to be true.

The kitchen door was unlocked, open a crack to the icy night air. She pushed it open the rest of the way, following the light. The television was on, too loudly, and for a moment she breathed a sigh of relief. Until she realized it was a game show. Phil hated game shows.

The living room was dark, lit only by the flickering light of the big color TV. Phil was lying on the dark carpet, unmoving, and Sam was kneeling over him. But Phil's carpet was pale beige, not an oval of deep red, surrounding him like an aura of death. And when Sam looked up and saw her, his face was twisted with such savage fury that she knew she was looking into the face of murder.

Chapter 7

For a long moment Elizabeth didn't move, paralyzed by shock, horror and a numbing sense of déjà vu. She had known what she'd find when she got there—the visions had teased through her brain, ignoring her efforts to push them away.

At first she could feel nothing but fear. Fear of a life spinning impossibly out of control. The man kneeling over Phil's lifeless body rose, slowly, stiffly, and she wanted to run away, as fast as she could, away from the smell of death and the face of murder.

He made no movement toward her, and her eyes met his, recognizing and accepting the hopeless fury in their black depths. If he believed she was responsible for Phil's death he'd kill her without hesitation. He hadn't trusted her for a moment during the past few days. Had his distrust pushed him far enough to believe she'd had a hand in this?

She should run. She should turn and race out of that house, away from him, before his damn judgment pronounced a death sentence.

And then she looked down at Phil. The only family, the only friend, she'd allowed herself, and he'd been ripped away with a savagery that was beyond shocking. And then there was no room for anything but grief, waves and waves of deep, slashing misery that tore through her. She stood there, trembling, and then she couldn't stand it anymore. She ran, but she didn't run away. Instead she went forward, stumbling into Sam Oliver's arms, clinging desperately, as she began to cry.

It had been years since she'd allowed herself to cry. The tears were harsh, painful, coming from deep within, and she felt Sam's arms around her, sensed their hesitancy, but she didn't care. She needed comfort; she needed the feel of a warm body, of life. She needed anything she could get, even the grudging solace of a man colder than the Colorado nights, as she wept through the storm of rage and despair that swamped her.

She didn't know when the mindless fury left him, when his arms held her more closely, when he picked her up and carried her from that room of death. She was aware of the cold sting of icy snow on her face, and then he bundled her into her car, the car she'd left running in her mad dash into Phil's house.

She didn't want to let go of him. She wanted to cling, to hide her face against the rough warmth of his shoulder; she wanted to cry until she fell asleep, and she wasn't sure if she ever wanted to wake up again. But he put her hands from him, folding them in her lap, and fastened the seat belt around her shivering body. When she looked down at her coat she could see the bloodstains from Sam's capable hands.

He didn't say a word as he pulled into the snowy street, his face cold and pale and grim. He drove very fast, dangerously so, but Elizabeth didn't protest, nor did she bother to ask where they were going. She didn't care. She was still in a numb, distant state of shock, and it took every remaining trace of energy she possessed simply to stop the tears.

She'd had years of practice at stopping them, and it should have been an easy enough matter to halt them once more, to shove her grief and despair back inside, down deep where no one else could witness them, particularly the cold, unfriendly man who was driving with such single-minded fury.

But the tears wouldn't stop. They had a life of their own, and having finally gained their freedom after two years of captivity, they weren't about to be penned up again. They slid down her cheeks, running into her collar, and when she leaned back they ran into her ears, her hair. It was too cold to cry, she thought dismally, her nose running. It was too cold to feel anything.

For some reason she hadn't expected him to drive her home. When the car slid to an abrupt stop, she looked up, dazed, at her tiny house in the woods, at the lights blazing from the windows.

Sam hadn't moved, hadn't turned off the ignition, and she wondered briefly if he expected her to get out of the car and leave him. Leave him in possession of her only means of transportation, while she spent the night alone in a house on the edge of nowhere, haunted by visions and memories and dreams of the future.

She had no energy to fight it. She reached for the door handle, but his hand covered hers, forestalling her. "Wait a minute." His voice was husky, raw, and she realized those were the first words he'd spoken since she'd found him kneeling over Phil's body. "Did you leave all those lights on?"

"I . . . I don't know."

"Did you leave your door open?"

She looked up, eyes narrowing through the blowing snow, and saw the crack of light from the thick kitchen door. "I don't know," she said again. "I don't remember much about the trip over to Phil's." She stumbled on his name, then righted herself. "I might have. I was so caught up in seeing . . ."

"I think someone's been here," he said, his emotionless voice cutting through her grief. "What do you think, swami?"

The faint, contemptuous edge to his voice did what he had no doubt intended it to. She glared at him, torn from her self-absorbed misery, and concentrated on the house. "I don't know," she said again.

"You don't know much, do you?" he countered. "What the hell good is your so-called gift if it can't tell you when your own house has been broken into, and it doesn't bother to warn you that a good man's going to be murdered until it's too late? I presume that's what sent you over to Phil's? A slightly overdue vision?"

"That's right. What sent you?"

He didn't say a word, but for a moment his hand tightened painfully on hers. "I just wanted to get away from you," he said, his voice mocking.

It should have stopped her questions. Instead it made her stronger, knowing he was lying to her. "Where's your car?"

"In a ditch somewhere. I hitched to Phil's."

"Well, you're not taking my car," she said. "Not unless I go with you."

For a brief moment his eyes met hers, something unbelievable flaring between them, vanishing before she could even comprehend it. "I have no intention of leaving you to be carved up like the others," he said evenly. "I just don't know whether you'd be safer waiting in the car or staying behind me."

"You think he's still here?"

Sam shrugged. "You tell me. Except that you can't, right? So we're just going to have to go with my instincts, poor as they are. And my instincts tell me that if the man who killed Phil is anywhere around, you wouldn't be safe in a locked car. So you're going to have to come with me. And you're going to have to stay right behind me, and be absolutely silent, and be prepared to do everything I say without a second's hesitation. Think you can agree to that?"

"Do you think it was the Colorado Slasher?"

"You mean, do I think Phil was killed by the same person or persons who's been killing the women around here? Yes. And I don't know if he's lying in wait for you. But I think he's been here."

Elizabeth shuddered, a very faint tremor shimmering across her chilled body. She couldn't tell if Sam was right or not—she'd been through too much in the past few hours to allow for any kind of emotional or psychic reserve. She could only do as he said and hope she'd put her faith in the right man. Otherwise, she was dead.

She thought she didn't care, but she did. She didn't want to die, and she especially didn't want to die at Sam Oliver's hand. For the first time in her life she wanted warmth and sunshine and laughter and love. But she knew full well that safety lay on the other side of a dark tunnel, and she'd have to traverse that darkness before she made it into the light.

"What are we going to do?"

"We're going into the house and see whether someone's been there. Whether someone's still there. If he is, then he's dead." His voice was flat, certain, and Elizabeth had no doubts at all. "If he isn't, we get a few things and take off. Come on." He released her, sliding out of the car, leaving it running. She followed suit, coming up behind him, unable to resist a nervous glance over her shoulder. The woods around her house seemed darker, the trees taller, menacing, moving in on her. Even the swirling snow seemed part of a conspiracy.

Sam had a gun in his hand. A large, efficient-looking gun, and she hadn't the faintest idea where it had come from. She hadn't felt it when she'd clung to him so desperately a short while ago. She'd always hated guns, but now, for the first time in her life, she viewed one with something bordering on affection. Not that she thought it would do any good. It didn't seem as if the man who had killed Phil Grayson could be stopped by something as mundane as a bullet.

For a moment she didn't comprehend what had happened to her house. Sam was too tall, his big body blocking her view as he moved, slowly, carefully, into the icy house. "Stay behind me," he muttered, his voice a mere thread of sound. "And close the door."

"But what if we need to run?"

"What if he needs to run?"

For a moment Elizabeth thought that was an excellent idea, and then she remembered Phil's body. She nodded, forgetting that he couldn't see her, but it didn't matter. He expected complete acquiescence, and she was smart enough to give it to him.

It took them less than a minute to ascertain that her house was trashed, shredded, and completely deserted. Sam began to curse, fluently and lengthily, as he picked through the ripped sofa cushions, the smashed furniture. "He's gone," he said flatly, tucking the gun back in the low-riding waistband of his jeans.

Like a zombie Elizabeth walked into the hallway, to the linen closet that had held the only things of value she owned. And then she stopped, sinking down onto the pile of shredded quilts with an animal moan of pain.

He'd ripped and destroyed every one of Granny Mellon's handmade quilts. The lace pillowcases, the stuffed feather pillows, the crocheted bedspreads, were mere ribbons of thread and material. He'd worked quickly, but efficiently, wiping out the only physical thing she cared about. She reached a trembling hand down to touch the remnants of a bear-claw quilt, and she saw the dark brown smear of dried blood across her fingers. Phil's blood.

She felt Sam's presence behind her, felt his impatience, but she didn't look up. "We have to get out of here," he said grimly. "He'll be back."

"Why?" She ran a desultory hand through the precious old cottons. "He's already destroyed everything."

"And taken the only thing of importance, that damn shoe. But he knows we saw it. He may have it, but he'll have to wipe us out, too."

There was one section, deep down beneath the pile of rags, that looked more or less intact. She began throwing the torn quilts aside, reaching down to pull out one small quilt that had been overlooked. It was small, in faded shades of pink and blue, in a tumbling-blocks pattern, and it had belonged to Elizabeth's mother, and to Elizabeth when she was a baby.

She clutched it to her breast like a talisman, feeling the earth shift and settle once more beneath her feet. "He doesn't have the shoe," she said.

She hadn't realized the sheer rage that Sam had been holding in check until he reached down and hauled her upright, yanking her around to face him. She still clung to the quilt with the devotion of a child to her security blanket, and she did her best not to quail in sudden fright. "What the hell do you mean?"

"I mean I took the shoe with me when I ran," she said, her fingers kneading the ancient material. "It's under the seat of the car."

"Hell," Sam said bitterly. "Let's get out of here."

She tried to pull away. "I need to get some clothes...."

"Forget it. He trashed your clothes, too. We'll get you something when we get there."

"When we get where?" She stumbled along after him, the quilt held tightly in her hands.

"Home," he said. "Washington."

Washington. Where Alan had drowned. "I don't want to go."

"Tough. You can't stay here—you'd be dead before morning. We're getting out of here now."

"But what about Phil...?"

"Phil's beyond help. If we're going to do anything about avenging him, we're going to have to get to Washington."

"Is revenge necessary?"

"Yes," Sam said bleakly. "Absolutely essential." And without another word he pulled her out of her wrecked house to the still-running car. And she knew as she handed him the Baggie-encased shoe from beneath the front seat and settled back for another dangerous ride through the snow that she would never see her house, her haven for the past two years, again. Pulling the crib quilt around her, she shut her eyes, unwilling to watch the house disappear in the swirling snow. Unwilling to say goodbye.

Muhammed Ali Reza watched them go. If he'd been a man with emotions he would have cursed, but emotions were a luxury for lesser men. He'd made a mistake—several, in fact—but he had every intention of righting them swiftly.

The policeman hadn't been much help. He'd been much better trained than Ali Reza would have suspected, and he understood pain. In the end it had been more of a formality than the hope of gaining any real information. He'd died well, and Ali Reza honored him.

The woman, when he killed her, would cry and scream and beg for mercy. She'd turn those devil eyes on him and fill them with tears; she'd plead and whine and moan. If he wanted to take his time with her he'd have to do something about her eyes first. He wouldn't be able to enjoy his work if she watched him.

There was no hurry. He knew where they were going—a simple search of Grayson's house had come up with a name and an address for the tall man. Besides, things were getting too hot in this miserably cold climate. Alarm bells were going to go off in the slow-working brains of the Denver police when a man turned up butchered in the same fashion as those other women. A man who was in a position to know too much about the killer.

It couldn't be helped. He'd considered burning the place, but he didn't have the proper equipment, and a fire might simply have called attention to Grayson before Ali Reza was ready for that to happen. And he'd been in too much of a hurry to find the woman, and the shoe. But in the end he'd missed her.

He'd learned patience, and thoroughness, years ago. He would put those two virtues into practice. And in a matter of days he'd be back in the warmth of Italy, with only wistful dreams to tease him. But first he had to make plans for Washington.

She looked like a whipped puppy, Sam thought, staring at his companion as she lay sleeping. He wondered how he looked. Probably just as bad. The flight attendants tended to eye him warily as they moved up and down the aisle, and they were very swift and generous with the Johnny Walker when he requested it. He'd seen that look in people's eyes before. He'd happened to accompany a divorced friend to the Washington zoo on custody day and found himself watching polar bears not long after the New York scandal of a child that had been eaten by one of the big white monsters. People were flocking around the tightly enclosed pen of the Washington polar bears, a crowd of voyeurs, and it was easy enough to guess what they were all thinking. You had only to look in their eyes, at their nervous, edgy expressions.

The flight attendant with the name Clarice printed above her generous chest was looking at him with just that expression. Fright, and a kinky fascination, and she leaned a little too close when she brought him his second Johnny Walker. If she was aware that the battered-looking waif asleep beside him belonged to him, she dismissed the notion as unworthy of her attention. Her smile was breathtaking, revealing perfect teeth, and her perfume was expensive and immediately recognizable. He hated it.

Elizabeth muttered something in her sleep, and he turned to look at her, dismissing Clarice's annoying attentions. Her normally pale skin was almost dead white, and he could see the salty residue of tears on her cheeks. The mauve shadows beneath her eyes had darkened, and her mouth was slightly open and vulnerable looking in sleep. At some point she'd braided her tangled brown hair and tucked it behind her, but it was coming loose, hanging over her shoulder. She was still clutching that damn quilt, wrapped up in it like it was a cocoon, and he told himself he should be irritated. Instead he was glad she was able to find at least a temporary peace. It was going to be a lot longer for him.

He hadn't expected her reaction. When she'd raced into Phil's house and stopped, staring at him, at Phil's body, with horror and shock and fear, he'd known that she had to suspect him. It would have been stupidly trusting not to consider that he might have done it, and the one thing he couldn't say about Elizabeth was that she was either stupid or trusting. Particularly toward him.

But he'd also known that if she'd run from him, if she'd accused him, he would have lost it. He didn't know what he would have done, and fortunately he hadn't had to find out. Instead of running, she'd turned to him for comfort, taking him completely off guard. In doing so she'd released his own grief. And he didn't know if he'd ever be the same again.

They'd lucked out when they got to the airport. He'd been fully prepared to order an Army plane, but he hadn't wanted to. He hadn't wanted the wait; he hadn't wanted the questions. There was more to this whole messy situation than met the eye, and he didn't know who would give him straight answers to straight questions and who might overreact if he got a bit too close to a sticky situation.

Paranoia had become second nature to him, and he trusted no one. Let's face it, he thought, I'm in the wrong business if I value any sort of mental health. But he'd made his choice decades ago, and it was too late to back out.

The commercial jet was the first to fly out since the storm abated, and even at three-fifteen in the morning it had been full. Too many people with delayed flights, he supposed, but he would have thought all those skiers would have hated to leave fresh powder. He hadn't skied in years, and he could scarcely imagine feeling free enough, lighthearted enough, to spend a day speeding down a mountain. Maybe he'd get a chance to do it once before he died. Maybe he wouldn't.

He pulled strings with ruthless efficiency, getting the two of them on that first flight, managing to keep the gun he had no intention of relinquishing to airport security. Right now he didn't trust anyone at all, and he wasn't going anywhere unarmed.

They'd land in Dulles sometime after dawn, then go straight back to his apartment while he figured out what the hell their next step was. And who he was going to trust.

"Sam?" Her voice was soft, scratchy, in the quiet jet, startling him out of his abstraction. He didn't remember her calling him by name before. Usually it was a scathing "Colonel Oliver." He liked the sound of his name on her lips. And he must be half drunk and half asleep to be thinking about such idiocy.

"Yeah?" he said, his voice cool and unencouraging.

"What's going to happen to Phil?"

Damn, he thought, trying to ignore the sudden cramp in his gut. It wasn't as if he'd forgotten. He'd just managed to block it for a while. "What do you mean?"

"I don't want him left there for too long." Her brown eyes were deeply troubled behind the thin-lensed glasses that he suspected she didn't really need. "I mean . . ."

"I know what you mean. I'll call in an anonymous tip when we land. Okay?"

"Won't they need us for questioning?"

"Not if we can help it. Not right now. They've botched up the entire investigation so far. They can just have one more unsolved murder on their books for a while. We'll get back to them as soon as we have a few answers."

She nodded, leaning back against her seat and pulling her faded quilt tighter around her. She was wearing one of her usual drab outfits, the pale colors washing her out even more, and he wondered for a brief, indulgent moment, how she'd look in something more vibrant. Something red.

"Are you all right?"

For a moment he couldn't believe her words. "What?"

"I asked if you were doing all right," she repeated patiently.

"No."

There was nothing she could say to that, no platitude she could come up with, but then Sam didn't really expect platitudes from her, or clichés. He expected the unexpected, like this sudden concern for a man she hated.

"I'm sorry," she said, her voice low and soothing.

He didn't want to be soothed. "I've seen it too often," he said, draining his Scotch. "Too many good men have died. Too many bad men have gotten away with it. I've lost too many friends. I didn't think I'd have to lose Phil, too."

"I know," she said.

She probably did. She knew too much, in that crystal ball of a brain she had. He didn't know whether Phil had told her anything about him, or whether she just closed her eyes and dreamed up stuff, but he had little doubt that he held very few secrets from her. He just wished he could return the favor.

"Go to sleep, swami," he muttered, flicking off the overhead light. "We'll be in Washington in another couple of hours, and we're going to have a lot to keep us busy. Better rest while you can."

She said nothing, and he could hear her even breathing in the dimly lit cabin. But he wasn't fooled. She wasn't going to sleep any more than he was. The moment he closed his eyes he'd see Phil's body, and he knew that was one vision they were doomed to share. Forever.

Chapter 8

Washington smelled different. The moment Elizabeth stepped out of the terminal she was assailed by the different scents, the different kind of cold. From the snowy cocoon of Denver she'd emerged, feeling like a battered moth, into the pollution and damp chill of the mid-Atlantic states, the East Coast that she'd grown to hate. She stood there on the sidewalk for a moment, swaying slightly, the crib quilt still clutched in her hands, her down coat hanging loosely around her. Her hair had come undone, and she was too bone tired to do anything about it, letting it hang down her back like a tangled curtain. If she had any sense at all she'd hack it all off. Alan had loved her hair, and she'd kept it long as some sort of memorial, or as expiation of her sin. But Alan was dead.

And so was Phil. She allowed herself a brief, nervous glance at the man standing beside her. An indomitable man, an emotionless, implacable, invulnerable man. No one could kill him, could they? No visions would come, haunting her, warning her too late. Life couldn't be that cruel.

She didn't stop to consider why she would care. Why Sam Oliver's death would be any crueler than Phil's, than Alan's. There were answers to that question, answers she wasn't ready to face. For the time being she wanted a shower and a bed, and oblivion for as long as she could grasp it. When she awoke she might be ready to face the unfaceable.

"Come on," Sam muttered, bundling her into a taxi. "I don't want anyone getting more of a chance to see us than they need to." He got in beside her, sitting close, and gave the address to the Pakistani driver before sliding the glass divider closed and leaning back.

"Why should it matter? He couldn't have followed us, could he? And even if he did, this is your home territory. You have backup, you have—"

"I have a hell of a lot of people I don't trust," he said flatly.

"Tell me something new."

His eyes narrowed for a moment as he surveyed her, almost as if he were seeing her for the first time. "I'm still alive," he said. "And all my friends are dead. Maybe there's something to be said for not trusting."

"And maybe there are some kinds of lives that aren't worth living. A life devoid of trust and caring is no life at all."

He stared down at her as the city of Washington whizzed by. The driver was safely cocooned in the front seat, humming along with the radio, and the two of them seemed isolated, apart.

"I haven't noticed you filling your life with trust and love," he said.

They were both too tired for this conversation, she thought wearily. Too much had happened; too many defenses had begun to crumble. "And who says my life is worth living?" she replied.

He considered that for a moment dispassionately. "I do," he said finally. "And, for that matter, I trust you."

It was grudgingly given, but nonetheless magnanimous. She knew he trusted her. He wouldn't be taking her to his apartment, he wouldn't be keeping her with him, if he didn't—at least to some extent. It was just hard for him to admit it. And she wasn't making things any easier.

"You don't mean to tell me that you actually believe in my gifts?" she said, too tired to resist bugging him.

"I wouldn't go that far. Let's just say I think you believe in them. And I don't think you're lying."

Elizabeth thought of Alan, and her vision of his death. And she thought of Sam, and his hand running up her red-clad thigh, she who never wore anything but neutral colors.

"Generous of you," she muttered cynically, because she was afraid to tell him how scared and grateful she really was.

"Hey, I'm a great guy," Sam drawled, sliding back in the seat and closing his eyes. The taxi smelled of cigarette smoke and sweat, and Sam's thigh brushed hers, resting against her absently. The faded quilt overlapped, its muted color echoing the aging blue denim of his jeans. She wondered whether he would wear a uniform now that he was back in the city, and how she, lackadaisical pacifist that she was, would feel about that. Would he get his hair cut even shorter? Would he become even more distant? More rigid?

What was she worrying about? She needed protection, safety, and she needed the military to provide it. If Sam Oliver started going by the book it would only be to her benefit. Wouldn't it?

And oddly comfortable silence filled the taxi, and she was just beginning to drift when it stopped, slamming her against Sam's strong body. She might just as well have run into a brick wall, she thought, pushing herself away and wondering briefly if she was bruised. She barely had time to look around her as Sam hustled her out of the taxi, down a flight of steps and through an elaborate security system, and it wasn't until he'd bundled her into the building that she managed to get her bearings.

"Where are we?" she demanded, moving away from him with her customary diligence. She couldn't afford to be too close; she couldn't afford to touch him, either accidentally or on purpose. It set off too many disturbing reactions.

"My place," he said, hustling her down a wide hallway and into an elevator. They rode up in silence, then walked down another anonymous hallway until he stopped and unlocked a door, ushering her in and triple locking the door behind them.

"Don't move," he ordered, stepping away from her, stalking through the apartment with the same air of distrust and menace as when he'd checked out that deserted cabin in the mountains of Colorado. She allowed herself a brief moment to mourn for the fact that he couldn't even trust his own home, and then he was back, tucking the gun that had appeared from nowhere into his waistband and shrugging off his parka. "We're okay. No one's been here."

"Why would they have?" she questioned, fascinated.

He shook his head. "I don't know. I just have a funny feeling about this whole mess, and until I get some answers I'm going to be damn careful." He reached for the quilt, and for a moment she clung to it, unwilling to relinquish it. But his hands brushed hers, setting off a swirling storm of reaction that frightened her, and she released it, stepping back, ignoring the question in his dark blue eyes. Ignoring the moment.

She looked around her, at the plain white walls unadorned by pictures, at the L-shaped modular sofa covered with white cotton. The only concessions to decorating were the heavy curtains and blinds on the wall of windows, now open to the bright morning sunlight, and Elizabeth knew perfectly well that those were in place for security reasons and nothing more. The only signs of human weakness were the TV and stereo and books piled haphazardly around. "And you mocked the way I live," she said, shaking her head.

"What's wrong with my apartment?"

"How long have you lived here?"

"Five years."

"It looks as if you moved in last week."

"I'm not a believer in acquiring possessions. Life's too short and uncertain to put your faith in things."

She sank down tentatively on the sofa. At least it was comfortable enough, if undecorative. "If you don't put your faith in things," she said, "and you clearly don't put your faith in your fellow man, where does it go? What do you believe in?"

He thought about it for a moment, standing there in the stark-white room, the early-morning sunlight streaming through the windows.

He needed a shave, she thought. He needed sleep. He needed . . . She wasn't going to make any more guesses as to what he needed. It was probably wishful thinking on her part, and dangerous to boot. Touching him was like touching an electric fence—you never knew when the current was going through, and whether you'd be knocked flat on your rear end when you least expected it.

He took the gun from his jeans and set it down on one of the white tables. "I believe in truth," he said. "And honor. Cold beer on a hot night. Strong whiskey on a cold one. I believe in trying your damnedest, even if you don't know what the hell you're doing. And I believe in love."

She stared at him, mesmerized for a moment, wanting to touch him, wanting to hold him, daring to risk the consequences. And then the name Amy Lee rose up between them like an unspoken curse, and she told herself he wasn't thinking of her at all. "Maybe there's hope for you after all." She managed to sound cool and distant, staring out the window, away from his thoughtful gaze.

"You'll have to check your crystal ball, swami," he drawled. "Find out if there's a happy ending for either of us."

"Even if I could, I wouldn't. What if the answer is no?" she said.

"It would be nothing more than I'd expect." He turned away, heading toward one of the open doors. "I'm going to go out after I take a shower."

She squashed down her sudden panic. "Can I come with you?"

"No. You're safe here. This building has excellent security, and if anyone's interested in us they'll follow me, not come after you. I don't think anyone knows we're here yet. You might as well get some sleep."

It wouldn't do her any good to beg. She had no choice but to trust him, to do as he said. If she did otherwise she'd be lost.

He left half an hour later, the rough stubble scraped from his incongruously handsome face, his eyes dark and wary, his uniform sitting far too comfortably on his tall, lean frame. Before he left he came over and put the gun in her hand.

She tried to drop it, but his fingers wrapped around hers, forcing her to hold the gun. "Do you know how to fire this thing?"

"I don't want to know," she said, gritting her teeth.

He ignored the protest, turning her hand over and forcing her to hold the weapon properly. "You pull this," he said. "And then you pull this. That fires it."

"No."

"Yes." His hands hurt her, pressing her small, softer hands against the cruel steel. "I need you too much to let someone kill you."

She stared up at him in sudden shock, misunderstanding him for a moment. As quickly as that absurd happiness flooded her it vanished into a dark cloud of common sense. "I won't let anyone kill me until you don't need my help," she said. "Now let go of me."

He didn't release her. "Will you use the gun?"

"If I have to." It was a lie, and they both knew it, and he cursed beneath his breath.

He moved away, and she dropped it on the sofa beside her, having every intention of hiding it under the cushion the moment he left. He was at the door when she spoke. "I'm going to need some clothes," she said. "We left everything behind."

"I'll pick something up for you. Don't answer the door, don't answer the phone, keep the curtains closed."

"When are you coming back?" She hated the plaintive note in her voice, but there wasn't much she could do about it.

"I'm not sure. Your best bet is to get some sleep. Take a long, hot shower, help yourself to the Scotch and go to bed."

"I don't want to," she said. "I don't want to dream."

"Honey," he said, opening the door, "sometimes we don't have any choice." And without another word he was gone.

She didn't know how long she sat on that stark-white sofa, unmoving. Long enough for the sun to rise and fill the barren room with blinding light. And then she finally stirred, tucking the gun under the cushion and climbing wearily to her feet. She moved slowly, following his instructions, shutting out the daylight and inquisitive eyes. And then she went in search of a bathroom and a bed.

The apartment was small, the right size for a man living alone. The kitchen was off to the left, stocked with beer, butter and Johnny Walker Red. A few tins of soup sat in a cupboard, along with a box of soft, stale crackers, but Elizabeth didn't want to eat. She wasn't going to touch the whiskey, either. Phil and Sam shared their affection for Scotch, and she didn't think she'd ever see Johnny Walker again without thinking of Phil.

The bathroom and bedroom were small and white. The bathroom even had a white shower curtain, and Elizabeth wouldn't have been surprised if the towels were white, too. Instead they were a surprise, a rich maroon, deep black and vivid turquoise—the only splash of color in the place. At least none were vibrant red.

The bed was huge. Elizabeth had never seen such a large bed in her life, and she couldn't resist smiling when she thought of Sam trying to cram his oversize body onto her sofa, particularly after he was used to sleeping in a room-size bed. The sheets were striped, and she breathed a small, illogical sigh of relief. That brief, erotic vision had no basis in reality, she reminded herself for the hundredth time. She never wore red. And the bed she'd envisioned had smooth gray sheets. Not stripes.

She took a shower in Sam's bathroom, washing herself with his soap, using his shampoo, drying herself with his thick maroon towels, wrapping herself in his essence. She'd never considered asking him to take her to a hotel, and she regretted it as she rummaged through his closets looking for something to wear. Of course he wouldn't have listened, so it was just as well she hadn't wasted her breath asking. Still, it would have helped assert her independence.

There was no way she was going to put on her own clothes again. She'd been in them for more than twenty-four hours—in those clothes she'd found Mary Nelson's death spot, gazed on Phil's murdered face. In those clothes she'd knelt amidst the ruins of Granny Mellon's quilts, and in those clothes she'd run away, with Sam Oliver at her back, guarding her. There was blood on her clothes, Phil's blood. And she wanted to burn them.

In the end she settled for a plain black T-shirt, so big it reached halfway down her thighs, and a pair of black sweatpants that threatened to trip her up. She put them on warily, remembering the vision that had engulfed her when she put her hands in Sam's gloves, but no horrible pictures forced themselves behind her eyes.

Climbing into the center of the huge bed, she took the comb she'd pilfered from the bathroom shelf and began trying to force some control on her waist-length hair. She fell asleep in the middle of trying to braid it, and for the next eight hours she didn't dream at all.

It was getting dark when Sam let himself back into the apartment. There were no lights, no noise, and he felt a sudden panic sweep over him. She wouldn't have been fool enough to leave, would she? No one could have come and taken her—they would have left some sign of their presence. Unless she was in the other room, her throat cut, her body butchered, as the others had been. He'd seen the police photographs, and they'd made little impression. He'd seen too many bodies to get worked up, but suddenly, vividly, he remembered the photos, the wounds, the pitiful ending of a human life.

His heart was racing when he stormed into the bedroom. In the darkness he could see the huddled bundle of humanity in the middle of his bed, and for a moment he, who didn't know the meaning of fear, was terrified to move. She was covered with the quilt from head to toe, and he knew that if he pulled that cover aside he'd be looking into her lifeless brown eyes, her cut throat a second red smile beneath her mouth.

He moved slowly, kneeling on the bed, and began to pull at the quilt. She didn't move, didn't make a sound, as he uncovered her still, pale, lifeless face. And then her eyes fluttered open, focusing on his face, and she smiled at him.

He couldn't figure out why she smiled. He'd always been a complete bastard to her, out of self-preservation as much as anything, and if she had any sense at all she'd ask what the hell he was doing, instead of smiling sleepily at him, so that instead of pulling away he wanted to wrap his arms around her, quilt and all, and drown in those sleepy brown eyes.

"How'd it go?" Her voice was husky, endearing, and he wondered what the hell had happened to him. How all his better judgment and defenses had flown out the window, so that all he thought about was touching her. But she didn't like to be touched, he knew that. Particularly by him. He just wished he knew why.

He sat back, moving away from her on the big bed, and turned on the light, flooding the twilit room with light. "Lousy," he said. "They lied to me."

"What did you say to them?" She sat up, brushing at her tangled hair with a desultory hand. He found himself staring at her hair, staring at her eyes without their customary shield of wire-rimmed glasses, and thinking things he shouldn't be thinking.

"*I* lied," he said.

She sighed. "Aren't you supposed to be on the same side?"

"Ostensibly. When you grow up you'll find that governments aren't to be trusted, even your own."

He'd hoped to provoke a reaction from her, and he'd managed. "Go to hell," she said, sliding off the bed, away from him.

She was too damn skinny, and his oversize black clothes made her look even more waiflike. He always preferred women with some heft to them. Amy Lee had always complained how fat she was with ten extra pounds on her frame, but he'd liked her that way. There was no way he wanted to touch a skinny little girl.

Except that she wasn't a little girl; she was twenty-nine years old, and if he believed her, she'd seen as much as he had of blood and pain and misery and death. Only she hadn't seen it firsthand. She hadn't ever been able to do a thing about it, to stop it, to avenge it, to make it better. All she'd been able to do was be a helpless witness. Maybe that was even closer to hell than what he'd been through.

"Something's going on, and they're not telling me," Sam said, stretching out on the big bed now that she'd left it, tucking the pillow behind him. He was bone weary, but he wasn't ready to sleep. Not yet. "They're sitting on the Derringer case and keeping it tighter than a drum. We call it a

need-to-know situation, and no one happens to see a reason
why I need to know."

"Why didn't you tell them?" She was trying to ram a
comb through her long, tangled hair, and she was pulling it.

"Instinct."

She stopped yanking at her hair to look at him in the
dimly lit bedroom. "Instinct?" she echoed.

"Unless you care to go into a trance and find out more,
you're going to have to accept that," he drawled.

"But . . ."

"I think they already know about Mary Nelson," he said
abruptly.

She turned to him. "Why?"

"Because those bastards have reported Phil's death as a
suicide."

"Suicide? There's no way . . ."

"Of course there isn't. The Denver authorities don't have
the capability or the motive to orchestrate that kind of
cover-up. Therefore, while I was pursuing my obscure little
lead, other people were after it, too."

She sat down on the end of the bed, near his feet, her long
hair forgotten. He'd never known a woman with hair that
long, never touched a woman with hair that long. Never
made love to a woman with hair that long. He knew suddenly that he was going to. "What do you think is going
on?" she asked.

It was lucky he was equipped with more than a one-track
mind. Part of him could think about sleeping with her, another part could be amazed at the very thought, while still
another concentrated on the Derringer situation, as they
were calling it. "I don't know. Either Mary Nelson is going
to stand in for Shari Derringer, or vice versa, and the Spandau Corporation is smack dab in the middle of it. What I
can't figure out is why they haven't called me in. There's no
one alive who knows more about Spandau than I do."

"Maybe they figure you're still emotionally involved."

He smiled sourly. "Hell, they know it. They also know I was in Denver, though no one asked a single question. They're waiting, watching, to see what I'm going to offer."

"They don't think you're involved?"

"They don't trust anybody, Elizabeth." He sighed, rubbing a hand over his eyes. "I don't want you leaving here." He didn't look at her, *couldn't* look at her. "Not for a while, at least. They followed me back here, but I don't think anyone was watching when we arrived. I don't know if they even know about your existence, and I think we'd be safer if they didn't. At least for now." He yawned, feeling so damn tired.

"Why don't you sleep?"

"Can't," he said, scooting down on the bed. "Too much to do. I've got calls to make."

"You're too tired."

"Maybe I'll just take a little catnap. Wake me in half an hour."

"Sure," she said, and he knew she had no intention of doing so. It didn't matter. He could program himself to wake up at any time he wanted, and he'd simply program himself to wake up in thirty minutes. Or maybe sixty. Maybe he deserved that much.

"I bought you some clothes," he mumbled sleepily. "And some food."

"I think I'd rather have the food at this point."

It was enough to make him open his eyes. "I've never known you to care about something as mundane as food," he observed. "Have you lost your death wish?"

She looked at him, her brown eyes troubled. "Oh, God," she murmured, clearly horrified. "I have." And without another word she left the room, closing the door behind her.

Chapter 9

Elizabeth ignored the pile of bags and boxes dumped inside the triple-locked-and-barred front door. She'd been telling the truth when she'd said she was more interested in food than clothes. Sam's soft cotton sweats were the most comfortable things she'd worn in years, and she was in no hurry to relinquish them for stiff, uncomfortable new clothes. She had no idea what he'd bought for her, but if he was running true to form she'd probably end up with a straitjacket and a chastity belt.

She wasn't going to think about it. About his contemptuous opinion of her and her dubious talents. She wasn't going to think about how comfortable she felt in his clothes, her naked skin where his had last rested. She wasn't going to think about Phil, either. She couldn't, without crying, and she didn't want to cry anymore. Her eyelashes were already bleached by the salty tears, and while she'd never been particularly interested in makeup she found she felt the sudden desperate need for mascara. Maybe a little blusher for her pale cheeks. And pale pink lip gloss.

She shook her head at her own foolishness, heading into the tiny kitchen. He'd left the bags of groceries on the spotless counter, and she began unpacking, trying to close off the eerie sense of déjà vu that was washing over her.

She'd expected the six-pack of Beck's Dark Beer to join the two bottles on the door of the almost empty refrigerator. And the frozen pizzas were no surprise, though she couldn't imagine how one human being could have such a limitless appetite for pizza. The French Roast coffee beans and heavy cream were more welcome but not surprising, and the thick red steak was enough to make any carnivore drool. Elizabeth wasn't sure whether she was a carnivore or not— vegetarian living had seemed an easy thing to fall into when she was living alone, but if one was going to partake of flesh, that steak looked worth the fall from grace.

She reached into the bottom of the bag, pulled out a jar of macadamia nuts and let it slip from her fingers.

She was lucky it didn't smash at her bare feet. The apartment and everything about it was upscale and first class, even if Sam had never bothered to move in in five years, and the kitchen floor was top-of-the-line vinyl with lots of cushioning. The jar bounced, rolled and ended up wedged under the refrigerator door. Elizabeth didn't go over and pick it up. She couldn't. Instead she reached for the other bag, warily, as if she expected to find a nest of spiders awaiting her.

All her fears were confirmed. The jar of macadamia nuts hadn't been a fluke. Along with the Dutch pretzels and beer nuts she could have anticipated were Granny Smith apples, a deli container of Chinese sesame noodles and a couple of ice cream bars. She leaned back against the counter, feeling the cool, hard Formica against her back, clutching it with nerveless fingers. He must have searched her cabinets. That was it. He must have memorized everything she had there. Except that she'd been all out of ice cream bars, and hadn't been able to buy more for weeks. And Granny Smiths were out of season—she was amazed he'd even been able to find them. How in heaven's name had he managed to come up with her obscure favorite foods?

The possible explanations were all equally unpleasant. It was farfetched but not impossible that they simply happened to share a taste for chinese noodles and Granny Smith apples. No, that couldn't be it. No one who ate beer nuts could appreciate the delicate nuances of Granny Smiths.

Another explanation could be that the research he'd done on her had been so exacting that it even cataloged her favorite foods. If her taste for macadamia nuts and ice cream bars had made it into some report on a bureaucrat's desk, what deeper, darker secrets had Sam been privy to? Did he know she'd once pushed Stevie Bishop into a muddy pond when he'd called her a spook? Did he know her aunt and uncle had tried to beat the devil out of her? Did he know she was a virgin?

He probably knew all of those things, particularly the last. She shivered in the warm kitchen. He kept the heat up higher than she was used to, and she found she was glad. She had a hard time getting warm nowadays, and Sam's bed didn't come equipped with an electric blanket.

Sam's bed. He'd sleep through the night, she was sure of it. Where was she expected to sleep? If only she'd thought of it, she might have appealed to his gentlemanly instincts and asked him to sleep on the sofa.

Fat lot of good that would have done her, she thought, picking up the jar of macadamia nuts and opening it, absently popping one into her mouth. Sam Oliver didn't have a gentlemanly instinct in his body, or if he did, it didn't extend to her. He probably would have told her to sleep on the couch, or share the bed with him.

Why did she think he would have said that? And why did she grow hot, then cold, at the very thought? What in heaven's name was she doing, thinking about sex, when her only remaining friend had been slaughtered less than twenty-four hours ago? What was she doing thinking about sex at all?

She looked toward the bedroom door. She already knew that he didn't snore. The walls in her house were paper-thin—she'd heard every deep breath, every time he'd turned over, every rustle and movement. As she was hearing them now.

She moved back to the bedroom door. The sun had set. The heavily curtained windows let in little light, and the room was almost completely dark. Sam lay stretched out on the bed, away from the pillows that she knew he never used. She was surprised he even owned any, considering the sparseness of his possessions. Probably bought them for guests, she thought sourly, not bothering to guess why the thought disturbed her so much.

Well, he could share his pillows and his bed with anyone he pleased. It didn't matter to her—after all, they were enemies, or at least antagonists, thrown together by their affection for Phil and their involvement in a series of violent deaths. She wanted to get away from him, far away, but she knew perfectly well she couldn't. At this point he was the only person who could protect her, the only person who would even begin to believe in the things she could see. She couldn't run, not yet.

She turned away, unwilling to look at him any longer. Part of his problem was that he was too damn good-looking. He was probably used to charming his way into anything, and women must fall for it by the dozens. He hadn't tried his charm on her, not since the first night when she'd realized he wasn't a ski bum on his way to Steamboat, and she could appreciate that. She'd prefer honest hostility to phony caring. But what she could have done with, right then, was some genuine caring. Someone to hold her, to frighten away the demons, to keep her safe.

She knew better. No one could save her from her demons—they came unannounced and unwanted, and they came from within. And no one could hold her, certainly not Sam. Another human's touch merely strengthened her visions. Sam's most of all. Sam brought the visions into sharp focus, when all she wanted was a fuzzy fade out.

She didn't know if she could sleep again. She felt restless, edgy, cold. She moved back into the living room, carefully skirting the shopping bags, and headed toward the bank of windows. She peered through the miniblinds into the twilight street below.

She wasn't used to crowds; she wasn't used to the city. The street was filled with cars, pedestrians, people hustling, people coming home from work. From her vantage point on the seventh floor they looked normal, innocuous enough, probably just a bunch of bureaucrats with mortgages and kids in braces. Those innocent-looking faces didn't hide a killer. No one was watching, waiting. Waiting for her.

"Get back from the window." Sam's voice was whiplash sharp, and she jumped back, letting the blinds crash against the glass.

"You scared me," she said accusingly. "I didn't hear you get up."

"I told you to stay away from the windows," he said. He'd stripped off his tie, and his khaki shirt was unbuttoned halfway down his chest. His hair was rumpled; he needed a shave, and he should have looked exhausted. Instead he seemed too alert, and the reasons behind that alertness unnerved her.

"Sorry," she said gracelessly. "I didn't remember. I'm sorry if I woke you. I thought you'd sleep through the night."

He didn't say anything, walking into the living room and sinking onto the sofa as he ran his hands through his hair. "I can't. A decent night's sleep is a luxury I can't afford. Did you sleep today?"

"For hours. I didn't even dream."

"Maybe you should."

For a moment she thought she hadn't heard him right. "I beg your pardon?"

"I said maybe you should. We aren't going to find out anything from the Pentagon, that much is for certain, and the Denver police and the newspapers are lying through their teeth. We can sit here and wait till Phil's killer shows up, or you can do something about it. Time for a trance, swami. Just a little séance, calling forth answers from the spirit world and all that."

She'd become inured to his mockery. "It doesn't work that way. I don't know why you're even suggesting such a thing. You don't believe I can see anything. You think I'm a liar...."

"If I thought you were a liar you wouldn't be here."

"Where would I be?"

He didn't answer, and she was just as glad. There was a ruthless streak in Sam Oliver that absolutely terrified her, even though she knew it wasn't directed at her, at least not right now. She knew he'd seen death, dealt death, without flinching. She wished she could be certain he would never hurt her, but on reflection that was simply a case of wishful thinking. His sense of honor and of what was right was absolute, and anything, anyone, might be sacrificed for it.

He leaned back against the overstuffed white pillows and looked at her. "Let's just say I'm getting desperate. Anything's worth a try."

"Forget it, Colonel Oliver," she said coldly. "I don't do parlor tricks."

She didn't know where she thought she was going. Maybe to lock herself in the bathroom for a few minutes, away from his unnerving blue gaze. He caught her by the doorway, catching her wrist and spinning her around against him. Again he'd moved so silently, so swiftly, that she hadn't been aware of his approach, and she stumbled, off balance, against him.

She didn't know where the panic came from, but it swamped her. She hit out at him, desperate, but he was far too strong. His hands were manacles on her wrists, bruising her as she fought him; his arms were iron bands around her as he yanked her body back against him. "Stop it," he hissed in her ear, but she was beyond caring, sailing into a terror that knew no peace. There was blood all around them; the harsh, metallic scent of it was in her nostrils, the wet, warm stickiness of it on her hands. She fought the vision, as she fought him, screaming, crying, whispering things she couldn't hear, until finally he shook her, hard, her head snapping back, her long hair flowing around them both in the dimly lit hallway.

She stopped her struggles abruptly, staring up at him in shock. She ached all over from the imprint of his strong hands on her wrists, the prison of his arms around her, but she knew she'd caused that hurt herself, fighting against him as he tried to keep her from hurting herself, from hurting him. She took a deep, shaky breath, letting it tremble from her body, letting it warm his bare chest in front of her. "I'm sorry," she whispered, staring at his open shirt, at his chest, no longer willing to meet his eyes.

"Better now?" His voice was a low rumble of sound, and she wanted to lean her forehead against that smooth-skinned chest, to shut her eyes and forget. Forget the past, forget the future. For once in her life to live only in the present. To float, dreamless, on that bed, the red dress flowing around them, her hair loose and streaming, his hand running up her thigh, bringing the full skirt of the dress with him, sliding higher, higher....

"Please let me go," she said, her muscles tensing.

"No." He was inexorable, determined, and frightening. "Something happens when I touch you, and I sure as hell know you're not fainting with desire, lady. What is it that you see? What frightens you?"

"Nothing," she said, closing her eyes, shaking her head, trying to shake the vision away. His hands tightened on her arm, the tiny pain forcing her eyes open again.

"What do you see?" he demanded, his voice urgent.

She couldn't fight it, or him, any longer. He knew, damn him. He knew his touch brought the visions into clearer focus. She didn't know how, or why, but his body was like an amplifier, boosting her power to frightening levels. "A man," she said, her voice nothing more than a raw whisper as she gave in to the icy currents sweeping around her. "A man with a knife."

His hands slid up her arms, but she was no longer fighting him. She stayed there, passive, cold, remote. "What does he look like? Is he here?"

"Not here. Someone else is coming. Someone else is coming for us. He's gone."

"Where?"

"I don't know."

"Where?"

"There's water. Cold, icy water, snow falling on curved boats," she murmured, peering through a dense mist. "A big empty house by the water."

"Damn." He released her, and the fuzzy picture vanished, like an out-of-focus television being switched off. "I can't do it."

She'd fallen back against the wall, dizzy, disoriented and so cold her teeth ached. "Can't do what?" she managed.

"Can't fall prey to your circus mumbo jumbo," he said bitterly. "I don't trust it, and I feel like a fool, trying to decipher what you're saying."

Her eyes focused suddenly. "By all means we wouldn't want you to feel like a fool," she shot back. "Your sense of dignity is so much more important than people's lives."

She was unprepared for the small, self-mocking grin that lit his dark face. "You think your visions can save people's lives?"

She remembered Alan, the dark waters of the Potomac closing over his head, and she shuddered, pushing that haunting vision away. "Maybe," she said. "Maybe one can save my life. And yours."

"If it comes in time. Your visions tend to go along the lines of hindsight. A little advance warning might be nice. Maybe Phil wouldn't be dead."

The pain was so sharp, so devastating, that the breath left her body. There was no way she could fight it, no defense against such cruelty. "Damn you," she muttered, turning away.

But even Sam Oliver had a conscience. When he pulled her into his arms this time he was gentle, and there was real regret in his voice when he spoke. "I'm sorry," he murmured against her hair. "That was completely uncalled for. Sometimes I'm a rotten bastard."

"Sometimes," she said, resting against him, not fighting. "I wish I'd seen it in time. If only..."

"Hush," he whispered. "It wasn't your fault." And she could feel the sound vibrate through his chest, rumbling in her ear. She closed her eyes, absorbing the feel of him, the warmth and scent and strength of him, knowing her danger, knowing and ignoring it. For so long she'd avoided human touch, but all her frail efforts at self-preservation seemed to have vanished the moment she'd gotten off the plane at Dulles Airport. Or maybe it was the moment she'd looked down at Phil's body and turned to Sam for comfort.

If only her mind would stay blank. If only she could exist in a state of physical grace, the mental torments lost. If only...

It came slowly this time, sinuously, the vision that was almost more frightening than death and despair. For once she didn't fight it, flowing with it, allowing it to happen. They were on a bed. The red dress was the only splash of color in the room, against their skin, against his hands. The low-cut bodice of the dress was pushed down, exposing her breasts, and her hair surrounded them in a veil of secrecy.

Sam's arms tensed around her, and his hands held her. "What do you see?" he whispered, his voice low.

One last ounce of self-preservation caused her to pull away, but he was too strong. "Don't fight it, Elizabeth," he whispered. "Tell me. You're not seeing death anymore, are you? You're seeing life. You're seeing me. And you. Together. Aren't you?''

"No," she said, lying.

"You want me," he said. "You want me as much as I want you, and you're afraid to face it. You can see it, and you run away from it. That's it, isn't it? You're running from visions of life, not death.'' One strong hand came under her chin, forcing her head up to meet his. "Are you afraid of me, Elizabeth? Afraid of my hands on your breasts? My mouth on yours? My hands running under that red dress and touching you?''

She pulled away this time, and he let her go. She was shaking all over, but this time she wasn't racked with the desperate cold of her visions. She was hot. Hot all over, burning up inside. "You don't know what I'm seeing," she said. "You're just guessing."

"Am I right?"

"Go to bed, Sam," she said numbly, turning away, turning toward the kitchen. "You need sleep. Maybe once you're rested you'll remember you despise me."

"What about you? Will a good night's sleep teach you not to lie to me?"

Suddenly she'd had enough. She was being pulled in a thousand directions, inside and out; one more tug and she'd break apart. "If you don't go away and leave me alone," she said fiercely, "I'll leave. I'll walk out that door and never come back, and to hell with you and your delusions."

"Try it," he offered, and she wasn't fooled by his affable manner. She might get as far as unlocking one lock, if she was lucky. It wouldn't do her any good to wait until he slept, either. He'd been asleep when she'd gone over to look through the blinds.

He must have seen her reaction. "You might as well face it, Elizabeth. You're well and truly trapped. Here. With me. You may as well make the best of it."

"And what is the best of it?"

He appeared to consider her question for a moment. "That's for you to decide. You want to stay safe in your cocoon for a bit longer, and I suppose I'll let you. Sooner or later you'll have to come out, but I don't want to be the person to drag you, kicking and screaming, into life."

She looked around her, at the bare walls, the starkness of the place. "If this is your definition of life," she said, "I'm better off where I am."

"Maybe," he said. "But maybe we have no choice in the matter. Whether we like it or not, we're both going to change. Don't answer the phone, don't answer the door, don't go near the window. Understood?"

"Where are you going?" She didn't want him to leave her.

"Back to bed. You're welcome to join me."

"Stop teasing me!"

"I mean it," he said bleakly. "God help me." Without another word he left her, leaving the bedroom door open behind him.

She stood in the hallway without moving, still flushed with that unaccustomed heat. And then she walked, slowly, thoughtfully, back to the living room, sinking down on the uncomfortable sofa. She sat there for a long time, keeping her mind blank as darkness closed down around her, and only the street noises outside the apartment reminded her that other people still existed in the world. And it wasn't until she was ready to drift back into a troubled sleep, when the utilitarian digital clock read eleven forty-three, that the most obvious thing hit her, the one thing that had been nagging at her, teasing her, keeping her unbalanced and off center.

She got up and went over to the pile of shopping bags, flicking on the hall light as she went. It didn't take her long to find it. Amidst the lacy underwear that was a size too small for her, the clothes that should have been worn by someone very different from Elizabeth Hardy, was the red dress.

She was still clutching it when she went into the bedroom. Sam was awake, lying across the bed, his head resting on his crossed arms. The pillows were beside him, waiting.

He was wearing jeans, and nothing else, but she knew that. She stood in the doorway, clutching the dress against her, and there was no way she could mitigate the accusation in her voice.

"How did you know the dress was red?"

Chapter 10

Sam moved, flicking on the bedside light. "I don't know what you're talking about," he said. And she knew he was lying.

She walked into the room, to the side of the bed, and tossed the red dress down on him, so that it spilled across his nude, tanned torso with a splash of color that was somehow shocking. "You said I was seeing your hands on my red dress. I've never owned a red dress."

"You do now. I must have been imagining you wearing it."

"Don't lie to me. This isn't just a red dress that you bought on a whim!"

"Isn't it? Why not?" His voice was soft, taunting.

"Because I've seen it, and you know it. I've seen you and me, and that damn dress."

"I thought you could see the future, swami," he drawled. "Your hookie-pookie voices must have known I'd buy that dress."

"No."

"No?" he echoed. "What's your theory, then?"

"That was more than just a good guess." It took all her resolve, but she leaned over and placed her hands flat on his warm chest. The muscles tightened beneath her fingers; the tension began to flow. "I think you see things, too."

He put his hands over hers, warming them, imprisoning them against him. There was no answering warmth in his voice, only a bleak kind of despair. For a moment he said nothing, looking up at her, and she waited for him to lie to her.

"Yes," he said finally. "I do."

"Damn you," she said, ripping her hands away from him and stumbling backward. "You liar. You hypocritical, sneaking bastard. All this time, mocking me, treating me like a cross between the village idiot and a criminal, all this time you've known exactly what I've been going through."

"Not exactly." He was unmoved by her anger. His long fingers touched the red dress, which still lay spilled out across his lap, and his voice was distracted. "I don't have your gifts. Assuming, of course, that yours are really all you say they are. I just get little snatches of things. Glimpses, not clear views. Phil thought it was just a well-developed case of instincts, but it's a little more than that. Unfortunately."

"And you don't like that," she said. "You don't appreciate your gift at all—you despise it."

"Yes."

"And you take out your frustration on me."

"Yes," he said again, his hands stroking the red dress.

She stood still for a moment, knowing what was going to happen, knowing she'd have to make one last effort to escape. She could see no future for the two of them together. And she was afraid, mortally afraid.

She made it as far as the door. She'd forgotten he could move so fast. One moment he was lying stretched out on his huge bed, covered with the flowing red material, a few seconds later he'd caught her by the front door. Caught her with his large, strong hands, imprisoning her arms. Caught her with his big body, pressing her smaller, frailer one up against the heavy door. Caught her with his mouth on hers, hot and wet and demanding.

She held herself very still, feeling like a trapped butterfly. She didn't want his kisses, didn't want the implicit demand within them. A demand she knew she would answer in another minute. No one had ever kissed her like that. Alan's kisses had been chaste and gentle and wooing. No one had ever taken her and forced a response from her.

She brought her hands up between them to push him away, but once again her fingers touched his bare skin, his smoothly muscled chest, and she was lost. She tipped her head to one side, to give him better access, and let him kiss her.

He lifted his head and stared down at her in the darkness of the hallway, his eyes glittering and strangely savage. "Kiss me back, damn it," he said harshly, setting his mouth back on hers. And she did, opening her mouth to his, sliding her arms up and around his neck, pulling him down to her.

It shouldn't feel this way, she told herself. A simple kiss shouldn't make her feel lost and dizzy and floating. Except that Sam Oliver's kiss was not simple at all; it was complex and hungry and overwhelming, and her shy, untutored attempts to respond only seemed to feed his hunger. And her own.

When he pulled away she was disoriented, dazed, aching. The visions she'd feared hadn't even come close. She'd only had room for the sheer, visceral response of her body against his. And she wanted more. She reached for him, but he was already gone, and it took her a moment to realize that the phone was ringing.

He was standing by the phone in the living room, breathing deeply, as he barked into the receiver. "What is it?" Elizabeth stayed where she was, trying to call back some semblance of sanity, trying to regain her normal heartbeat, her normal breathing patterns. She was glad she wasn't the person on the other end of the phone, on the receiving end of his abrupt fury. Except that if she were, she'd be out of reach, and he wouldn't be able to touch her and make her brains melt.

"You're kidding me!" Sam was saying, his voice only slightly mollified. "When did this happen? I see. What's the official story?" He waited, listening, and his response was brief and colorful. "And they expect people to believe that? Okay, I know. Keep me posted. Yeah, I won't yell at you." His eyes met Elizabeth's for a brief, pregnant moment. "No, I won't be doing anything important."

She felt the relief and disappointment flood through her. Her mouth still throbbed from the pressure of his; her body still shivered with an icy heat everywhere he'd touched her. But that was as far as it was going to go. She wondered why.

Maybe he'd taken pity on her. She doubted it. Sam Oliver didn't have a merciful bone in his body. And he knew she wanted him just as much as he wanted her. The problem was, he knew what to do about it. And all she wanted to do was run and hide.

At least that wasn't necessary. The moment had passed, and he had other things to do. She was safe from his desires. Her desires. For now.

He hung up the phone, reached over and turned on the light, flooding the stark room with brightness. "Have you eaten anything?"

She thought back to the macadamia nuts, the Chinese noodles, the Granny Smith apples. All her questions were answered. He hadn't needed to rummage through her cupboards. He'd already rummaged through her mind. "No," she said.

"I'll make us something," he said. "Or order in pizza. It's going to be a long night."

"Why? What happened?"

He stopped in front of her. "Guess."

She shut her eyes, partially in irritation, partially because she didn't want to look at him. To be tempted by him.

"I'm not playing any more parlor games with you, Sam," she said. "I don't know what happened."

"They found Shari Derringer's body."

He was still surprised that he'd told her the truth. Elizabeth was so caught up in guilt and misery and her own tormented dreams that she probably could have been fobbed off with some likely story. But he'd suddenly gotten sick of lying to her. Sick of lying to himself. He hadn't told anyone about his dreams, his brief, uncomfortable glimpses of the future, in years. Not since Amy Lee, for all the good it had done her. He didn't know why he'd chosen Elizabeth Hardy of all people to confide in. Maybe he felt he owed it to her.

"I don't eat animal flesh," she said with just a trace of haughtiness when he'd pulled the steak out of the refrigerator. He'd put on a shirt, not because the apartment was cool, but because she wouldn't look at him without a shirt on, but he hadn't bothered to button it up. He liked watching her eyes slither away from him, try to concentrate on someplace safe. She wouldn't look him in the eyes; it gave too much away. She clearly didn't want to look at his mouth, and he could understand why. He found her soft, pale mouth completely distracting himself. She didn't want to look at his chest, and below the belt was out of the question. So her gaze tended to concentrate on his nose, or his left ear, or his bare feet.

Sooner or later he'd make her look at him. But for now he wasn't going to push it. "You'll eat red meat," he said calmly, "and like it. You're too skinny, and you're going to need all the strength you can muster over the next few days."

"I've been a vegetarian for the past two years," she said, staring over his left shoulder.

"You've been a neurotic hermit for the past two years, too," he said. "Life has changed, lady. Welcome to the real world. Rare or medium?"

"Neither."

"I refuse to cook a steak well-done in my apartment," he said, shoving it under the broiler.

"I'm not going to eat it. The Chinese noodles will do me just fine."

"You're probably the sort of person who has broccoli on her pizza," he said in total disgust.

"It's delicious."

"That's practically sacrilegious."

"If you happen to worship pizza, maybe."

He found himself grinning, and she began to smile back. As quickly as it had come the smile vanished, leaving her closed back in on herself. But it was a beginning. He had every intention of making her smile more. Maybe even making her laugh. And laughing with her.

She turned away from him, staring at the stainless-steel sink with great concentration. "Are you going to tell me more about your phone call?"

"Over dinner," he said. "While you eat your steak."

He thought he was going to have more of a battle. While he did the cooking she found a card table he never used and set it in the living room, and when he brought the steak in he saw that she'd put sharp knives at both places. He put her plate down, handed her a cold beer without asking and sat down opposite her.

She stared at the rare steak for a long moment, and he controlled his own hunger, waiting. "Do you have ethical problems with killing animals?" he asked.

"No. Animals kill each other for meat."

"Do you hate the taste?"

She shook her head, still hesitating. "It smells delicious. I just haven't been interested in food recently."

"You haven't been interested in life recently." He cut a small piece and held it out to her, across the table. "Come on, Eve, take a bite. It's about time to leave the Garden of Eden."

Her eyes met his finally, and he almost wished they hadn't. There was pain in their deep brown depths, and sorrow, and fear. And, most terrifying of all, there was the faint stirring of hope. Then she leaned over and took the steak with her strong, white teeth.

He turned his attention to his own meal once she began to eat, tipping his bottle of Beck's Dark down his throat. Maybe he was making a very dangerous mistake, dragging her back into the harsh, cruel world. That look in her eyes could very well turn into something even worse. It could turn into love, and then he'd be in a real mess. Despite what he'd told her, he didn't believe in love, not anymore, and he didn't want to. But he suspected that was exactly what Elizabeth Hardy needed. The belief in love, and happy endings. Just the sort of things he couldn't give to her.

Who the hell did he think he was, interfering with her tight little cocoon? He'd never been a knight on a white charger, rushing in to rescue the sleeping beauty. He should let her doze on, her emotions in a coma, and let someone else wake her up.

Except that he couldn't leave her alone. If he did, she'd be dead. So might he, for that matter. Anyone who could take out Phil Grayson, even ten years into his retirement, had to be a formidable opponent indeed.

So the two of them were bound together. And even if he knew he should back off, should keep his hands off her, he knew that within the next forty-eight hours he was going to make love to her. And heaven help them both.

She'd eaten nearly half her steak before she spoke. "Well?" she said. "Are you going to tell me?"

It took him a moment to realize what she was talking about. "Shari Derringer's body was found this afternoon in a quarry in eastern Virginia. She'd been raped, her throat was cut, and she'd been dead for approximately ten days."

Elizabeth put down her fork, and he didn't blame her for losing her appetite. "Mary Nelson disappeared ten days ago."

"So she did. Shari's been positively IDed. She was in pretty rough shape, with her face bashed in, but her father identified the body, and the dental records matched."

Her eyes widened. He wondered briefly where she'd left her wire-rimmed glasses, and if she actually needed them for anything other than a barrier between the cruel world and her own frailties. "Then it must be her."

"Unless the secretary of state and the FBI are lying," he said blandly, continuing to eat.

"Is that possible?"

He shrugged, reaching for his beer. "What do you think?"

"I don't know. I thought you would."

He drained half the bottle, setting it down with a snap. "Distrust our government? The people I've spent more than half my life working for?" he mocked. "How could you think I'd be that cynical?"

"I wonder."

"Funny thing, though. When Shari disappeared she was wearing a white linen suit. It wasn't very white when her body was found, but it was definitely the same outfit." He paused, watching her.

"Go on."

"Are you waiting for the other shoe to drop?" he inquired in a dulcet voice.

"Sam, get on with . . . what?" His words finally sank in, and her eyes widened as she stared at him.

"That's right. She was only wearing one red shoe. And no one could find any trace of the other one."

"Damn," she said unexpectedly, and reached for her untouched beer.

"They're saying she's the victim of a random killer, of course. And that she's been in the quarry for the past ten days. No chance of her taking a little detour by the way of Colorado."

"Maybe the killer could have kept the shoe as a souvenir? I mean, if I'm wrong, maybe it really was a random killer, and he's been crisscrossing the country, committing random murders.''

"All right, we'll consider that scenario. If he happened to have some sort of shoe fetish, why would he leave that shoe behind at the cabin, then? If he collected footwear from his victims you'd think he'd hold on to it, not let it get shoved underneath a deserted cabin.''

"Maybe once he got Mary Nelson's shoe he didn't need Shari's.''

He just stared at her in fascination. "You have a sick mind, do you know that?'' he said finally.

She took another generous slug of her beer. "No, I don't. I just happen to have been witness to a few sick minds. I know the way people can think.''

"Is that the way this killer thinks? Did he just happen to kill Shari Derringer and Mary Nelson? Is he a shoe fetishist?''

She shook her head. "I don't know. I don't think so, but I really don't know.'' She drained the bottle, then stared at it in surprise. "I don't like beer,'' she said.

He tipped back his chair, watching her out of hooded eyes. "Your fall from grace, swami. You've tasted red meat and survived, you enjoyed a beer, you've kissed a man and wanted more. Pretty soon you'll start wanting to put on the red dress, and then who knows how it will end.''

"You know how it will end,'' she said, reaching for her tangled sheaf of hair and attempting to braid it. "So there's no way on earth I'm going to put that dress on. Return it to the store. And the clothes you bought me were too small. I wear a size ten, not eight.''

"You may wear a size ten, but your body is a size eight, or smaller. Take it from a man who knows. Your clothes are too baggy.''

"My clothes are comfortable. Besides, what does it matter to you what I wear?''

A small, wry grin lit his mouth and he swallowed the obvious answer. She was tired; she was reeling from all the unexpected occurrences of the past thirty-six hours. He could only push her so far and so fast. It was time for a decent man to back off. He just wasn't sure how far his decency extended.

"What's going to happen next?" she said, and again he thought about her. About him. About them. He couldn't afford to do that, couldn't afford to let himself be distracted. Their lives were on the line, and if he was busy thinking about getting between her legs and not about who might come knocking at his door, who might be bugging his phone, who might be putting a knife in his back, then he was putting them both at risk.

"I go in to work tomorrow. I find out the details on the official line on the Derringer case, and I see what I can ferret out. I'm good at ferreting things out, and I have friends who trust me. Hard as that may be for you to believe."

"That you have friends or that people trust you?" She'd wrapped a piece of string around the end of her thick chestnut braid, but she still didn't look like the pale schoolmarm he'd first seen in Colorado. "Neither surprises me. Phil was your friend, and Phil trusted you. He wasn't someone who gave his trust or friendship lightly."

"Therefore I'm trustworthy?" he suggested.

She managed a tiny smile. "I didn't say that."

"Or a worthy friend."

"Maybe," she said. "Are you my friend?"

There was a leveler, he thought wryly. He took friendship seriously. In a world where love and God didn't exist, friendship took their place. If he decided he was Elizabeth Hardy's friend it meant he'd be chained to her for life. And that was something he didn't want to risk.

It also meant he couldn't go to bed with her, not if he thought it might hurt her. And, damn it, he knew that it would, sooner or later.

She was waiting for an answer, a simple answer to a simple question. She'd put her life in his hands, and she wanted to know if he was her friend.

He considered saying, "Sure," but he couldn't do it. Couldn't placate her with an easy lie, particularly since she probably wouldn't be placated.

"I'm not your enemy," he said, unable to come up with anything closer to the truth. She was going to run again; those beautiful brown eyes would probably fill with tears, and he'd have to stop her. Have to touch her. Hold her. His body tightened at the thought.

But she didn't run. Didn't cry. This time her eyes met his without shrinking, and she nodded. "I suppose that will have to do. I appreciate your not lying to me."

If he'd felt like a sleaze before, now he felt like the worst sort of monster. And he had no excuse to touch her, none at all. "Where do you want to sleep?" he asked abruptly, as if that hadn't been on his mind all evening. For days, even. "The bed's big enough, and I don't thrash around much. If I did, I never would have survived on your torture chamber of a sofa."

"I think it only fair that I endure your uncomfortable sofa as penance," she murmured.

"You're safe in the bed with me as long as you don't wear a red dress."

"You think so? Only red turns you on?"

God, why did he feel suddenly lighthearted? "Any chance I could convince you of that?"

"Not a snowball's chance in hell."

He wondered what would happen if he touched her. Part of him wanted to find out. At least if he touched her, if he took her to that bed she seemed determined to avoid, he might be able to stop being obsessed by her. He might be able to stop thinking about her when he should be thinking about who killed Mary Nelson and why Shari Derringer's father was willing to have everyone believe his daughter was dead.

That was simply an excuse. He could think of a million reasons to touch her, to stretch her out on that big bed and make love to her until she shattered and all her secrets simply washed away. A million reasons to do it, and one reason not to. He was afraid she might start to matter. And he couldn't let anyone matter.

"You can have the pillows," he said, covering the sudden disturbing thoughts with a lazy yawn. "You think you'll be able to sleep?"

"Yes."

"All right. Just do me one favor."

"What is it?"

He kept his hands on his side of the table, fighting the impulse to touch her. "Don't dream."

"Can I get you anything else, Mr. O'Donnell?" In first class they knew your name, and this 747 just now winging its way over the Atlantic Ocean came equipped with very pretty, very blond flight attendants who probably would have cleaned his shoes with their tongues, they were so eager to please. Muhammed Ali Reza looked up and smiled.

"No thank you. I think I'll just nap." He slid down into his comfortable seat and closed his eyes. He'd never thought he would mind the weather, but he'd been too cold for too long. He was glad to be leaving his little problem behind, much as it galled him to accept assistance. It wasn't as if he couldn't have handled Oliver and the woman. It wasn't as if he didn't want to, with a desire quite unlike his usual sangfroid. That had been a warning signal, one he'd heeded. When something began to matter too much, he pulled back. Sending Kempton in to finish the matter showed that he was above such mundane emotions. Efficiency, that was all that mattered.

He shifted, and the gun dug into his ribs. He would have preferred his knife, but he only used one kind of knife, and it was of cold metal. The gun beneath his armpit was made entirely of plastic, undetectable by airport security. But very deadly, nonetheless.

He had no intention of using it. He simply wanted to get back to the decrepit, supposedly deserted blue house on the

Rio Benedetto and warm up. But there was no way he'd go anywhere without a weapon. Life was too capricious.

No, he'd warm his bones and wait for Kempton's report. And then the Spandau Corporation could finish its work, no matter what silly games the United States government tried to play. And never again would he set foot in a place as cold as Colorado. Even if it meant leaving his recent, enjoyable activities to the Kemptons of this world. Warmth, that was what he needed. Bright Italian sunlight.

"Are you staying long in Venice?" the chirpy stewardess asked, leaning over him. His fault for being too charming. He hoped that the next time one of his confederates blew up a plane she'd be on it.

"Not long," he said, his faintly Irish accent perfect. He was lucky—with his dark looks he could pass for any number of nationalities, but he particularly preferred Irish. It was more of a challenge. "Just a short vacation. I'm meeting my girlfriend."

The wattage of the stewardess's perfect smile dimmed noticeably at the mention of his fictional girlfriend. "I hope she packed warm clothes," the woman said. "It's snowing in Venice."

Chapter 11

When Elizabeth awoke the next morning the apartment was flooded with a murky half-light fighting its way through the miniblinds, and Sam was gone. She woke up stiff and sore and aching, cursing the uncomfortable sofa. She was also bored and edgy and nervous, cursing her house arrest—and famished.

Sam had left a pot of coffee warming, and she offered a silent prayer of thanks as she poured herself a huge mug. She ate cold spicy chinese noodles and leftover steak, then moved on to macadamia nuts and a Granny Smith apple as she wandered through the empty apartment. She was tempted to top it off with an ice-cream bar, but even her newfound appetite had its limits. It was only seven-fifteen in the morning. She'd wait till nine to start on the ice cream.

Whoever had shared Sam's pillows had left some perfumed face cream in his medicine chest. While she didn't want to smell like his previous lover, she was a little tired of smelling like deodorant soap, and she took a long, leisurely shower, then rubbed herself all over with the cream. It was only as she was heading back to the kitchen and her promised ice-cream bar that she realized she'd thought of the perfume woman as a previous lover. Who said she was in the past? Elizabeth chided herself. And who was supposed to be the future?

She told herself that she had no choice but to put on the lacy underwear Sam had bought her. Her own serviceable cotton was dirty, and she had orders not even to attempt finding the laundry room in this anonymous apartment complex. She had no intention of washing her underthings out in the sink and leaving them draped around his bathroom. Besides, there was no way he was going to see the lacy things she was wearing. Was there?

He was right, of course. Size eight fit a lot better than size ten, and even that was a little baggy. He'd tossed the red dress on a chair when he'd gone back to bed, and she carefully avoided it, afraid even to touch it as she pulled on the jeans and cotton sweater Sam had bought her. At least she had to give him credit for more or less following her usual tastes for the rest of her clothes. She lived in jeans and cotton sweaters. These were slightly different. The jeans were stone washed, soft and clinging, even brand-new. And the cotton sweater, instead of one of her preferred neutral colors, was a deep rose color that made her skin look warm and her eyes sparkle. There was no way she could fault him on his choice, but deep down she suspected he'd picked that color on purpose. Just as he'd picked the red dress.

Ice-cream bar in hand, she wandered back into the living room and the complex audiovisual setup that seemed to be the only purchase Sam had made. She'd owned a television in Colorado, a small black-and-white model she'd used to check the weather reports when a storm was due. Savoring the rich, creamy ice-cream bar, she picked up one of the remote controls and aimed it at the television, preparing herself for a long, boring day.

That was before she discovered the music-video channels. She stumbled on them by accident, flicking past news stations and game shows and sitcoms from the 1970s, and paused, enraptured, as the wonders of rock's latest sex symbols paraded in front of her. She cautiously turned the sound up, but clearly Sam's apartment was either sound-proofed or surrounded by working tenants, for no one banged on the wall, ceiling or floor. By eleven o'clock she began to dance, her long veil of hair swinging around her. Never in her life had she danced. Her aunt and uncle had considered music and dancing just more tricks of the devil, and Granny Mellon hadn't been blessed with anything as complicated as electricity. By the time she was on her own and met Alan, she'd learned to beware of men putting their arms around her, and she was too inhibited to dance alone.

Not today. The door was locked, and only Sam had the keys. The windows were tightly sealed, with no chink of light, and if the place was bugged, all they'd hear was loud music and a few artistic thumps.

She ate sausage pizza and beer nuts for lunch, washed down with one of Sam's beers, and went back to dancing for the afternoon. By the time Sam came home she was in love with at least two different singers and longing to look like a third. She was also exhausted, anxious and feeling more alive than she'd ever felt in her entire life.

She was so happy to see him, and to smell the Chinese food he brought with him, that she ignored his bad temper as he slammed in the door once she'd unbarred it and stomped into the kitchen. After dumping the white boxes down on the counter, he stormed out again without a word, this time heading into the bedroom and slamming that door shut behind him. A few minutes later he emerged, dressed this time in jeans and an aging black sweatshirt with a faded orange tiger on the front and the words Princeton University almost obliterated. That was something new, she thought. He didn't strike her as the sort of man who would have gone to Princeton.

"Hi," he said, the first word he'd spoken since he arrived home.

"Bad day?" she inquired, wondering if she should be a proper housewife and make him a drink. She hadn't been a proper housewife at all; she hadn't even bothered to make the bed.

"To put it mildly." He solved the problem by making his own drink. "Do you want one?"

She shook her head. "Anything new?"

"Too much. And too little." His eyes suddenly focused on her, on her flushed face and loose hair. "Why are you wearing those glasses?"

She reached up and touched the wire frames. "Because I need them."

"You didn't need them yesterday," he growled. "Take them off."

"Don't be absurd...." He'd already snatched them off her face, holding them up to his own fierce blue eyes and peering through them.

"These are practically clear glass," he said.

She grabbed for them, but he was much taller, and he held them out of her reach. "Give them to me. I need them."

"Forget it," he said. And without another word he crumpled the fragile wire frames in his big hand, letting the thin glass lenses pop out.

She took a deep breath, wondering how far she'd get if she hit him, which she very much wanted to. Not very far. He was much bigger, stronger, and if she touched him, he'd touch her back. And there would be no end to it, red dress or not.

She took a step backward, calm once more. "Just because you had a lousy day," she said, "doesn't mean you have to come home and torment me."

He dropped the ruined glasses on the counter, and if there was a trace of regret in his usually cool eyes, he didn't let it surface for more than a moment. "Sorry," he said briefly. "How'd you spend your day?"

"Dancing."

He laughed, thinking she was kidding. "Did you watch the news?"

"Absolutely not."

"No wonder you're in such an uncharacteristically cheerful mood," he grumbled, opening one of the boxes of Chinese food and dumping it on a plate.

"I'm usually a lot more cheerful than you are," she replied, taking another box and unearthing egg rolls.

"That's not saying much."

"No, I suppose it isn't. We don't make a very jolly couple, do we?" she said, unwrapping the chopsticks.

"I wasn't aware that we made a couple at all."

Elizabeth could feel her face flame brightly, and she was glad they were in the artificial light of the kitchen. She ducked her head, concentrating on the pork lo mein. "I was speaking in general terms," she said.

"I couldn't find out a damn thing," he said, slamming his plate down on the counter. "They've closed ranks, come up with their neat, nice story, and there's not even a hint of dissension in the whole lot of them."

"Except for you." She hoisted her body up onto the counter and continued eating.

"Are you crazy? I know how to play the game, follow the company line. I acted like I believed the whole rotten cover-up as much as the next guy. That's the only way I'm going to find out what really happened. On top of everything, some turkey from the Bureau is breathing down our necks, my neck in particular."

"The Bureau?"

"FBI. They don't get along too well with Army Intelligence at the best of times, and this isn't the best of times. The particular agent they've sent over has always been an especial nemesis of mine, and he's using this chance to climb all over me."

"Why?"

"They know I was in Colorado. They knew enough to cover up Phil's death, just like they're pulling a fast one on the Derringer case. They want to know what I know."

"Why don't they just ask?"

"Because they know I won't just answer," he replied, setting down his plate and taking another long pull on his Scotch. "Not until I get an idea of what's going on. Not until I have some assurance that we're not expendable, you and I, for the greater good."

"Sam, the U.S. government doesn't sanction killing innocent citizens just for the sake of some bizarre scheme."

He didn't say a word, didn't argue with her, and somehow his silence was even more chilling than any words could have been. "I don't care, I don't believe you," she said stubbornly. "If we're in danger it has to be from some foreign agent infiltrating our government."

"Maybe," he conceded, pouring out the rest of his drink and rinsing the glass. "Frankly, I think that scenario is even more farfetched, but the only way we can survive is to consider every possibility."

"Maybe your FBI nemesis is a foreign agent," she suggested, trying to lighten the situation.

He managed a brief smile. "I should be so lucky. Life doesn't tend to be that convenient. The bad guys too often turn out to be your best friends. And the so-called good guys are the creeps." He moved across the kitchen, and before she realized what he intended he'd taken her half-empty plate of lo mein from her hands and set it out of reach. She considered fighting him off with the chopsticks, but set them down docilely enough, waiting expectantly.

"Do me a favor," he said, standing in front of her. "Touch me."

She scuttled back on the counter nervously. "What?"

"Put your hands on me, Elizabeth," he said. "And close your eyes. Think about Shari Derringer."

"Why?"

"I want to know if that really is her body that everyone's identified beyond a shadow of a doubt."

"What makes you think I can just summon up an answer?" she hedged.

He took her hands and placed them on his strong, tight shoulders. "You know the answer to that as well as I do. Your visions increase when you touch me. Let's see if we can make them work *for* you, instead of against you. Think about Shari Derringer."

She wanted to pull away, but she did no such thing. She could feel his hips against her knees, and she obligingly spread her legs around him to allow him closer. She'd tried to summon up answers before and never had any success. But she'd never had someone to help her, someone beside her, someone to take the frightening energy that flowed between them and put it to use.

She closed her eyes, letting her hands rest on his shoulders, emptying her mind of everything but Shari Derringer. She'd seen pictures of her, in gossip magazines when she'd been to the dentist, occasionally on the news when she'd been waiting for a weather report. She tried to summon up that blond, perfect face, but all that came was Mary Nelson.

And then the cold came, sliding into her bones like tiny icicles, turning her blood to slush. She began to tremble as the smell of fear and death surrounded her. She tightened her hands instinctively, holding on to Sam as if he were the only solid, safe thing in a world that was adrift with madness, and let the layer of ice come, coating her body, glazing her eyes, encasing her in a cold sheet of icy rime. She was shaking so hard she couldn't understand why the ice didn't shatter and break, but it was too thick, too encasing. She couldn't look at Sam, couldn't open her eyes, but she found herself wondering if the ice had spread to him, covering and immobilizing him. Whether they'd be found, blue and frozen, years from now, locked together in an icy embrace.

"Shari Derringer." His voice came from a long distance, and she wanted to shake her head, shake away that nagging, insistent name. It would be wasting her time; she knew it. She was at the mercy of forces stronger than her cowardice—forces from within, her tormenting inner voices; forces from without, from the insistent man with his hands covering hers, holding them in place on his wiry shoulders. Having no other choice, she concentrated on seeing Shari Derringer's dead face, and for a moment it came clearly into focus, those beautiful, flat-blue eyes laughing, that perfect pink mouth curved in a smile, that long, glorious blond hair rippling down her naked back as she grinned her smug pleasure at her unseen voyeur.

And then her face began to alter, to pale, to melt. The blue eyes grew grayer in color, filling with fear. The nose changed slightly; the mouth opened in a silent scream of death. It was Mary Nelson, an innocent housewife from Golden, Colorado. Mary Nelson who lay dead, identified by a lying father and a lying group of authorities, by dental records belonging to another woman. Mary Nelson who wore Shari Derringer's filthy white suit and one red shoe.

She felt his hands release hers, dropping down to her arms to support her. She felt limp, weak, and she collapsed against him, too drained to hesitate. His arms came around her, and she was scooped up with surprising gentleness and carried through the darkened apartment.

She didn't want him to leave her, but she was too shaken to cling, as she wanted to, when he set her down on the middle of the huge bed. She lay very still, her arms at her sides, her eyes open, trying to focus on the white-painted ceiling, the shadows from the bathroom flitting back and forth. She tried to think of rock videos and solitary dancing, but all she could see was Mary Nelson.

She felt the bed sag, but she didn't turn to look. A cool, damp cloth covered her eyes, but they couldn't shut out Mary Nelson's terror. She lay without moving, absorbing the cool dampness on her face, the weight of a body on the bed beside her. She lay waiting.

She lost track of time. It could have been minutes later, or it could have been hours, when she sat up, letting the washcloth drop onto the unmade bed. Sam was sitting cross-legged among the tangled sheets, his dark blue eyes shadowed and intent and very patient. She wouldn't have thought patience would be one of his qualities, but she found he could be limitlessly still.

But even his patience had an end. "What?" he said, reaching for her hand.

"No," she said, scuttling out of his reach. "Don't touch me. Not for a moment. Please." Her skin felt hot and prickly; the thought of another human touching her, the thought of Sam touching her, was unbearable.

He moved back, away from her, out of reach. Beyond temptation, she thought vaguely, wondering why he'd be tempted to touch her. She knew what she looked like. Visions that strong were few and far between, and when they finally left her she looked and felt like a drowned rat, a helpless piece of flotsam washed up on a polluted beach. She wanted to turn over, to burrow back into the covers and hide from the vision, from Sam, from her own damnable gifts.

Slowly her breathing returned to normal. Slowly the prickling, icy terror left her skin; the leaden, heavy weight began to lift. She raised her eyes to look at Sam, and she was startled to see his concern, his own dark anger directed far from her.

"It's Mary Nelson, isn't it?" he asked, his voice rough and low. "Not Shari Derringer lying on a slab in the top-security morgue in Langley."

She nodded, the effort paining her. "Did you see it, too?"

"Not really. Not clearly. Just glimpses. More than I usually see, however. Whatever happens between us increases my own...abilities. The question is, where's Shari Derringer? What happened to her?"

"She's somewhere safe, laughing," Elizabeth said, lying back again, the lukewarm washcloth clutched tightly in her hand. "Waiting."

"Waiting for what?"

"I don't know. I don't think I want to know."

Sam slid across the bed, turning on the bedside light and flooding the room with a harsh glare that hurt her eyes. "You don't have any choice in the matter," he said. "Nor do I. Whether we like it or not we're involved, and our only weapon is knowledge. We can't tell the good guys from the bad guys, Elizabeth. And the only scorecard we have is you."

"Isn't there anyone we can trust?"

"A few people. People I've worked with for years, people like Phil. I'll have to be careful in my questions, though. I don't know why they're lying, or what they hope to gain, but two people aren't going to be much good going up against the concerted efforts of the FBI, Army Intelligence and the State Department. We're going to have to be very, very careful."

"Why would he lie?" she murmured, half to herself.

"Who?"

"Her father. MacDonald Derringer. Why would he lie about his own daughter's death? And what about her mother? What has he told her?"

"They're divorced. A rather messy case, as I remember. He's probably enjoying making her miserable."

"But what about when she shows up? What are they going to say then?"

"Beats me," Sam said, lying back against the pillows. "I imagine that little Miss Derringer is involved in something so nasty that Daddy Dearest will do anything to keep it under cover."

"Why would you think that? I know with your rampant cynicism you'd be bound to believe the worst, but who's to say that she isn't a hostage? Terrified for her life, kept in a closet like Patty Hearst ... ?"

"It's not my rampant cynicism. It's just a sense I have, that other people have had for the past few years, that Shari Derringer has made some interesting friends and acquired some bad habits. Besides, you saw her laughing."

Elizabeth shivered for a moment, the memory of Shari Derringer's girlish glee unnerving. "I may have been seeing her from another time," she said, trying to be fair. "She may not even know about Mary Nelson. She may just have disappeared with a not-too-savory lover, and everyone's jumped to the wrong conclusion."

"Do you believe that?"

"Not for a moment," she admitted. "I just hope I'm wrong."

"Hope away. In the meantime, we'd better lie low. I'm not going in tomorrow. I'm going to check in with a few old friends who know who to lie to. Besides, I want to keep away from the chief spook."

"Spook?" Elizabeth echoed, yawning.

"Slang for agent," he clarified. "My nemesis. A harmless idiot named Kempton. If I can just keep out of his way I'll be a lot happier."

"At least he's harmless," Elizabeth murmured, wondering if she dared close her eyes. "It's the nonharmless variety we have to worry about."

"I'm counting on you to warn me."

Her eyes flew open. "Don't count on me for anything. I've told you, I can't program what I see. I had no idea anything was going to happen to Phil until I . . ."

"Until you what?"

"Until I put on your gloves," she admitted reluctantly.

She couldn't read the expression on his face. She wasn't sure she wanted to. "You see," he said, his voice neutral. "Something happens between us."

"I don't want it to."

"Tough. We're not in a position to worry about niceties," he growled. "Close your eyes and go to sleep. You look like death warmed over."

"What a horrible thing to say!" She shivered at the thought.

"I'm a horrible guy sometimes, haven't I warned you? I've got a few phone calls to make." He slid off the bed, not touching her.

"I can't sleep here," she said, not sure she even had the energy to stand. She not only looked like hell, she felt like it, too.

"Sure you can. My couch is a hell of a lot more comfortable than yours."

"It couldn't be," she said flatly.

"Bad night?" His voice held no sympathy. "You could have spent it in here."

She ignored the suggestion. "Wake me up when you're ready to go to bed and I'll move to the couch," she said, closing her eyes against the bright glare of what was actually a low-wattage light bulb. She could barely manage to say another word.

"Sure thing," he said, but she knew he wouldn't.

"You don't call me swami anymore," she said sleepily, snuggling her face into the pillow.

"Sorry. You're having a mellowing effect on me. Good night, Elizabeth."

There was no answer. She was already sound asleep.

Chapter 12

When Elizabeth woke up she had no idea what time it was. Despite Sam's arrogant assertion, she really did need her glasses, at least occasionally, and the dull red glow from the digital clock beside her refused to coalesce into numbers. She could always move closer and peer at it, but she wasn't ready to do that. She wasn't ready to move at all.

It was probably sometime after midnight but well before dawn. She had the washed-out, weary feeling she always had after one of her sessions, yet this time she felt oddly different. Probably because her visions had been different, she thought, staring up at the ceiling, moving nothing but her eyelids. Usually these things moved slowly, building in intensity. That brief, horrible glimpse into another world had been the psychic equivalent of a quickie. Fast and hard and emotionally devastating, all in an abnormally short period of time.

She shouldn't have woken up at all. She should have slept for hours, days even, recouping her strength. And yet her strength already seemed to be flowing back, her strength and her interest in life. A few hours ago she'd looked and felt like a corpse. Now life and blood were stirring in her, coursing through her, and she found herself wondering if Sam had left any Chinese food behind. If he'd drunk all the dark beer. If the red dress was still draped across the chair at the foot of the bed, and if it would fit her as well as the lace underwear Sam had bought her.

It took her sleep-muddled brain a moment to realize she was still wearing that underwear. The pale peach bikini panties and lace-trimmed bra that subtly enhanced her meager curves. She was wearing the fancy underwear and nothing else.

And she wasn't alone. That deep, steady humming noise in the back of her brain wasn't a furnace, wasn't the cosmos humming along. It was the steady, quiet breathing of the man who was asleep beside her. The man who'd managed to strip off most of her clothes without waking her up and then covered her with her grandmother's baby quilt.

She turned her head slowly to look at him. His eyes were closed, his breathing deep and even. At least he wasn't naked. He was wearing a white T-shirt and a pair of navy-blue jockey shorts, and she'd managed to hog all the sheet, leaving him exposed in the warm apartment air. She lay there staring at him, curiosity and a certain lassitude keeping her from moving.

She'd known his legs were long, but she hadn't realized how long. They were covered with a light dusting of dark hair, and his bare feet were long and narrow. She let her eyes skim past the jockey shorts, determined to be matter-of-fact in her perusal. She'd never had the chance to simply observe a man's body before, and in her current state she found it fascinating. The baggy white T-shirt had ridden up, exposing his flat stomach, and she realized he had hair there, too, riding down his abdomen and disappearing in the low-slung briefs. He didn't have much hair on his chest—she already knew that—and while she told herself she hadn't really noticed, she decided she was glad about it. She liked the smooth, muscled skin of his chest. But she also liked the hair on his stomach and legs. She even liked his feet.

Never in her life had she slept with a man, not even platonically. Alan had understood her fears, her misgivings, and he'd been gentle, deferential, counting on her to let him know what she could or couldn't take.

There wasn't a deferential bone in her current companion's beautiful body. He wasn't going to be gentle, wasn't going to wait until she was ready and able to withstand the psychic assaults physical intimacy forced on her. When he decided it was time he was going to take her. And she, poor, lovesick fool that she was, would go willingly.

God, she was spacey, she thought. To have even entertained the notion that she was lovesick was a clear sign that she was bordering on lunacy. That session in the kitchen must have affected her more strongly than she'd thought. Love had no place in their relationship. Love had no place in her life at all. And it didn't look as if it belonged in his, either.

She wondered if the hair on his stomach would be soft or scratchy. A stupid question, but she couldn't get it out of her mind. She wondered whether, if she touched him, the visions would come flooding back. Would Mary Nelson's face float before her, reproachful and lost? Or, even worse, would Shari Derringer laugh at her?

She rolled onto her side, but he didn't stir. His eyelids didn't quiver; his breathing didn't alter. She watched him, coming to the uncomfortable, inescapable conclusion that he was better looking than both of her new rock star loves. Combined.

She let her hand slither across the mattress toward him. And then, before she could chicken out, she touched his flat stomach, gently.

The hair was downy soft. The skin beneath it was hard and warm. No bloody visions swept through her head; no erotic visions teased her. It was just skin, and muscle, and hair, and . . .

And a hand clasped tight around her wrist with the speed of a striking snake. She looked up guiltily into his dark eyes. "You're awake, then," she said, feeling like a fool. Her sensitive fingers were still pressed against his stomach, and the grip around her wrist was neither punishing nor painful. It was, however, inescapable.

Her hand was too close to the edge of those navy-blue briefs. All she had to do was stretch her fingers and she'd touch them. All he had to do was exert the smallest amount of pressure. She couldn't move, wouldn't move. But she found herself perversely hoping that *he* would.

"There's a line in an old blues song," he said, his voice a husky rasp in the darkness. "If you don't want my peaches, honey, don't shake my tree." And he released her, waiting.

She pulled her hand away as if burned, unable to miss noticing that what lay beneath the navy-blue briefs had grown. She'd done that, and the thought both fascinated and terrified her.

Sam made a frustrated sound in the back of his throat and rolled over on his stomach. "Go back to sleep," he growled.

She didn't move. She didn't want to sleep. She wanted to move across the seemingly vast expanse of bed between them and put her arms around him. She wanted to press her face against his broad, strong back; she wanted his strong body pressing down on her, blocking out the terrifying world. She wanted comfort and oblivion. But he wanted too much in return. And not enough.

She pulled the striped sheet up to her chin. She should offer to share it with him, but she wasn't going to say a word. She wasn't going to touch him, and she certainly wasn't going to share her covers with him. She should get off the bed and go sleep in the living room, but she knew she wasn't going to do that, either. He might be waiting for her to make the first move, but he'd have to wait for an eternity. And she knew Sam well enough to know that his patience had definite limits. If he wanted her, he'd have to come to her. He couldn't force her to come to him.

She didn't want to dream, so of course she did. Not about the two interchangeable blond women, thank heavens. Not about blood and death. She dreamed about sex. She dreamed about Sam's hands on her skin; she dreamed about flushed responses and burning needs that threatened to suffuse her entire body. She dreamed about his long, hairy legs entwined with hers; she dreamed about his flat stomach pressed against her. She dreamed about desire spinning out of control, and she awoke with a convulsion and a cry, to find she was alone in the bed, damp and shaking.

It was after ten in the morning. Sam was gone, and this time he hadn't left her any coffee. This time she didn't turn on the television—even the video channels had occasional news reports, and she didn't want to listen to a pack of lies while they ran Shari Derringer's smiling face across the twenty-five-inch screen.

She made her own coffee, ate cold spareribs and egg rolls, and wandered around the apartment, missing him. Trying to remind herself that she was mad at him.

The phone rang several times, but she obeyed orders and didn't go anywhere near it. She hoped Sam remembered that he'd told her not to touch it. She hoped he realized it would be impossible to get in touch with her. What would happen if he was in an accident? She'd heard stories of faithful dogs starving to death while their beloved master floated in a coma. She was already getting a little tired of obeying Sam's autocratic orders. If he didn't come back tonight she was out of there.

She didn't even bother trying to braid her hair; she just let it hang in a tangled mane down her back. The first thing she was going to do when this mess was resolved was get it all cut off. She felt like a butterfly, emerging from her cocoon, and she wanted to shed both the weight of her hair and the weight of her guilt as she emerged in the light. She also seemed to be more than mildly interested in shedding the weight of her outmoded virginity, but at least a small por-

tion of self-preservation had remained so far. She wondered when that, too, would disappear.

It was midafternoon when she heard the knock on the
door. She'd succumbed to the television, taking refuge in
soap operas, and the peremptory knocking on the door
made her jump. She was halfway there, ready to unfasten
the chains, when she realized that hadn't been Sam's prear-
ranged knock. Someone else was outside the apartment
door.

She stopped where she was, immobilized. Unfortunately
she'd turned the television up too loud—whoever was out
there wouldn't believe the apartment was deserted.

The knock came again, sharp and insistent. She tried to
remember the downstairs security arrangements when they'd
arrived a century and a half ago. If she remembered correctly they'd been reassuringly stringent. Whoever had gotten as far as Sam's seventh-floor apartment was either very
determined or very lucky. Neither alternative was reassur-
ing.

"Miss Hardy?" a voice called through the thick wood-
and-metal door. It was a smooth voice, with a faintly
Southern accent, and Elizabeth told herself it was no one to
fear. No one knew she was there unless Sam had told them.
Therefore, whoever was out there must be someone she
could trust.

She still didn't say anything. Self-preservation had become a strongly ingrained habit, and she waited, waited for
more reassurance from the man on the other side of the
door. "Miss Hardy," he said. "Elizabeth. I need to talk to
Sam. I know he's not there right now, but he said he'd meet
me here at three. He said you'd let me in."

She still didn't say anything. Sam had told her to let no
one in—he wouldn't have sent someone there to meet him.

Of course, he hadn't been getting much sleep, either.
Maybe he'd had no choice but to make this arrangement,
and maybe he'd tried to call her and warn her, and of course

she hadn't answered the phone. Just as she hadn't answered the door.

"Look, Elizabeth," the man said. "I couldn't have gotten this far if it wasn't okay. I just need to get in there to wait for Sam. It's dangerous for me in the hallway. He told me to tell you it was okay. For Phil's sake."

Phil's name, Phil's memory, was like a punch in the stomach. Sam would have known it would affect her this way—he couldn't have chosen a better password. She moved toward the door on leaden feet, guilt and sorrow overwhelming her.

She still had enough common sense to keep the chain on the door when she opened it. The man on the other side was short, round and balding, with a faint resemblance to Truman Capote. No one who looked like Truman Capote could possibly be dangerous, but Elizabeth decided she still had to be careful.

"Who are you?" she asked.

"One of Sam's co-workers," he said. "He's decided to trust me, much as he hates to. Here's my ID." He handed a wallet through the door, open to his official identification, complete with photo. The spook, Elizabeth thought. FBI incarnate. She'd hoped she would go through her life without ever having to meet an FBI agent, but life had changed.

She handed the wallet back. "All right, Mr. Kempton," she said. "I believe you're who you say you are. I still don't want to let you in. Why don't you go out and wait in your car? It's almost three anyway. You can see when Sam arrives."

"Lady!" The man's voice lost any claim to Southern charm, and he sounded faintly, normally exasperated. "If you think Sam is going to waltz in the front door you're out of your mind. There are people watching this place. I didn't come in the front door, either, and I sure as hell am not going to go back out and provide target practice for a bunch of crazies. Let me in, damn it, or my blood will be on your hands."

She'd had Phil's blood on her hands. Literally. She was suddenly very, very cold, and she told herself it was the guilt. Before she could think again she slid the bolt back and opened the door.

There was a faint film of sweat on his lined forehead, and he seemed genuinely relieved that she'd let him in. He let his small, observant eyes seep over her, but there was no undue curiosity in his gaze. "Miss Hardy," he said, "you are one tough customer. Got any coffee?"

She wouldn't have thought an FBI agent would be so unprepossessing. He was shorter than she was, and a good deal rounder, and his pale pink hands looked soft and useless. Maybe looks were deceiving. "I suppose so," she said, trying to muster a certain amount of graciousness, unable to rid herself of a nagging worry. Sam had told her not to let anyone in, and she'd gone and done it. And not just anyone. He'd told her that he hated having Kempton breathe down his neck. Now the man had encroached on his home territory, and Elizabeth could only hope he wasn't lying. And that letting him in hadn't been the worst mistake of her life.

Despite Sam's doubts, she knew her government couldn't sanction innocent people being threatened, coerced, hurt, much less murdered. If Agent Kempton was lying, the worst he could be doing would be trying to ferret out information from her. And there simply wasn't that much she could tell anyone, apart from her dreams.

She made him instant coffee, taking the last cup of the real stuff for herself. She could see him through the kitchen doorway, wandering around the living room, not touching, not sitting, just taking everything in. She watched him, knowing she had no doubt at all that he was who he said he was. Knowing that, she was frightened anyway.

"Thanks," he said, accepting the coffee with a shy smile. "You like Washington better than Colorado?"

She kept her face bland. "I don't know. I haven't seen much besides the airport and this apartment." She didn't volunteer the information that she'd lived here before Alan died. If Kempton was as efficient as he should be, he'd already know that.

Apparently he didn't. "It's a great little town," he said. "If you can stomach the politics." He took a sip of the coffee and beamed at her. "Just the way I like it. How'd you guess?"

Stupid, stupid, stupid, Elizabeth berated herself. She smiled into the little man's beady eyes, distrusting him, suddenly frightened of him. "I'm psychic," she said, and he laughed.

"Have you known Sam long?" he inquired in the most casual of voices, wandering away from her to look out the window. She almost warned him not to touch the blinds, but something kept her silent. She watched as he poked through the narrow shades. Watched as he did it three times in quick succession.

She shivered. "The heat in these new buildings is rotten, isn't it?" she said, hoping he'd agree, hoping her sudden chill was the fault of the heating system.

He turned and looked at her in surprise. "I think it's rather warm," he said, setting his half-drunk coffee down on the glass-topped coffee table.

She was going to have to touch him. She knew that, and still she balked. There was no way she was going to know if she was trapped in Sam Oliver's apartment with a killer if she didn't touch him, and there was no way she could bring herself to do it.

It wouldn't matter. If he was a killer she wouldn't be able to escape. The door was once again triple locked—by the time she got the chains and locks unfastened he would have finished her. She might as well pretend nothing was wrong and let him do it when she wasn't expecting it.

Except that she couldn't do that, either. A few months ago she could have accepted her death with equanimity. Not anymore. Like it or not, she'd come alive in the past few days. She couldn't give that up without a fight.

"More coffee?" she inquired, draining hers.

"This is fine," Kempton said. "Why don't you have a seat? I wanted to ask you a few questions."

"I'd rather wait until Sam comes home."

His friendly smile faded slightly. "Suit yourself," he said, putting his hand in his pocket as he sank down on the uncomfortable sofa. She knew what was in that pocket. Not the knife that had brutalized Phil, that had murdered Mary Nelson and the others. It was a gun, with a silencer. And he was biding his time.

She was crazy. "I'm going to have some more coffee," she said, walking very carefully back toward the kitchen, all the time acutely aware of what a perfect target her narrow back would make. The soap operas were noisy; the remote control was near his small, plump hands. All he had to do was turn back to the video channel, turn up the volume and shoot. No one would ever hear a thing.

When she reached the kitchen, out of his sight, she put her hands on the counter and took a deep, shaking breath. She must be crazy! He was harmless; she was imagining all sorts of ridiculous bloody scenarios. He wasn't going to hurt her; he just wanted to pump her for information, and she'd been fool enough to let him in and give him that chance. He could even take her in for questioning, or put her in protective custody, she supposed. At least, she didn't know enough to stop him if he decided to do just that.

She had to touch him. She'd turned to head back to the living room to do just that, when she heard the sounds of rock coming in place of "The Days of Loving." And he'd turned up the volume.

She had very little time. Sam existed on convenience food and takeout pizza—she'd already discovered that he didn't have a decent knife in the entire place. He'd left his gun for her, but it was in the bedroom, out of reach. Once she stepped out of the kitchen she was going to be in deep trouble.

Except that she wasn't safe in the kitchen. She could feel his approach, even if she couldn't see him. He'd gotten tired of waiting for her; he was coming after her.

The cast-iron frying pan was still sitting on the stove. She moved swiftly, without thinking, picking it up and swinging it in an arc as Kempton stepped through the kitchen door.

He went down in a limp heap, blocking the doorway. Her sweating, trembling hands still clutched the heavy frying pan, and she could still feel the sickening impact as she'd crashed it against his head.

What if she was wrong? What if he'd come to say he'd like another cup of coffee after all? What if she'd killed an innocent man?

She could hear someone singing in the background, and she almost laughed hysterically. She fought back the urge, moving closer to the unmoving body blocking the kitchen door. She touched him with one shaking hand, but he didn't move. The sense of evil was wrapped thickly around both of them, like toxic gas, but she didn't know whether it was her own evil, from killing an innocent man. Shifting the heavy frying pan into her right hand, she started to turn the poor man over.

He moved swiftly, shifting around and aiming the gun directly at her throat as his eyes blazed with madness and fury. It was already too late. Without thinking she'd swung the frying pan again, and the gun went skittering across the floor as he crumpled beneath its lethal force.

She hadn't expected there to be blood, she thought, standing there, the frying pan held limply in her hand. She let it drop, knowing without question that she'd have no more need for it. Stepping over the dead body, she stumbled down the hallway and into the bathroom. There, collapsing on the floor, she began to vomit.

She'd lost track of time when she heard Sam at the door. She couldn't get up and let him in. To do so would mean passing the body in the hallway, and that was one thing she couldn't do. She'd wait in the bathroom until hell froze over before she went anywhere near what was left of FBI agent Kempton.

She could hear Sam calling her name through the opening allowed by the chain. She should answer, and she tried, but her voice only came out in a weak croak. She tried to rise, bracing herself on the toilet seat, but her body collapsed beneath her, and she leaned back against the wall, panting. He'd have to find some other way to get in.

She heard the splintering of the wood with vague satisfaction. He must have ripped the latch out of the door frame. He was calling her name, and there was a satisfying desperation in his voice, one that almost sounded like love. She tried to answer, but he was making so much noise that he couldn't hear her. And then all was silent.

He must have found Kempton, she thought distantly. Maybe now he could hear her....

She managed a small croak of sound, but it was enough. Sam filled the bathroom door, looking huge and terrible as he stared down at her. "Are you all right?" he demanded. "Did he hurt you?"

"No," she whispered. "Yes. I mean, I'm all right. I'm just . . . a little shaky."

He closed the bathroom door behind him, shutting out the smell and feel of death, and moved toward her. "Who killed him?"

She needed him to touch her, to hold her, but she didn't know how to ask. And then she found she didn't have to because he pulled her up from her cramped position on the tile floor and into his arms, holding her tight.

"I killed him," she said, her face pressed against the rough texture of his scratchy cool jacket.

His hands were soothing, comforting and everything she ever needed. "Good," he said. And for the first time the horror and pain began to recede.

Chapter 13

Sam was efficient—frighteningly, blessedly efficient. He left her in the bathroom long enough to close the door from the bedroom into the hall, hiding the ugly sight of Kempton's blood-soaked body, before returning, scooping her up and carrying her to the wide, soft bed. He set her down carefully, one hand still touching her, as he reached for the telephone, punching one of the preset buttons.

She hadn't expected to get comfort from his touch. For the past week she'd shied away from his nearness, simultaneously drawn and repelled by the effect he had on her. She had grown accustomed to the spiraling tendrils of desire, something she'd never experienced before, when he touched her. She'd also grown to accept the sudden, shocking flashes of blood and death and danger, clearer, more disturbing, than ever before. But she wouldn't have thought just the slight pressure of his arm against hers would send warmth and serenity flowing through her, pushing away the horror and death.

"It's me," he said into the phone, his voice deep and abrupt. "Yeah, I know. I've got a package for you to dispose of." He waited a moment, and whoever was on the end spoke too softly for Elizabeth to hear. "No bullets. Head trauma. Lots of blood. Maybe an hour...?" He cast a questioning look at Elizabeth, who nodded, feeling queasy again. "Been dead an hour. No, not me, man. A friend."

A friend, Elizabeth thought. He hadn't been able to call himself that last night. But he was her friend today, her savior, and she trusted him to rescue her from this horrible mess. She didn't know for sure how it had happened, how she'd gotten from her safe little house in the Colorado woods to a blood-soaked apartment in Washington. And she didn't know how she'd escape. She only knew that Sam, her friend, would take care of it.

"We'll be out of here by then," Sam said, no longer looking at her. "See if you can manage a fire to destroy evidence. No, I'm not telling you how to do your job. Just trying to be helpful. Oh, and Danny...it's someone we know. Kempton."

He hung up the phone, sitting there for a moment, unmoving. His eyes drifted back to hers, and they were dark with concern. "Are you okay?"

"I suppose so."

"We're getting out of here. You just stay put—I'll pack."

"Where are we going?" She didn't really care; she just felt she should make an effort not to be so passive.

"Leave that to me. Someplace where the Kemptons of this world can't find us. That bastard. I had no idea he'd turned. No, scratch that. My instincts told me he had. I just didn't have anything concrete to go on. You sure he didn't hurt you?"

"He didn't touch me." She watched as he threw clothes in a suitcase. She almost said something when he threw the telltale splash of red in among the khaki and cotton, then thought better of it. She'd thought the dress was the color of blood. Now she knew better. Blood was dark red, thick

and viscous, evil in its slow, seeping power. The dress was
flame-red, life at its most intense. If she ever got out of this
mess she'd wear nothing but bright red.

"Ready?" he asked, and she wanted to shake her head,
to scuttle away, to hide. She had no choice. She was going
to have to pass the kitchen door, with its ugly mess sprawled
into the hallway. She'd have to step over him to escape. It
was the only reason she'd still been holed up in the bathroom. If she'd had any other route to the outside she would
have been gone into the night, and there would be no one to
help her.

"Ready," she said, shivering slightly.

He picked up the heavy suitcase in one hand, then reached
down and scooped her into his arms with the other. "Hide
your face," he said, and she did, burying herself against his
strong shoulder as he carried her through the apartment.

She told herself that she couldn't smell anything. She told
herself that he wasn't really there, that if she buried her head
against Sam's strong shoulder and concentrated, she could
push Kempton's bloody fate out of existence. Of course,
he'd met that bloody fate at her hands. She trembled
slightly, and Sam's arms tightened around her briefly,
comfortingly. And Sam Oliver wasn't a man for comfort.

She felt him close the door behind them, and he set her
down carefully on the hall rug. She hadn't seen the corridor since he'd first brought her there, days ago, and she was
vaguely shocked at the bland normalcy of the place. In the
distance she could see a couple leaving, and for a moment
she tensed.

"I know them, it's all right," Sam muttered, only a thread
of sound issuing from his mouth. Looking down at her, he
brushed the hair from her face. "You look a little the worse
for wear," he said wryly.

She didn't want to look down. She was certain there was
blood on her clothes, and if she saw it she knew she'd start
screaming. No, he wouldn't let her leave with bloody
clothes. Looking down, she realized she simply looked

rumpled; the khaki pants and peach-colored sweater looked slept in. "Sorry," she said. "I've never been one for high fashion."

"You look fine," he said, suddenly soothing. "You just look like we spent a busy hour in bed before leaving."

That stung her. She could feel an unaccustomed heat flood her face, and she would have glared at him if she'd had the energy. She did manage a mild retort. "You mean if we'd spent an hour in bed I'd have tear marks on my face?"

He leaned closer, and his hand reached out to stroke her skin, sliding down the V-neck of her cotton sweater, and his voice was sinuous. "Darling," he murmured, "there are all sorts of reasons to cry, good and bad."

The warmth from her face spread to her body. She could imagine it, see it, lying beneath him, wrapped around him, her face streaked with tears as she felt a pleasure so intense it bordered on pain. She stumbled back from him, shocked at herself for entertaining such a vision so soon after she'd killed a man, shocked at him for deliberately inspiring it.

He grinned at her then, unrepentant. "That's better," he said. "Life's a better thing to think about, anytime. He was a murderer, and he would have killed you without compunction, and then he would have waited and killed me."

"Would he have?" She shook her head. "I can't imagine he'd take you off guard."

"It's nice to know you have such faith in my abilities. Normally he wouldn't be able to. But in this case I imagine he would have draped your body artistically in front of the door, counting on my reaction to overwhelm me long enough for him to get me."

"And would it have?"

"I've seen a lot of people die, Elizabeth. A lot of people I cared about. And I'm still alive."

"So if you'd seen my dead body you would have been wary first, sorrowful later."

"This is a morbid discussion."

"Hey, it's been a morbid afternoon," she snapped back. "You want the truth?"

"Always," she said, not sure if she really did.

"If I'd walked in the door and seen you—and believe me, he wouldn't have killed you nicely—I probably would have lost it. For one crucial moment I wouldn't have been able to do anything, and he would have killed me. Ten years ago I could have taken it in stride. Right now I've seen too many deaths, too many bodies, too many friends taken out. I'm not going to let it happen to you. And neither are you. Whether you can admit it or not, you want to live. You don't want some crazed terrorist slitting your throat. You want to live."

She looked up at him in silence. The long hallway was deserted now, the contents of the apartment forgotten. He was absolutely right: she did want to live again, and that knowledge was almost as hard to take as the memory of what she'd done. She felt a sudden, shocking impulse, one she knew she would never indulge. And then she did, reaching up and kissing him, hard, on the mouth.

She was moving down the hallway before he could reach for her, and by the time he caught up with her, she was standing by the elevator, a bland expression on her face. He took her arm as they stepped into the elevator, a casual gesture that covered its own protectiveness. He punched the first-floor button, and she looked at him in surprise.

"We're going out the front door?" she questioned.

"Yes."

"Won't someone see us? Follow us?"

"Yes," he said again. "I'm hoping everyone will see us and follow us, the good guys and the bad guys. As if we even knew who was who."

"I suppose it would be naive of me to ask why?"

"I don't want anyone around to watch when Danny gets rid of Kempton. I'd rather they were busy trying to see where we're going and leave the path clear for the dirty work."

"And what if they catch us?"

"They won't." The words were simply spoken, and she believed him.

The elevator descended smoothly, the doors swooshed open and Sam handed her a pair of dark glasses. "Better wear these," he said.

"I thought you said it didn't matter that I'd been crying."

"It doesn't. But your eyes look terrified. Anyone who took a good look at you would know you were under extreme pressure. I don't want to get picked up for kidnapping, wife beating or something equally bizarre. Put the glasses on, keep your eyes on me and smile, damn it."

She bared her teeth in a semblance of a grin. "Lovely evening," she said in a deliberately artificial voice.

"Peachy," Sam growled, leading her off the elevator toward the revolving door. "My car is only a little ways down. Unless someone's towed it, of course. Then we're up a very nasty creek without a paddle."

"You parked in front? In a no-parking zone?" she demanded, aghast.

"Smile," he reminded her, his own cheerful expression a travesty. "I was in a hurry."

"Why?"

"I knew you were in trouble."

"How?"

"Don't ask me, swami. Consult your crystal ball."

They were just the words she needed to hear. Her shoulders went back, her head went up and righteous indignation filled her even as she realized he'd done it on purpose. The words had done what he'd wanted them to. She was too angry to worry about all the observant eyes following her progress. All she could concentrate on was making it to the car and giving Sam Oliver a piece of her mind.

The silvery-gray Audi hadn't been towed. After dumping the suitcase in the back seat, he bundled her into the front, leaning over and giving her a showy kiss that landed on her jaw, not her mouth. "Look like you're enjoying this," he muttered. "I just hope to hell they haven't had time to bug the car while I was gone."

"What if they have?" she asked, smiling up at him with a perfect parody of adolescent passion.

"Bitch," he murmured genially. "If they have, we're going to have a damn hard time shaking them. We'll find out soon enough. If they're still on our tail after half an hour we'll have to be more creative."

"What if they planted a bomb instead of a bug?"

"I don't think they had enough time."

"And if they did?"

He slid into the driver's seat. "Then I'll be damn sorry you never wore the red dress." And without even flinching he put the key in the ignition and turned it.

The car wasn't rocked by an explosion. The engine began to purr, like a cream-fed kitten, and Sam pulled out into the early-evening traffic with just the right combination of aggression and care. Elizabeth slid down in the sinfully comfortable seat and took off the dark glasses. "Anyone following us?"

Sam was whistling under his breath, something fast and tuneless, as he glanced in the rearview mirror. "Two cars. One a Buick, probably FBI. Another Mercedes. That's probably Kempton's confederates. I don't know if they're aware of each other, but my guess is they're not. That'll work to our advantage." He kept up his sedate pace, stopping politely for the traffic, still whistling that damn nonsong.

"I'm going to sleep," Elizabeth said, making sure her seat belt was fastened before she crossed her arms across her middle and shut her eyes.

"You think so?" There was an edge of humor in his voice. She'd heard that edge before, and hated it.

"I survived that drive down the Colorado mountains when the Toyota was chasing us, didn't I? I imagine this will be a piece of cake in comparison."

"Maybe. I'm not as good a driver as Phil was."

"At least a Toyota isn't following us."

"Was Kempton the man in Colorado?" He turned swiftly, unexpectedly, and Elizabeth was thrown against the leather-covered door.

"No," she said without pausing to think about it. Not that thinking would have given her a more reliable answer.

"Did he have anything to do with Shari Derringer's kidnapping?"

"Shari Derringer wasn't kidnapped."

He slammed on the brakes, and she was catapulted forward, the seat belt restraining her just inches from the windshield. In the distance she could hear the echo of screaming brakes as whoever followed them stopped short. He was moving again, faster than ever, before he said something. "You think she went willingly?"

"I think she was part of the whole nasty thing. I don't know why—I haven't seen anything clearly—it's just a sense I have."

"You think she knew about Mary Nelson being butchered to take her place?" They were going quite fast by then, and Elizabeth gave in to temptation and looked in the rearview mirror. The Mercedes and the American sedan were keeping pace with Sam's Audi, but just barely.

"Yes," said Elizabeth. "I think she knew."

Sam's reaction was short and obscene. "No wonder they're covering up. If sweet little Shari is that deeply involved they might have to do anything to keep things quiet. This administration isn't in the mood for another scandal. Hold on." He skidded around a corner, and Elizabeth had the notion they'd done it on two wheels.

She held on, closing her eyes and letting him concentrate. The Audi was extremely comfortable—she wouldn't have thought a high-speed chase could be so smooth. Of course, the only other deadly ride she'd been in had been down an icy Colorado mountain, with a Toyota trying to run them off the road, so that anything with a decent suspension on a paved road was bound to be an improvement.

"We've lost the Buick," Sam said minutes later. "The Mercedes is hanging tight."

She stirred, looking over at him. The sun had set, and they were on their way out of the city. She had no idea where they were, or in what direction they were heading, and she really didn't care. "Will the Buick go back to the apartment?"

"I don't think so. There's no need. They know we're gone, and they've searched my place any number of times, whenever the mood strikes them. No, I imagine they'll go back and try to figure out our destination."

"Will they be able to?"

"I doubt it." He was driving at a surprisingly sedate pace for the time being, and she could feel the powerful lights of the Mercedes burning into the back of her head. "In the meantime, Danny's probably taken care of everything. If they decide to go back to the apartment, they won't find anything."

It took all of Elizabeth's courage to speak. "Sam, he bled onto the hall carpet...."

"It'll be gone. Every trace, in record time. Danny's one of the few people left I can trust, and he'll do what I ask him, and do it perfectly." He glanced at the digital clock on the dashboard. "And it's about time to get rid of the Mercedes. I want to get to a phone and start getting some answers." He stepped down on the accelerator, hard, and the Audi shot ahead.

There had been an advantage to that hair-raising trip down the mountain, Elizabeth thought, biting down on her lip and clutching the armrest. There were no other cars involved, just the Toyota and Phil's car, and the icy highway. The roads in Washington were bare and paved, and there were no dangerous cliffs or hairpin turns. But there were cars of every shape and description and speed. Elizabeth shut her eyes and prepared to die.

The ride in the Audi was no longer smooth, and it certainly wasn't silent. She could hear the blaring of horns, the squealing of brakes, the occasional crash and tinkle of broken glass as someone, not them, wasn't able to stop in time. Sam drove his elegant sedan like a race car, downshifting, gunning the motor, sliding through narrow openings in the traffic flow as if he thought he was on a motorcycle. Elizabeth leaned back, still clutching the armrest, and prayed for it to be over.

She was aware of the silence first. Not silence, exactly, just the absence of traffic, of squealing tires and honking horns. The Audi was smooth once more, and slowly, cautiously, she opened her eyes.

They were beyond the noise and traffic of the city, heading into the countryside on secondary roads. The traffic had thinned out around them, and there was no ominous black Mercedes looming up behind them. "We've lost them?" Elizabeth asked.

"I think so. Unless they planted a homing device, we should be okay."

"And if they have?"

"Very simple," said Sam. "They would have had to plant it on the car. Therefore, we change cars."

"That simple? We just change cars?"

"I could always go over the car and try to check. I couldn't be sure, though, not in the darkness and with the lack of equipment. Better to be safe than sorry. Hungry?"

The thought of food made her weak with longing, and then she remembered just why her stomach was so empty. "No," she said.

"Tough. You probably threw up everything in your stomach, and you need sustenance. We'll stop at a convenience store and pick up something."

"No red meat," she said, shuddering.

"No red meat," he agreed. "Macadamia nuts and ice-cream bars for the pacifist vegetarian."

"Don't mock me. Unlike professional soldiers, I'm not used to killing," she said stiffly.

"Got something against the military?"

"No," she said. "I just think warfare isn't the best career to devote yourself to."

"Spare me your bleeding-heart liberal garbage," he said warily. "It would be great if peace just happened, but it doesn't. It takes armies to work out an equitable peace, like it or not."

"I don't want to talk politics," she said stiffly. "We aren't going to agree on anything, so why bother?"

"To keep your mind off other things," he said flatly.

"It won't work."

"I realize that. We'll simply have to deal with it when we get to where we're going."

"Where *are* we going?"

"You'll see." He pulled up to a convenience store and turned off the car. "Keep down. I'll be out in a minute. If anyone comes near, lock the doors and lean on the horn."

"I thought you said we'd lost them."

"If we can change cars, they can, too. I don't think they're anywhere around, but the way you stay alive in situations like these is to be aware of all the possibilities."

"Have you been in situations like this before?"

He paused as he climbed out of the car. "Too many times," he said wearily. "And, damn it, this is the last."

She watched him go. She could see him through the glassfront of the store, watching with an odd combination of disgust and deep-down tenderness as he bought frozen pizza and beer nuts. He seemed to be taking an inordinately long time paying for the food, and the bleached blond teenager with the bubble gum in her mouth was flirting like crazy, staring up at him out of huge eyes like he was some movie star, Elizabeth thought grumpily.

No one slowed down as they drove by; no one pulled in beside her and pointed a gun through the tinted-glass window of the Audi. There was no one near the isolated store but the teenager, Sam and her.

He came out moments later, keys in his hand. The wrong keys. Yanking open her door, he beckoned her out. "Come on."

"Where are we going?"

He didn't answer for a moment, grabbing the suitcase from the back seat and slamming the door behind him. "Changing cars," he said. "I traded with Marcy Lou."

"Marcy Lou?" Elizabeth echoed, not caring if she sounded like a jealous witch. "You know her?"

"I do now. She's the proud owner of a 1987 Audi. While we are blessed with her boyfriend's aging Datsun pickup." He gestured to a rusting orange monstrosity parked halfway behind the store.

"The boyfriend won't mind?"

"Would you?"

"I guess not. What if there *is* a homing device? Won't she be in some danger?"

"I know you think I'm completely conscienceless, but I do draw the line at risking innocent teenage girls. I explained the situation and suggested she leave the car there till morning. If no one bothers it, she'll be safe."

"And you're really going to give her your car?"

"I'm not into material possessions."

"So I noticed," she said, thinking of his apartment as she climbed onto the high seat of the truck. It sagged beneath her, and the cab of the truck smelled of stale beer, diesel fuel and marijuana. "You think this thing will get us there?"

"We don't have far to go."

"To go where?" she prodded again, but he simply shook his head, starting the engine. It was a far cry from the gentle purr of the Audi. It was more a dyspeptic cough and splutter, but it started, then ran bumpily. They pulled out onto the two-lane highway. Elizabeth turned to watch the Audi with a trace of nostalgic affection, wondering whether the teenager inside would appreciate it. She was still watching when the car exploded, bursting into a sheet of flame.

Chapter 14

Sam didn't turn, didn't slow down, didn't stop the rattling old Datsun. He kept his face turned to the front, not even bothering to find out whether Marcy Lou had been outside checking on her new luxury car.

Elizabeth watched in relief as the astounded, bleached-blond figure raced out of the store, clearly unharmed. The car was burning steadily, but there didn't seem to be any other explosion, and apart from the shattered storefront windows, nothing else seemed in imminent danger.

She slid around in the bench seat of the Datsun and stared at her companion. "No one was hurt," she said. "Not that you seem to give a damn one way or the other. Did you set that bomb?"

That got a reaction out of him, if only brief disgust. "No."

"What if that girl had gotten killed?"

"If she had, there wouldn't have been anything I could do. I didn't know the car was rigged. Kempton's associates were even more professional than I expected. I wouldn't have made the trade if I'd thought it would kill an innocent bystander. But the bottom line is that it didn't, and I'm not going to waste time and energy bewailing the close call. It almost got us, Elizabeth. I'm spending my time being damn glad we dumped it in time."

"You're absolutely heartless, aren't you?"

He didn't even bother to glance at her this time. A fire engine was racing back toward the convenience store, sirens blaring and lights flashing, but he kept his eyes straight ahead. "Maybe," he said. "I do my best."

There was nothing she could say to that. When she'd first met him she'd been convinced he was as ruthless and stony-hearted as his cold eyes. She'd learned she was wrong about that, wrong about him. Despite the layers of protective toughness wrapped around his lean body, inside there was a heart that hadn't withered and died at all. It beat, strongly, warmly. Maybe it even beat for her.

She leaned her head back, sliding down in the seat and wincing as her unpadded backside hit a spring. The Datsun was quite a comedown from the Audi. The late Audi, she thought with a trace of nostalgia.

The sound of the sirens faded in the distance, and before long Sam turned off onto a back road. She opened her mouth to ask him where they were going, then shut it again. She'd asked him several times already, and he hadn't answered. There was no reason to think he'd be any more forthcoming now.

"Won't the police be looking for this truck?"

"Yup."

"Won't they find it?"

"No."

She gave up. She couldn't force him to distract her with aimless chatter, so she had no choice but relive the afternoon in her brain. She wished she had any alternative, but her mind kept replaying it, looking for a way out, looking for a reprieve or a justification. She had no doubt at all that Kempton had been planning to kill her. No doubt that he'd planned to hurt her very badly before he did so. It still didn't make what she'd done all right.

She shivered slightly, closing her eyes. It had started to rain, a steady, soaking drizzle that matched her mood. In Colorado it would be snowing. In Colorado her only friend was dead, and her home was no longer her haven. As far as she could see, she had no place to run to. The memory of too many bodies would follow her, tormenting her dreams.

She'd lived with tormenting dreams all her life. It was nothing new; she would learn to cope. But for now, just for a little while, she would have given anything for a little oblivion.

She'd fallen asleep. Sam hadn't thought she would. Her entire body had been strung so tightly that he'd been afraid she would shatter at the slightest sound or touch. As usual, he'd underestimated her toughness. She'd survived his own rough handling of her, and she'd survived the explosion without going into the hysterics he would have expected of a lesser woman. She *was* angry at him, furious at his endangering that silly, gum-chewing teenager. What she didn't realize was that they were endangering anyone they came near. Her very existence was a major threat to certain people, those who knew her abilities and those who only suspected. He didn't want to be the one to tell her. She was already carrying burdens enough on those slender shoulders.

Damn Kempton and his ilk! Sam could have killed him easily enough, could even have enjoyed wrapping his hands around the man's thick throat and watching his piggy little eyes bulge out. He'd killed often enough that he could do it—when it needed doing.

But Elizabeth was a different matter. To have forced her to commit a bloody act of violence was beyond cruel, it was the sort of thing that could destroy someone as quiet and gentle as she was.

Except that she wasn't as quiet and gentle as she seemed. Beneath that nunlike demeanor was the heart of a lion, one who could kill if her life was threatened and not be destroyed by the act. She was going to have a hard time of it tonight, though; he knew that. And he knew what he was going to do to distract her from the memory of Kempton's blood-soaked body. Whether she liked it or not, he had every intention of finally making love to her, finally staking his claim on her slight, deceptively fragile-looking body. Though he fully expected her to like it quite a bit, once she got used to the idea.

She didn't wake up when he reached the east gate and punched in the proper security sequence. The rain was beating down steadily, a comforting reminder that the icy-cold ground was going to give way to spring flowers before long. He wanted to see her in spring, with warm sunlight beaming down on her long curtain of hair. He'd spent too much time in the cold and darkness with her.

It took another fifteen minutes, driving along rutted, rain-soaked roads before he pulled up in front of the tiny house. Years ago it had served as a gate house for a grand estate. The main house had burned down in the forties, and the new one had been built at the opposite end of the four-hundred-acre parcel of land. This place was inviolate, out of the way of prying eyes and nosy neighbors. No one would be able to find them—even the few people he trusted didn't know where he was. And they didn't know about Elizabeth's existence. For the next few days they'd be quiet, and safe, while they figured out what their next move should be.

The place was locked up tight, dark and unwelcoming. He considered leaving her sleeping in the truck while he went and opened it up, but he thought better of it. She'd been through enough in the past few hours, the past few days. She didn't need to wake up, abandoned, in a strange place.

"We're here." He reached out a hand to shake her, planning only a brief touch, but her skin seemed to call out to him. He grasped her arm gently, his fingers caressing her through the thick cotton sweater.

She lifted her head, her eyes dazed and unfocused for a moment, and he was sorry he had to bring her back to reality and remembrance. He knew the moment it came back from the way her brown eyes darkened, her vulnerable mouth trembled slightly, and a stricken look passed over her face. Then it was gone, and she was sitting up briskly, rubbing her arms against the chill in the air.

"Are we here?"

"Yes."

"Are you going to tell me where 'here' is yet, or do I have to guess?" The asperity came into her voice quickly, and he almost smiled. She was still fighting. He liked that.

"'Here' is a remote gate house on a secure estate in Virginia," he said. "No one followed us, and no one can find us here. For the time being we can catch our breath and see what we're going to do next."

She nodded, accepting his words at face value. "Will I be charged with Kempton's death?" she inquired in a deceptively casual tone of voice, her face hidden as she reached for the raincoat at her feet.

"No. I don't expect Kempton's body will be found, and there's such a thing as habeas corpus. If he is found, it'll be a completely convincing case of accidental death. There's no way you'd be implicated." The rigidity had come back to her shoulders, and he knew what was going through her mind with a sudden clarity that was no longer surprising to him. "You don't like that, do you? You want to pay for your imaginary sins."

"Killing a man isn't an imaginary sin," she said, sitting up and meeting his wrathful gaze.

"Self-defense isn't a real one. I don't want to sit in a cold truck and argue about it. You need something to eat, I need something to drink and we both need a warm fire and a good night's sleep. Come on." He didn't look back as he climbed out of the truck and hoisted the suitcase with him.

She could sit in the truck and freeze for all he cared at that point. If she was recapturing her death wish, far be it for him to talk her out of it.

She was right behind him, shivering slightly in the rain, as he went through the complex convolutions that guaranteed the tiny house's security. If she thought the safety code a bit excessive for a country retreat she didn't say anything. Maybe she needed a drink, too.

The place smelled musty and closed up, and it was too damn cold. The first thing he did was crank up the electric heat, at least for the time being, and turn on lights. The gate house was surrounded by tall, enshrouding trees, and the warm yellow light would penetrate only a few yards into the rain-soaked darkness. For now they were safe.

Elizabeth was standing in the middle of the one large room, taking in the comfortable furnishings, the old quilts and honey-pine furniture, the American primitives on the wall and the threadbare Oriental carpet on the polished oak floor. The walls were whitewashed plaster, and the narrow flight of stairs leading to the sleeping balcony and the bathroom was edged with a wrought-iron railing lifted from the ruins of the burned-out manor house. She'd be wondering who lived here, he thought, heading for the galley kitchen and dumping the food down on the counter. She'd be wondering who had put the loving care into the woodwork, painstakingly stripping all those layers of paint to reveal the glowing wood beneath. Who had patched and plastered the old walls, who had bought the old, comfortable furnishings, who had hung the austere primitive paintings and the one surprisingly lighthearted Chagall print. And she'd be wondering who he knew who'd be willing to lend him this place.

She stood in the doorway, watching him. Her long hair was still hanging loose, and she was paler than he'd ever seen her. But her eyes were bright with curiosity. "This is yours, isn't it?"

He didn't know why he was surprised. He hadn't managed to fool her yet. "How'd you know?"

She shrugged. "Just a sense. I knew this place, and yet I'd never been here before. And then I realized I knew you, and this place *is* you. Not that barren apartment in the District."

"That's a nice, sentimental thought, but it's not true." He made her a drink, weaker than his own, and handed it to her, expecting her to demur. She took it, her fingers touching his without flinching this time. "The apartment in D.C. is as much a part of me as this place is. I just developed the habit of keeping parts of me compartmentalized."

"Convenient," Elizabeth murmured, sipping her whiskey and grimacing. "I don't want to eat anything."

"You're going to." He handed her a jar of macadamia nuts, then turned back, rummaging through the bag. "They didn't have any ice-cream bars. You'll have to make do with Popsicles."

"I'll survive," she said, wandering back into the main room.

"I know you will," he murmured, staring after her for a long moment. "I know you will."

He managed to get her to eat a slice and a half of pizza, two handfuls of macadamia nuts, and to drink another, milder glass of Johnny Walker Red. She needed the slightly numbing effects of the booze, needed to dull the memory that flashed in the back of her brown eyes. But he didn't want to get her drunk. Even he had his standards, and those didn't include taking a reluctant, drunken woman to bed. He'd take a drunken woman, or a reluctant one, but he wouldn't attempt the combination. Besides, Elizabeth needed a kind of comfort even good Scotch couldn't provide. So, for that matter, did he.

He let her wander around exploring the place while he built a supplemental fire in the wood stove. Electric heat was too damn expensive, and this country retreat was a luxury he really couldn't afford. He also couldn't afford to live without it.

He knew she'd found the bathroom. He knew she'd found the only bed the place boasted, smaller than the king-size bed in his apartment, cozier. He'd never shared that bed with anyone. He wondered if he'd feel cramped. Somehow he didn't think so.

"Sam." She was leaning over the loft balcony, and her long brown hair was hanging down. He thought of Juliet; he thought of Rapunzel. He thought he must be going out of his mind.

"Yeah?" he said, his voice neutral.

"I'm going to take a shower and then go to bed. All right?"

"Fine," he said evenly.

"Where do you want me to sleep?"

Silly question, he thought. "In the bed."

She didn't even argue. Maybe she thought he was too much of a gentleman to make a pass at her tonight of all nights. Or maybe she already knew what was coming. Either way, it didn't matter.

He washed up in the kitchen sink. He was on the phone when she came out of the shower, and he knew she could hear him. He wanted her to.

"Danny? We're safe. It doesn't matter where, but if you put your mind to it you could probably guess. Did you take care of our little problem?" He looked up and met Elizabeth's haunted brown eyes staring down at him. "Thanks, pal. I owe you one. You sure no one saw you? I don't want you taking the fall for this, either. Of course I have faith in your abilities. I wouldn't have called you if I didn't. There aren't too many people I'd trust. Yeah, you too. I'll call you tomorrow."

He set the phone down on the cradle. Her long hair was damp, curling around her pale, scrubbed face. She was wearing the nightgown he'd bought her, and for a moment he wondered why he'd chosen virginal white cotton.

He started up the stairs. She backed skittishly away toward the bedroom, and he stifled his momentary pang of guilt. "Danny took care of Kempton. A nice blazing car wreck in Silver Springs. It should be damn near impossible to pin anything suspicious on anyone. The fire should take care of most of the evidence, and there wasn't anything embarrassing like a bullet hole."

"Don't," she said faintly. "I don't want to think about it."

Her feet were bare. That was one of the first things that had attracted him to her. Her small, defenseless bare feet, and he still couldn't figure out why. She was nothing like the usual sort of woman he was attracted to. He liked her fragility; he liked her toughness; he liked her sweetness, and her bitchy side, too. For some reason he was drawn to her with an intensity that he could no longer fight.

"You can't stop thinking about it," he said, reaching the top step and walking past the bathroom toward her. "You're not going to be able to stop thinking about it until you face it squarely and accept it. You killed a man. The man deserved to die, and he was going to kill you. Case closed."

"Go away, Sam," she said.

"Look in your crystal ball, swami," he murmured, his voice a soft, wicked taunt. "Tonight's the night. You're not going to spend the next twelve hours wrapped up in a tight cocoon of misery while you replay the events of this afternoon. You're going to spend the night wrapped up around me."

"Sam," she said, and there was no missing the note of panic in her voice as she stumbled backward, away from him. "You don't understand." Her voice was breathless, terrified, and he put out his hands to catch her arms, to keep her from falling, to hold her.

"Why are you looking so frightened, Elizabeth?" he murmured, genuinely mystified. "I'm not going to hurt you. You know that. And you want me. You want me as much as I want you. I know you do. You know it, too."

"I don't . . ." she began, her voice shaking.

"Say no," he suggested affably, his fingers caressing her bare upper arms, soothing her. "All you have to do is tell me you don't want me, and I'll go back downstairs and sleep on the couch."

"I . . ." The words were stuck in her throat, and he pressed his advantage, leaning down and brushing her pale, frightened mouth with his.

"Can't say it, can you? We've spent too many nights sleeping on couches." He kissed her again, lingeringly this time, and her lips instinctively clung to his. He lifted his head, still keeping her trapped in his gaze. "Come on, Elizabeth, don't play games. It's not as if you . . . haven't . . . done . . . this before. . . ." He hadn't even finished the sentence before he realized the truth. He wanted to drop her arms and run. He wanted to get away from her, away from the trap of her vulnerability. But he couldn't. Couldn't move away, couldn't drop her arms, couldn't stop wanting her so much he thought he'd explode from it.

"You haven't, have you?" he whispered.

She wouldn't meet his eyes. She found her own bare feet fascinating, or maybe it was his she was looking at. She shook her head, a bare suggestion of a gesture, and tried to pull away.

He slid his hands up to cup her face. Pushing her gently against the wall of the loft bedroom, he pressed his body against hers, and he knew by the sudden widening of her soft brown eyes that she could feel his arousal. "Then it's past time you did," he said, dropping his mouth down on hers.

This was no gentle wooing. This was demand, pure and simple. And to his mingled surprise and satisfaction it was a demand she answered, sliding her arms around his waist and softening her mouth for his searing kiss.

She was all soft and shivery in his arms. The more he kissed her, the more he wanted. He wanted to drown in her mouth; he wanted to devour her; he wanted everything to disappear but the wet, hungry texture of his mouth and hers.

When he broke away she was looking dazed, stunned, vulnerable. Staring down into her hazy brown eyes, he knew that if he went one step further he'd never escape. Once he entered her virgin body he'd be tied to her for life. He told himself he should wait, think about it. Give her time to reject him, give him time to come to his senses.

He scooped her up in his arms and carried her the few short feet to the big old bed. It was a high one, covered with an old quilt. He set her down gently in the middle of that bed, and her long damp hair spread around her pale, waiting face.

He sat down beside her, his weight making the old bed sag. And then he leaned over and turned off the light, plunging the room, the cottage, into a velvet darkness lit only by the fitful flickering of the firelight in the fireplace down below.

He didn't know where to start. He didn't know if he could touch her without terrifying her; he didn't know if he could take that white cotton nightgown with its row of tiny buttons off her without tearing it from her. He didn't know if he could stroke her, arouse her, bring her pleasure, before the raging demands of his own body overwhelmed him and he buried himself in her. For the first time in his life, his woman's pleasure mattered more than his. He just wasn't sure if his body realized it.

Maybe he should pick a fight with her, he thought, lifting one slender hand and holding it in his. Hers was cold, icy, but he knew it was only from nerves. If he picked a fight with her, he could take her in anger, getting the whole thing over quickly. And then maybe she'd cease to have such power over him.

But he couldn't do that. He'd already gone too far down the road to deliberately hurt her. Not in this way. Sex was one weapon he wasn't going to use, not with her. There was no turning back. He wasn't going to have sex with her tonight. He was going to make love to her. And he wasn't going to stop until she realized what she'd been missing all these years.

"Sam?" Her voice wasn't much more than a whisper in the darkness, and her small hand turned in his, catching his larger, stronger one. Holding it. Holding it for comfort. For protection against the demons of the dark. Despite the fact that he was one of those demons.

He could see her face in the pale light, a dim oval with dark, shadowed eyes. He'd turned the light off for her, knowing she'd be shy. And for him, not wanting to be reminded of how very vulnerable she was. It didn't matter. He could see her clearly, even in the darkness. And she was his.

Chapter 15

Elizabeth lay in the dark without moving, her hand held tightly in his. A thousand times she wanted to open her mouth and say, *No, I don't want this.* To tell him she needed more time. To beg him to leave her alone.

He'd probably do it. For all his coolness, his unsentimental, hardheaded approach to life and most particularly to her, she knew he didn't want to hurt her. That he would go back downstairs and leave her if she asked.

His hand was callused, hard against her own soft skin, and his fingers closed over hers, capturing her. She could see his expression in the firelight filtering up from below, and he looked almost regretful. And just slightly brutal.

And then he moved, slowly, gracefully, covering her body with his, his hips resting against her, his broad chest pressing against her small, sensitive breasts as his hands cupped her face. "Maybe I shouldn't do this," he said. "But I can't stop unless you stop me." He waited, his mouth poised above hers, and his breath was soft and warm on her upturned face.

"Don't stop," she said, her hands reaching up around his back, sliding underneath his loose cotton T-shirt to his smooth, warm skin. "Don't stop."

He groaned in the back of his throat, and then he kissed her hard, his mouth opening over hers, his tongue diving deep. She kissed him back, with passion, with desperation, with fear. She knew there was no turning back at this point, and she didn't want to turn back. But she was still afraid of what lay ahead.

He felt hard and heavy and dangerous against the fragile cradle of her thighs. She wondered whether it would hurt. She wondered whether he'd be gentle or rough. Most of all, she wondered if she'd be torn apart by visions of bloody death, or torn apart by pleasure.

He rolled to his side, giving him more access to her. The nine tiny buttons at the neck of the demure nightgown gave way beneath his deft fingers, and the coolness of the night air against her skin soon gave way to the wet warmth of his mouth on her breast. She gave a little cry, but he ignored it. It was surprise, surprise at the effect his mouth had on her, surprise at the warmth and dampness between her legs. The aching longing in the pit of her stomach was nothing new, but the tingling in her skin, the tightening of her breasts, the hot flush that covered her skin, were all unexpected.

His hand covered her other breast, its rough texture curiously arousing against the softness of her skin. She seemed to swell and harden against him, and she found she wanted to kiss him again. Wanted to quite desperately.

He took her hand in his and brought it down, down to rest against the zipper of his jeans, against the bulge of male flesh beneath it. He held her there for a moment, his longer fingers covering hers, pressing her against him, showing her how to caress him. When he released her she kept her hand there, her fingers touching and exploring the hard ridge of flesh. She liked the feel of it against her hand. She liked the safe barrier of the jeans between them. And then suddenly the denim frustrated her, and she wanted to feel his skin, his softness and hardness, his male flesh, in her hand.

She couldn't manage the zipper. She'd hoped to tug it down gently, almost surreptitiously, but it stuck, and even a discreet yank wouldn't release it. She thought she heard him laugh, only the whisper of a sound, and then he sat up, taking the hem of her nightgown and pulling it over her head, leaving her wearing nothing but white cotton underpants that seemed absurd. She didn't even know why she'd put them on in the first place—she never slept in underwear. Maybe she'd hoped they would offer her some sort of protection.

"The zipper's stuck," she said, not meeting his gaze, controlling her strong desire to cover her breasts. She knew perfectly well they were too small, that someone like Sam would prefer a chesty woman, with voluptuous hips and . . .

"Your breasts are perfect," he said, his voice a deep, sexy rumble. "And it's no wonder my zipper's stuck." He unfastened it himself, and she kept her eyes on his face as he slid his jeans off and pulled the dark T-shirt over his head. She knew he was wearing nothing, but she couldn't quite bring herself to look. Her shyness was overwhelming, even when he lay back down beside her and pulled her into his arms.

"You'll have to tell me what you like," he said in her ear as his hands cupped her breasts. "You'll have to tell me what gives you pleasure, what frightens you." He ran his thumbs lightly over her hard, sensitive nipples, and she moaned. "Did you like that?" His mouth followed his thumbs. "Did you?" he whispered against her skin.

"Yes." It was just a breath of sound as his mouth lingered on each breast for too brief a time and then trailed lower across her flat stomach to the lace-trimmed edge of her panties. And then his mouth touched her, right at the juncture of her tightly closed thighs, and his breath fanned through the cotton, warm and damp and impossibly arousing.

He nibbled at her through the cloth with lips and teeth and tongue, and she put her hands on his bare, strong shoulders, wanting to push him away, clinging to him instead as she trembled beneath his touch.

Before she realized what was happening he'd slipped his hands inside the cotton briefs and pulled them off. His mouth was on her, touching her, and he'd managed to move her legs apart, to give him better access. The strangled protest died in her throat as the first flames of a deep, dark passion began to build. She couldn't begin to imagine what he was doing with his tongue; she didn't want to know, and she didn't want it to stop. She was writhing beneath his practiced mouth, and his hands on her hips were holding her still as he teased and tormented and pleasured her with such exquisite care that all shyness and doubt and sanity melted into the darkness, and she felt she was reaching, reaching for something so distant that she couldn't even see it.

And then she was there. She heard the strangled cry, almost from a distance, and knew that it came from her. But she was beyond noticing anything. Her body convulsed, shattered, and every bone, every muscle, in her body tightened, dissolved, disappeared, and the shock wave swept over her.

She tried to pull herself back together again. She was frightened, mortally frightened of what had just happened to her, frightened of the darkness, frightened of that intensity of feeling that was almost painful in its pleasure. Her eyes couldn't focus; for a moment she didn't know where she was. And then she realized that Sam's arms were around her, Sam's body was pressed against her, his heartbeat almost as rapid as hers, his hands gentle, comforting, wiping the tears away from her face, pushing the curtain of hair away from her. She kept her face down, away from him, unaccountably shy, but he ignored it, tilting her chin up and kissing her gently on the lips.

"I'm going to hurt you." His voice was harsh in the stillness, and she suddenly felt the tension thrumming through him, the iron control keeping his body rigid. "I don't want to, but . . ."

She put both hands on the sides of his face and kissed him. "Hurt me," she said. "Just do it."

She trembled when he touched her, and for a moment she tried to close her legs to him again. But she couldn't. He murmured soft words in her ear, love words, sex words, words that made no sense and made her feel shy and proud and sexy. She was very damp, she knew that, but she was also very tight, and she wondered how much he really would hurt her.

She reached down and touched him, that combination of silk and steel that would soon be a part of her. He was damp, as she was, and pulsing with desire. He held himself very still as she explored him, running delicate hands across the ridges and veins of him. She hadn't realized how big he was. And she realized he might hurt her quite badly.

For some reason she couldn't bring herself to worry. She felt empty, aching inside, and she wanted him. Wanted him on top of her, pressing her down into the soft mattress, wanted him inside her, filling her with this pulsing male power. She wanted not to be afraid anymore. Of anything.

He must have sensed her readiness. Moving over her, he knelt between her legs, his strong, tense arms supporting his weight as he rested against the center of her. "Bite your lip," he whispered, pressing against her, into her, gently. "Scream."

"I don't want to. . . ." Before she'd finished speaking he'd done it, sinking deep into her, pushing past the fragile barrier with only a momentary spasm of pain, resting deep inside her, holding very still.

She was breathless for a moment, from the sharp pain and from the impact of his invasion. For a brief second panic swept over her as she lay trapped beneath his strong body. She didn't struggle, only tried to withdraw mentally, drawing in upon herself, but he wouldn't let her. He caught her chin in one strong hand, forcing her to look at him, and his eyes were dark with regret and a glaze of passion that astonished her. "Don't," he said, his voice raspy. "Stay with me. Don't leave."

She'd forgotten he knew her so well, forgotten that he was privy to her innermost thoughts in a way only she could understand. Her fingers were clutching the sheet beneath her, and it took her a moment to relax her desperate grip. Another moment to touch him, to feel the warmth and heat of his smooth skin, and know that it was going to be all right.

"That's right," he murmured, reaching down and pulling her legs around his narrow hips. "It's going to be all right," he said, his voice low and soothing and hypnotic. "It's going to be just fine."

He began to move, and she automatically tensed, expecting more pain. But there was none, just the graceful glide of flesh and dampness and heat and longing. She didn't notice when her hands began to cling to him; she didn't notice when she began to follow his movements, the simple, elegant rhythm that was building to something far beyond elegance. Their bodies were slippery with sweat, and she could sense that his control was about to shatter. She wanted to savor the moment, to lie there and take his pleasure into her, but she'd reckoned without his determination. That same dangerous rawness was building once more, with even greater intensity, and she was afraid of it, afraid of its power, afraid that if this time she lost herself, she might never come back.

"No," she whimpered, not knowing what she meant. "I can't...I don't want..."

"Yes, you do," he whispered, his voice harsh, and fitting his hands between their bodies, he touched her.

It was darkness; it was terror; it was the deep, endless limits of outer space with no light or breath or life, until he shuddered, losing himself within her, catching her as she fell through the velvet, limitless night, holding her tightly in his arms, keeping her safe. She could hear the maddened thudding of his heart against her, and she didn't know where his heartbeat ended and hers began, where his body ended and hers began. She didn't know where his life ended and hers began. Everything was permanently, inextricably, eternally entwined.

She knew she was crying. She didn't want to, but she couldn't help it, and soft, silent sobs were shaking her still-trembling body. He was holding her tightly against him, and at some point he'd rolled on his side, taking her with him, and her hair was wrapped around them like a shawl. In the distance she heard the phone ring, and she burrowed her head against his chest, whispering, "Don't answer it," as she hid from his too-observant eyes.

"I wouldn't think of it," he said, the words a deep vibration beneath her ear. Slowly, gently, he untangled his body from hers, even as he still held her tight. She knew he wanted to look at her, but right then she couldn't bear it. All she could do was burrow against him and cry.

He was a patient man. He waited until the tears faded into an occasional hiccup and sniff; he waited until the shudders faded almost entirely from her body, waiting until the tension and resistance left her muscles and he could carefully push her face back as he soothed the damp hair away from her. "Are you all right?" he asked, prosaically enough, and she didn't know what to answer.

"No," she said, trying to turn away.

This time he wouldn't let her. "Did I hurt you? Was I too rough? Elizabeth, for pity's sake..."

"Shut up," she said fiercely. "Just be quiet for a moment, would you? Or if you have to say something, tell me it was one of the most wonderful experiences of your life. Tell me I'm beautiful. Tell me you love me."

The words hung in the air between them. "It was one of the most wonderful experiences of my life," he said slowly, deliberately, and she believed him. "You're beautiful," he said. And nothing more.

It was more than she'd expected—more, probably, than she deserved. It wasn't his fault that her life had undergone a metamorphosis in the past few days, culminating in his bed. It wasn't his fault that she'd been fool enough to fall in love with the first man she'd ever slept with.

Her emotions felt raw, her body still trembled, and her heart felt ripped and battered. "I need some sleep," she said, hoping he'd leave her. Knowing she'd hate him if he did.

"I know," he said gently. He wasn't a gentle man, a patient man, but he'd been both with her tonight. He'd been a loving man, but he didn't love her. And she didn't know how she was going to survive that simple fact.

"Come here," he said, a foolish thing, since she was already draped over his body like a limp rag doll. Very carefully, very deftly, he arranged her against him, so comfortably that she was asleep almost before she realized it. Asleep with his unloving body holding her tightly. Asleep with his unloving hands gentle on her skin. Asleep with his unloving mouth resting against her hair. Asleep.

It was a small bed. She spent the night wrapped in his arms, and when she'd finally accepted that fact, she slept soundly. He'd pulled the quilt over them, afraid she'd wake up chilled and miserable, and kept her tight against him, transferring his formidable body heat to her slender frame.

He'd heard the confusion, the misery, in her voice. And he didn't know what to do, apart from lying to her. And lying would have done no good, either. She would have known the truth. He wasn't a man who knew how to love any longer. But he could care for her.

She'd been frightened by the intensity of her response. He'd been awed by it. He'd been hoping to give her at least some pleasure; he hadn't expected her to be swept away by it. And he certainly hadn't expected his own reaction to match hers.

Magic. Hookie-pookie garbage, maybe. It could have something to do with that annoying, almost mystical link they shared. More likely it had to do with hormones and a happy coincidence. They were well suited to each other, despite outward appearances. They were good in bed. Period.

She turned to him in her sleep. She reached for him, her lips murmuring his name, her hands touching him, her face rubbing up against him like a hungry kitten. He wanted her again, with an intensity that surprised him. But the least he could do for her was let her sleep.

He lay in the darkness, listening to the rain beat down on the roof, listening to the sizzle and crackle of the dying fire. It was hours later when she stirred. The rain had ended sometime during the night, and the early light of dawn was streaking through the roof window overhead. She opened her eyes and looked up at the blue sky and the bare branches overhead. And then she looked into his own blue eyes, and she was very solemn.

"You're in trouble," she said.

"Am I?" The quilt was covering her breasts. He pushed it down, casually.

"I could get addicted to this," she said faintly.

"I hope so." Her body was faintly pink in the early-morning light, and her nipples were hard. Probably from the coolness of the air, but he could hope. "I'll do my best to keep you hooked. Unless you wanted to become a nun again." He started to push the covers down farther, but this time she caught them, pulling them up to her neck.

"Don't be snide," she said. "It doesn't become you."

"That quilt doesn't become you. Take if off."

"I'm a mess. I need a bath, I need clean clothes, and I need to talk to you."

"Um-hm," he agreed lazily, kissing her eyelids. They fluttered shut just in time, and he moved his mouth to her ear, nibbling at the soft lobe. She liked that, arching her back slightly, and he was sorry he hadn't tried that last night. "What about my needs?" he murmured softly.

"I can just imagine your needs." Her voice was tart.

"You don't need to imagine," he said, pressing against her. His mouth caught hers gently, and he kissed her slowly, thoroughly, lovingly, doing his best to give her everything he could but the words. When he drew back her eyes were faintly glazed, her lips parted and her cheeks flushed.

"Maybe," she said very carefully, "our needs aren't so far apart."

"Besides," he said with a wicked smile, pulling away the quilt before she could cling to it, "I happen to like messy women."

Muhammed Ali Reza looked at the woman lying in the narrow, filthy bed. She was asleep, but just barely, and he knew that within an hour she'd be awake and ravenous again. He'd never known a woman with such an appetite for sex, such as unceasing craving for constant erotic adventures. And he wondered if there were other women in the U.S. like Shari Derringer. Perfect little ladies with the souls of whores.

Her cravings disgusted him; her body defiled him. He wouldn't go anywhere near her, except that she didn't know how to take no for an answer, and he couldn't kill her. She also had one other advantage. Her enjoyment of pain was almost equal to his enjoyment of inflicting it.

But for now he'd had enough. The raw, red marks on her body no longer had the capacity to excite him. Besides, he had other things on his mind. He'd been told that Kempton hadn't checked in when he was supposed to. Ali Reza hoped he was just being thorough before reporting, but he had the gloomy feeling that Kempton had failed.

What harm could two Americans do, far away in Washington? To be sure, he'd found out that the man, the one he'd instantly distrusted, was a professional with impressive credits. An old enemy of the Spandau Corporation, he was an adversary to reckon with, but what could he do when he knew nothing? And there was no way he could know anything important—Ali Reza was too careful a man for that.

And there was the woman with the ghost eyes. He'd wanted to shut those eyes out of superstitious fear and an attention to details. But really, what could she know? He'd read the papers, known she was supposed to be a psychic who could see things other people couldn't. He didn't believe in such things. Still, he wished he'd managed to tidy up that small matter.

When this was over, when things were still in a diplomatic shambles, he'd take a quick trip back to that accursed country and track down Elizabeth Hardy. Otherwise he had the feeling she'd haunt him for the rest of his life.

Of course, Kempton might have managed it. But the more time that passed since he was supposed to check in, the more Ali Reza accepted the fact that he had failed. So it was up to Ali Reza once again. And there would be no more mistakes.

The American stirred in her sleep, and he saw a smear of blood on the dirty sheet. He shrugged. It was convenient of her stupid father, of her idiotic, pride-drugged nation, to go along with the deception. The embarrassment and public outcry would be all the greater when the mission was finally accomplished. Mary Nelson had served her purpose, providing an identity for Shari Derringer to travel under. It was even more delightful to have her serve as Shari Derringer's corpse.

He had no doubts at all as to whether they actually believed Shari was dead. She hadn't been discreet those past few months in Washington, and they knew the information that lay in the back of her mind, festering there. Much as the U.S. government would like to believe that Shari Derringer's dangerous knowledge lay buried with the corpse found in the quarry, their forensic knowledge was too advanced.

But there was no way they could have any idea where Shari was. They'd been too careful for that. Every clue would lead the searchers on a wild-goose chase to a dead end. By the time they found Shari Derringer, all hell would have broken loose. And if he had his way about it, she'd be publicly, spectacularly dead.

Chapter 16

It was midafternoon before Elizabeth woke up. Sometime during the long hours of the morning the fitful sunlight had disappeared, and a steady drizzle was beading on the slanted glass skylight. She was alone in the bed, but she could hear Sam moving around downstairs, could smell the delicious scent of coffee.

She'd get up in a moment, run herself a deep bath in the old-fashioned claw-footed bathtub and try to soak some of the aches and pains away from her body. She tried to summon up a trace of self-pity for the shape she was in, but none came. Despite the discomfort from parts of her she'd barely acknowledged existed, she felt warm and safe and absolutely wonderful.

She let herself drift, knowing it could be dangerous, letting it happen anyway. God knows it wasn't a vision, she told herself. Just daydreaming. Wishful thinking. What a cozy house this was. Big enough even for a baby. One, at least. Two would need an addition. And there would be three.

She scrunched down in the big soft bed, wiggling her toes, and she let the fantasy play out behind her eyelids. The images were vague, soft-colored and comforting, and she wanted to float in them, safely removed from real life.

It took no effort at all to know that the quilt beneath her fingers had been lovingly made by an old black woman in South Carolina. Her granddaughter had sold it to a Washington antique shop to support her upscale life-style. Elizabeth could feel the love and caring in the tiny stitches, and she wondered if the granddaughter knew what she'd traded away so carelessly. Probably not. She wouldn't be privy to the strange strands of knowledge that twisted and filtered through Elizabeth's brain. If only all her visions, her snips of knowledge, were as gentle.

A flash of red intruded among the misty, impressionistic pastels, and she could see the red dress again. She could also sense urgency, even a trace of fear, and she tried to reach it, to focus on it. A rattle of dishes from the floor below made it vanish, and she was just a sore, aching woman alone in a messy bed.

She headed into the bathroom, pinning her tangled hair on top of her head. It was going to take hours to get the snarls out. She should never go to sleep with her hair wet, she reminded herself. Not that she'd actually slept. And not that it was the act of sleeping that had tangled it.

She slid into the deep, warm water with a sigh of contentment. Lovemaking wasn't quite the peaceful, passive activity she'd envisaged. But, of course, she'd only contemplated it with Alan, a man so gentle and undemanding that he hadn't done more than give her a few delicate kisses, once he'd understood her fears.

Sam had understood her fears, then overridden them in his usual high-handed manner. And while he'd been gentle, he'd been rough, too, delightfully, arousingly rough in just the right way. She found her body growing warmer than the tepid bath at the memory, the anticipation.

The red dress was hanging on the back of the bathroom door. She found herself smiling wryly as she realized he'd hung it there on purpose. She might as well wear it. The lack of it hadn't protected her. Though that was probably because she hadn't wanted to be protected. Not from Sam. Not from her own suddenly overwhelming needs.

The last twenty-nine-year-old virgin bit the dust last night, she thought, looking at her toes peeping up from the steaming water. And Sam was absolutely right—it was past time. And almost more important than the mind-shattering, body-dissolving pleasure she'd received at his clever, hard hands, was the knowledge that her mind hadn't gone sinking into bloody visions. There had been no one in the bed but Sam and Elizabeth. No other heroes and villains, interfering. And she wondered why.

She waited until the water grew cool and her skin grew pale and wrinkled before she climbed out. She was just toweling herself off when she heard the phone ring.

Sam was still talking when she stepped out onto the balcony overlooking the living room, wearing the red dress and nothing else, her long hair fastened in a loose bun at the nape of her slender neck. She knew the moment he saw her—his eyes looked up and met hers, and she was shocked at the brief flare of possessive sensuality in their depths. And then he returned to his phone conversation, effectively shutting her out as she wandered down the narrow stairs. She tried not to listen, and indeed, he didn't say much, just made a few noncommittal grunts as she headed for the kitchen area and the coffee.

She heard him hang up, without anything as civil as a goodbye. When she turned he was still sitting on the comfortable old sofa, and his expression was remote, thoughtful and faintly grim.

"Who was it?" she asked, sinking down in the chair opposite.

"Danny."

"Is it bad?"

"Depends on how you look at it. Kempton's been found, and they're treating it like a vehicular accident. I doubt anyone will waste much time on it, and if they do, Danny knows who to call to put a stop to it. The police are on the lookout for the pickup. Marcy Lou didn't take too kindly to the Audi blowing up, and her bosses didn't appreciate having the store windows shatter."

"I can't say I blame them. What are we going to do?"

"Nothing. They won't find the pickup here. We're safe behind one of the best security systems in the world. No one can get in here, and I'll ditch it before we leave."

"Why?"

"Why what?"

"Why one of the best security systems in the world? Do you have that many enemies?"

"Probably. However, it's not my security system. I couldn't afford such a rig. I happen to own twelve acres of a larger property. The owner of the rest pays for the security system."

"Who?"

"Nobody you would have heard of. He was my boss in the old days, and he's one of the few men I trust. He's very old now, and just about crippled from a series of strokes, but there are still people who'd give anything to kill him. The security system keeps them out. It'll keep people away from us, too."

"All right." She accepted the information, albeit unwillingly. "What else?"

"What do you mean?"

"Your friend Danny wouldn't have called without something more than that. What is it?"

A small, wry smile lifted the corner of his mouth. "How could I have forgotten? You'd be hell to be married to. No one could ever lie to you."

She kept her face impassive. He'd said it on purpose, testing the waters, and she had no intention of reacting. "Keep it in mind," she said. "What else?"

"Mary Nelson flew from Kennedy Airport in New York to Orly last Friday."

"So that's why. They wanted her identity."

"It makes sense. I doubt if the missing-persons report made it all the way to the East Coast, and if it did, it certainly wasn't high priority. No one would have picked it up if Danny hadn't had a friend run a computer check."

"Are we sure it's the same person? Mary Nelson can't be that uncommon a name."

"True enough. But Danny was able to track down the clerk working the desk that day, just on the off chance he'd remember. And he did. For one thing, she paid cash. No one pays cash nowadays, and that caught his eye. For another, she was very pretty and very flirtatious. As a matter of fact, the clerk told Danny that he got the impression she would have gone beneath the counter with him at the drop of a hat. Which, believe me, sounds just like Shari Derringer."

Elizabeth shook her head. "Orly?"

"The Paris airport . . ."

"I know that," she said, sipping at the coffee. It had been sitting too long, and it was dark and strong and oily, and it went zipping through her veins like wildfire. "I just don't think she's in France."

"Danny's working on that. Apparently she took another flight to Frankfurt, but we don't know what happened next. He'll be calling back in another hour. He told me he'd shoot me if I didn't answer." Again he smiled, and that hungry look was back in his eye.

"You'll answer. I intend to start eating and not stop until everything in this house is gone. Did you finish the pizza?"

"Every bite. There's soup, frozen steak, beer nuts and crackers."

"I may draw the line at beer nuts," she said, heading back toward the kitchen, wondering if he was going to say something, wondering if he was going to follow her, wondering if he was going to touch her.

Instead he stretched out on the sofa. He was wearing a pair of drawstring gray sweatpants, and they were drooping down around his narrow hips. His dark blue T-shirt had seen better days, but he'd managed to shave while she slept. He was watching her out of hooded blue eyes, and she could feel that telltale flush rise again, across her exposed chest, up to her cheeks.

He seemed to have every kind of Campbell's soup known to man, and she started opening cans haphazardly, trying to ignore him. "You know," he said, his voice conversational, "I always thought I'd give anything to see you in that red dress."

She turned, leaning against the counter. "And?"

"I'd much rather you took it off." His voice was low, sexy and compelling.

"Dream on," she said, turning back to her soup.

"I'll do more than that," he said, starting to rise from the sofa, when the phone rang once more.

With a shrug he answered it, though his greeting was nothing more than a barked, "Yes?" And then he did sit up, tension radiating through his lean body.

Elizabeth turned off her soup. It didn't take special gifts to guess this was new trouble, nor psychic abilities to know she wasn't going to get to her soup for a while. She stood at the edge of the threadbare Oriental carpet and listened, watching him out of steady, troubled eyes.

Sam dropped the phone back into the cradle with a short, explicit curse. "Danny," he said briefly.

"What's happened?"

He leaned back, watching her out of hooded eyes. "Why don't you tell me?"

For a moment she misunderstood, and it was like a slap across the face. "You can't still think I could be involved . . . ?" she began, her voice raw with pain.

He shook his head, unmoved by her hurt. "No. I'd know if you were. I mean, why don't you summon up your crystal ball? We've reached a dead end, Elizabeth. Mary Nelson flew from Frankfurt to Amsterdam, and then she disappeared. No trace of her, and there's not going to be."

"How do you know that?"

"Danny asked the right people. So it's up to you to find her."

"I can't."

"Or Phil's death goes unpunished."

"I told you . . ."

"Not to mention Mary Nelson, the other women in Colorado and God only knows who else. Whatever these people are doing is worth killing for, and they're not going to stop. When it's over there's no telling how many people will die, innocent people. Children. And if you aren't part of their original plan, once they've finished whatever it is they're doing, they'll come after you. And me. And the next time they won't make mistakes."

"How many times do I have to tell you it's not that simple?" The raw edge in her voice sounded too close to tears, but there was nothing she could do about it. He'd seen her cry, felt her tears. There was no way she could ever convince him of the myth of her invulnerability.

He was off the couch in one fluid movement, and she wanted to run. Instead she stood her ground, chin raised defiantly as he stalked her. "You forget. We did it before, in the apartment. We can try it again."

She backed away from him. "Maybe I've lost my powers," she said, her voice a little hysterical. "Isn't there something about witches losing their powers when they lose their virginity?"

"No," he said, catching her arms in his strong, hard hands. "They lose their powers when they fall in love."

She knew he was testing her, taunting her. "That lets me out, then," she said.

"Of course, only virgins can catch unicorns," he pulled her closer with a gentle little tug. "Were you planning on going unicorn hunting?"

"No. I don't want to do this, Sam." She pulled, but his hands were inexorable. "I feel too...too fragile. Give me some time, and we can try it. Please."

"Time is one thing we don't have." If there was regret in his voice there was none in his hard, impassive face. When she tried to pull away he caught her, turning her in his arms so that her back rested against his chest, and his arms were crossed in front of her, holding her tightly. "Close your eyes and watch, Elizabeth. What do you see?"

There was no breaking free. His arms were like iron bars, holding her against him, and everywhere her body touched his, she could feel heat. Danger. Darkness, pain and anger. She struggled briefly, but it was a waste of time. Sinking back, she let the fight drain from her body. And let the tension rush in, like the returning tide.

They came, sharply, abruptly, and she wanted to scream in rage. She didn't want to give Sam what he was demanding from her. She would give him her body, her heart, her life. She couldn't give him her visions.

"Don't fight me, Elizabeth. Don't fight it. Let it work. Go with it. Listen to it." His voice was a slow, seductive purr, rumbling from the center of her back, speaking through her heart. She bit her lip, hard, but she couldn't fight it any more. Redness was everywhere, not the bright flame of her dress, but the dark, foul blood seeping through everything. Waterways dark red with the stuff. Canals of blood.

She hadn't realized she'd said it out loud. Maybe she hadn't. "Canals of blood," Sam repeated in a low, hypnotic voice. "Then she's still in Amsterdam."

She shut her eyes, leaning her head back against his shoulder. "Blue," she said. "The house is blue, and old, rotting. He's with her. There are others. Evil. Cold." She began to tremble, and the heat emanating from Sam's body burned her.

"Who's there?"

"The killer. Phil's murderer. Except that they're all murderers," she said, the words hurting her throat. She opened her eyes to stare straight ahead, not seeing the whitewashed walls, the primitive paintings, the rainy Virginia twilight. "I see your blood. Covering me."

This time it was Sam who pulled away. "God, Elizabeth," he muttered, shaken.

But she was beyond noticing. It was so cold, so icy, that she knew she'd never get warm again. She could crawl into the fire that Sam had built, curl up in the heart of it, and her ice would put it out. He was going to die. She was going to watch it. And she couldn't bear it.

"I can't let it happen again," she murmured, not even aware she was talking out loud.

He was standing a few feet away from her, visibly shaken. "Can't let what happen again?"

"I'm not going to watch anyone else die." Her eyes met his calmly. "I watched my parents die in a fire. I watched them scream in agony and terror. I watched as our house burned down around them, even though I was fifty miles away at my grandmother's house. No one believed me. Not my aunt and uncle—at least, not until the police called them. And then they became convinced that I was possessed. And you know how you deal with possession, don't you? You beat it out of the child."

"Elizabeth . . ."

"I was seven years old. They beat me every day, until my mother's mother, Granny Mellon, came and took me away from them." She could hear her voice, light and detached, coming from far away. "I stayed with her until I was seventeen, and then she died, too. But that was all right. She was very old, and she was ready to go. But Alan wasn't."

"Alan?"

"I was going to marry Alan. He was going to love me and take care of me, and he was the kindest, gentlest man I've ever known. I loved him, and when I saw his death I told myself it was just a horrible nightmare. And I didn't warn him. I was too much of a coward to face it, and he drowned in the Potomac one icy day, trying to save a stupid dog.''

"And you ran away to Colorado," Sam said softly.

Her mouth curved in a bitter smile. "This is no surprise to you, is it? Even Phil didn't know much about my background, but you have access to a person's soul, don't you? You knew about Alan. About why I ran away."

"I knew about Alan Spencer. I didn't know you'd seen his death, or felt guilty about it. What makes you think you could have changed things?"

"If I can't, why do I bother? I don't want to be a policeman, a judge and jury. I don't want to find the bad guys. I want to stop the bad things from happening."

"Elizabeth," he said gently, "you can't. Bad things happen. Bad people are everywhere. The only thing you can do is find the bad people and stop them before they do more harm. You can't change the past. I'm not convinced you can even change the future."

"Then I'm not going to do anything," she said stubbornly. "I'm not going to sit back and watch you die."

"Why not?"

"Don't ask stupid questions."

"All right. But we don't know whether we can keep it from happening. What if we can? What if the only chance I have of surviving is having you with me, helping me?"

"What if the only chance you have of surviving is not being able to find that house? That sick woman and that evil man?"

"I'll find them. You know that. Sooner or later, I'll find them."

"But I won't be there to watch."

He shook his head. "Or maybe they'll find me. And you'll be there, in your red dress, covered in blood. And it might be yours, not mine."

"Is that supposed to be more incentive?" she cried. "Maybe I'd rather it was my blood."

He moved so swiftly that she wasn't expecting it, pulling her into his arms with unaccustomed gentleness. "I thought we'd gotten rid of your death wish," he murmured, his mouth too close to hers. "Maybe I'll have to remind you that you don't want to die." He kissed her, a brief, hungry kiss that left her confused and aching for more, but he still didn't release her.

She reached up and put her narrow hands on either side of his dark, handsome face, and she left all her defenses shattered at her feet. "I don't want to watch you die," she said very clearly.

"I don't want to die. Help me, and we'll both make it through."

She couldn't resist him. Even if part of her was convinced that she was helping him to his death, she couldn't withhold what he wanted. He must have felt the sudden acquiescence in her body, for his smile was brief and triumphant.

"You'll help me?"

"I'll help you."

"Do you know exactly where this blue house is?"

"No. I'll recognize it when I see it, I expect."

"So." If he regretted coercing her into helping him, only his dark blue eyes suggested such a thing. "We'll leave as soon as we can. Probably not until tomorrow—we'll need fake passports, and those take a certain amount of time. I still don't know who I can trust. I think right now we're on our own. At least this way we won't have to watch our backs."

She nodded, too drained to summon up enthusiasm. "I'm tired," she said, her voice low and flat. "I think I'll go up to bed. Alone."

He just looked at her for a moment. "That's probably a smart idea. I've got phone calls to make, things to take care of. I wouldn't want to disturb you. You'd better eat first."

She shook her head, pulling away from him and starting back toward the narrow stairs, her body leaden. "Tomorrow."

"All right. The Dutch are famous for their food. We'll fill you up with cheese and cream."

She paused on the steps, pushing her loosened hair back. "That's very nice," she said dully. "But Shari Derringer is in Venice." And without another word she continued upstairs and crawled back between the rumpled sheets.

Chapter 17

It was past two in the morning when Sam came up the narrow flight of stairs and into the bedroom. He looked down at her sleeping face, the faint stain of tears beneath her eyes, and told himself what a bastard he was. It had little effect. He'd always known he was a bastard—it took a hard man to survive what he'd survived. There was no room for gentleness, for sympathy, for giving someone else the benefit of the doubt, or any other benefits, for that matter. He was in a tight spot, with just about nothing on his side. The only advantage he had was her gift, talent, curse, whatever you could call it. And even if it tore her apart, he had to make her use it.

He could tell himself it was for her sake as well as his own, but it wasn't much comfort. He would have forced her anyway, even if her own life wasn't in danger. He would have used her if he'd needed to, coldhearted bastard that he was. He already had one woman's death on his conscience. He wasn't about to get squeamish over Elizabeth's misguided affections.

He couldn't stop thinking about Amy Lee. He'd been sitting down in the empty living room, staring at the fire, thinking of the other woman he'd betrayed by his devotion to duty. He'd loved Amy Lee more than he'd ever thought he was capable of loving, and he knew he'd never feel that way again. It didn't matter that he felt more tied up and drawn to Elizabeth Hardy in a shorter time than he had with his wife. It didn't matter if the feelings were sharper, deeper, more tormenting. He didn't want to believe in love anymore. He couldn't. And he couldn't live with what might happen to someone he fell in love with.

Amy Lee had been all of twenty-five when those bastards had gotten her. Cheerful, happy and trusting, she'd known that he would never let anything happen to her. But he and Phil had gone racing off on a wild-goose chase, and while they'd been gone, people they'd been after had taken her hostage. And before Sam had even heard their demands, they'd killed her.

He'd lived with that guilt for more than ten years. He wasn't about to let anything like that happen again. He knew her death wasn't his fault, but his love for her had made the guilt real and inescapable. He'd decided then and there that if he didn't care about anyone, didn't trust anyone, then he couldn't be responsible for anyone. And never again would he have to be torn apart by grief and guilt.

He looked down at the woman sleeping in his bed. She'd come so damn close in such a short time. Too close already, and he knew that if anything happened to her, he wouldn't be able to stand it.

She didn't know why he was closed up inside. She had her own grief and guilt about Alan, but it was nothing compared to his anguish, his responsibility, for Amy Lee. And he wasn't going to tell her. She was just going to have to think he was a coldhearted bastard who, no matter what he'd said, was incapable of loving.

Maybe sometime he'd be able to talk about Amy Lee. Maybe, when that time came, he'd be able to let go.

It was funny, though. He couldn't remember what she looked like anymore. So much time had passed, and now, when he tried to summon forth the face of love in his mind, Elizabeth Hardy's pale face appeared.

He needed to put some walls between himself and the woman lying in his bed. He needed to get on with what needed doing and not waste his time worrying about what effect it was having on her mental and emotional well-being.

Besides, he already knew her emotional well-being was shot to hell. She'd convinced herself she was in love with him. He'd known that was inevitable, once he took her to bed. Either that or she'd hate him. He'd hit the jackpot this time. She both hated and loved him. Or so she thought.

She'd grow out of it, he thought coolly. A little more time around him, a little time realizing there were other men, better men, kinder men, gentler men, out there, ready to fall in love with her if they had any sense at all, and she'd be gone, leaving him in the dust—where he belonged. He had no reason to feel guilty. Not in the long run, at least. He'd woken Sleeping Beauty, and when she was ready, she'd be gone without a backward glance.

And he wouldn't give a damn. He'd watch her go, speed her on her way, dance at her wedding, dandle her babies on his knee, play golf or softball with her husband, maybe even get invited for Thanksgiving dinner. The perfect uncle, and she would have forgotten they'd ever shared a passion so intense it was almost frightening.

But he wouldn't forget. He slid into bed beside her, carefully, not wanting to wake her. If he woke her he'd make love to her, and while her body would want it, her mind wouldn't. He could control his own tumultuous needs, but not if she opened those vulnerable brown eyes and looked at him. As long as she slept he could tell himself that he'd make it through. She'd find someone worthy of her, and he'd be back in his solitary life.

But he wouldn't forget. And he'd give a damn. And if she thought he'd smile and dance at her wedding she was out of her damn mind. . . .

She turned in her sleep, sighing, and reached out for him. Her hand brushed his chest, and she moved closer, snuggling up against him for a comfort he couldn't give her. And then she opened her eyes and looked at him, her expression troubled and waiting.

He didn't move. He didn't dare. She smelled of flowers, of spring rain, of him. He wanted to bury himself in her body; he wanted to wrap her long, long hair around their entwined bodies, tying them together. He waited. Waited for her to tell him to leave the bed. Waited for her tears and anger. Waited for her to close her eyes and go back to sleep.

Her mouth against his was soft, damp, still tasting faintly of toothpaste. Her tongue against his lower lip was shy, delicate, probing, and he thought he'd explode if he didn't drag her into his arms and complete the tentative kiss. His muscles ached with the force he used to control himself, but he lay back and let her taste his mouth, responding gently, just enough to encourage her.

She rose up on one elbow, and her hair fell around them, a thick curtain of silk that he wanted to capture and bury his face in. "What took you so long?" she whispered against his mouth.

"You told me you wanted to sleep alone."

"And you thought I meant it?"

"No. I just thought you might need a little time to realize you didn't."

He waited for her anger. Instead she smiled, a slow, sensual smile that made his bones ache. "I'm a quick learner," she said, pushing the quilt down. And he realized she was still wearing the red dress.

He didn't think about visions, either hers or his. He didn't think about destiny, or fate, or what was going to happen to them in the next few days. He didn't even think about what a bastard he was. All he could think about was her long legs under the red dress.

He slid his hand up her thigh, bringing the dress with him. Her eyes were very dark, glowing in the paleness of her face, and he moved his hand higher, touching her.

She was wearing nothing under the dress, and she was damp, ready for him. That knowledge tore away the last of his tenuous control. He rolled over on top of her, pushing her down into the soft mattress, letting her feel how much he wanted her. She wound her arms around his neck and kissed him, full and deep, with a reckless abandon that answered his own. He'd already dropped his own clothes on the floor beside the bed when he'd climbed in, and he began to fumble with the red dress, wanting her smooth and naked against his. But she wouldn't let him, catching his hands and placing them on her breasts beneath the silky red fabric. The skirt was up to her hips, and his fullness pressed against her, ready to explode.

"Wait," he groaned against her mouth. "You're not..."

"Yes," she said, pulling him against the cradle of her thighs, until he rested against her, throbbing, waiting. "Yes, I am," she whispered.

With a muffled moan he slid into her, hard and full and deep, and for a moment he thought he might explode with the wonder of it. He held himself very still, trapped deep within her glorious body, and he could feel the shimmering pulses of desire rippling around him, clutching at him. He wanted time; he wanted to be able to pleasure her, to seduce her, to bring her to that startling ecstasy she'd felt last night, but suddenly his body was raging out of control, ripped apart by the tremors shaking him. He clutched the sheet beneath them, but his large hands caught the red dress instead, and he was lost, driving into her with a mindless need that banished all thought but the woman surrounding him and his own desperate search.

He was half-mad with it. He could feel the bed shake beneath his pounding thrusts, could feel her body, damp and trembling beneath him, but he couldn't stop. He'd die if he stopped. And then he heard her scream.

He lifted his head from the cradle of her neck to watch her, transfixed, as her eyes glazed over and her body went rigid in his arms. She was wrapped tightly around him, holding on to him as if to a lifeline, and he could feel the spasms rippling through her body, tearing her apart. And then he was with her, driving into her one last time, pouring himself into her, filling her emptiness, losing himself in the wonder of her womanness, before he collapsed on top of her.

It was a long time before he could move. He was shivering with reaction, covered with sweat, damp with it. His hair was damp; his face was damp; and he wiped the water from his eyes, telling himself it wasn't tears. He started to pull away from her, suddenly panicked that he might have hurt her, but her arms held him tightly against her with unexpected force, even as her face was turned away from him.

He had no doubt at all that those were tears on her face. "Did I hurt you?" he whispered.

"No."

"I don't know what happened," he said, lifting his head slightly to look down at her, wishing that this time of all times he could see what was in her mind. "I just couldn't control it any longer."

She reached up and touched his face with one faintly trembling hand, reached up and touched the tears he refused to acknowledge. "You don't have to control everything," she said softly. "Sometimes you can let things just happen and trust it will be all right."

"What if I'd hurt you?"

"I would have yelled," she said.

"You did." He realized with sudden wonder that she could blush.

"That was different," she said sternly. And then she reached up around him, and he felt the silky strands of her endless hair wrapping around their bodies, just as he'd imagined. "Go to sleep," she said. "We have a long day tomorrow."

He moved off her, careful not to dislodge the imprisoning strands of hair, and pulled her tight against him. He still felt oddly disoriented, and he didn't know what he could do about it. Sleep was probably the only thing that would help.

He closed his eyes, letting the last remaining bits of reaction drain from his body, keeping her tight against him. He was almost asleep when she spoke. He knew she was going to say it. He could feel her own tension; he knew she wouldn't be able to sleep until she said it. He wished there was some way he could stop her, but he knew it was hopeless.

"Sam." Her voice wasn't much more than a whisper, and he wondered whether he could pretend to be asleep. And then he remembered exactly who and what Elizabeth Hardy was. With his body wrapped around hers, there was no way he could keep secrets from her.

"Yes?" He kept his voice nothing more than a sleepy mumble, hoping to discourage her.

It didn't. "I'm in love with you." The moment the words were out the tension left her body, and she sighed, snuggling up against him like a sleepy kitten.

He lay without moving for a long moment, pondering the kindest way to respond. "I know you think you are," he said gently. "It's only natural to think you're in love with the first man you sleep with, but it's just an animal instinct. Love doesn't have anything to do with it, and if you try to convince yourself it does..." He was interrupted by a quiet, unmistakable snore. Elizabeth had fallen soundly asleep.

So much for rational explanations. He pulled her closer, sliding his hand under the red dress until it cupped her breast, letting her curtain of hair drift over his chest. He'd tried to explain it to her, and she'd had the temerity to fall asleep. And it wasn't until he was almost asleep himself that he realized that in all the nights and days he'd spent sleeping with her, she'd never emitted anything like that ladylike snore. She'd been faking, to shut up his rational explanations, damn her. And he found he was smiling as he fell asleep.

They made love more gently in the early-morning hours, the red dress on the floor, her long hair wrapped around them like a silken mantle. They made love just after dawn, this time with her on top, her hair rippling around her slender, flushed body, and she thought she could never get enough of him. They almost made love in the shower, until he noticed the slight wince of pain she tried to hide from him, and instead he insisted they behave like rational adults and only neck a little beneath the hot stream of water.

When she finally made it downstairs her legs were still slightly trembly, and her stomach was so empty she thought she might faint. Sam put a huge plate of bacon and eggs in front of her, loaded her with coffee and watched her eat with a troubled, proprietary air.

"I don't know why I was so famished," she said finally, draining her second cup of coffee and pushing her curtain of hair over her shoulder. "I used to go days without eating in Colorado."

"You've been getting more exercise." There should have been at least the suggestion of a leer accompanying that statement; instead he seemed merely distracted.

"So I have," she said calmly. "What's the problem?"

"There's no problem. Danny came by while we were asleep. He brought passports and clothes for both of us. We should be leaving in about an hour if we're going to make it. We're flying out of Kennedy in about seven hours. To Venice."

She ignored the tightening of fear in her stomach. "How'd they manage to do a passport of me without a picture?"

He grimaced. "Bingo."

"That's the problem? You couldn't get a picture?" she guessed.

"No. Never underestimate my resources. Danny got a look at your file photo, found a model with similar looks and had it done, all within a matter of hours. Here." He tossed it to her, his eyes grave.

She opened it, looking into the eyes of a woman who might have been her twin. It was an eerie sensation, and she realized why the Germans wrote those horror stories about doppelgangers. Somewhere in the Washington area was a woman who looked like her, down to the small nose, large eyes and vulnerable mouth. She was also a woman with very short hair.

She closed the passport and looked up at Sam. "Couldn't they have found a wig?" she asked mildly.

"They tried. It looked too fake."

She reached behind her, twisting her thick long hair in a rope. "Got any scissors?"

It took him a moment. "Sure," he said casually, strolling into the kitchen area and opening a drawer. In a moment he returned with a very serviceable pair of shears.

She leaned over, presenting her fragile neck to him, feeling absurdly like Mary Queen of Scots on the scaffold. She waited, but he made no move to come closer. Finally she looked up, into his tormented eyes, and a small core of hope began to form inside her.

"I can't do it," he said, tossing the scissors down on the sofa beside her and walking away. A moment later he'd slammed out of the cottage, leaving her alone.

She hadn't cut her hair since Granny Mellon died, almost twelve years ago. It had been her only vanity, her one beauty, and a matter of pride that she almost hadn't realized existed. And its loss was the first tangible sign that Sam Oliver wasn't as emotionally remote from her as he thought. Picking up the scissors, she headed toward the bathroom, smiling as she went.

She didn't know when he came back. She had to take her time with the hair—seven hours to a flight from Kennedy didn't allow for a visit to a hairdresser to fix up any messes she made, so she cut carefully, strand by thick strand, until it lay in a pile around her bare feet.

The woman who looked back at her from the mirror was someone else. Not the eerie clone from the passport photo, not the lost ghost of Colorado. The woman in the mirror was new. Someone strong, and hungry, and in love. Someone who was finally, completely, alive. Someone who had every intention of staying that way, and keeping her man alive, too.

She was dressed in a khaki jumpsuit, her short hair brushed back, when she went back downstairs. Sam was standing in the kitchen, and he didn't move; he simply stared at her.

For a moment she panicked. What if he no longer found her attractive? What if her antiquated hair held some sort of magic charm? What if...?

He crossed the room in a few long strides, his hands cupping her shorn head, pulling her face up to his, her mouth to his, kissing her with an intensity that washed away the last of her self-doubts.

She wanted to say it again, to tell him she loved him, but she kept silent, knowing it would trouble him. Instead, when he lifted his mouth from hers, she smiled up at him. And to her amazement he smiled back.

"Let's get the hell out of here," he said gruffly. "Or it'll be hours before we get back out of bed."

It was cold in Venice. Elizabeth pulled her coat more tightly around her, resisting the urge to huddle against Sam's broad, strong body as the vaporetto sped them along the crowded canals. She'd expected warmth and sunshine in Italy, not gray skies and a chilly drizzle that came from both sky and canal and drenched her thin cloth coat. Fool that she was, she'd expected romance from Venice, not this horrible sense of impending doom that grew stronger and stronger. She'd expected beauty in Venice. Not the seedy, sagging dwellings, and the god-awful smell of diesel and sewage and dead fish.

"Anything look familiar?" Sam murmured in her ear. It wasn't a low, affectionate murmur. The water bus was crowded, and Sam didn't trust anyone. Neither, for that matter, did she.

The damp winter air was cold on her exposed neck. She still wasn't used to her short hair—it made her feel curiously light-headed, almost dizzy. Too many dark and horrible things had crowded around her during the past week; too many time zones had been passed. Life had become strangely unreal, and as they plowed through the murky waters of the ancient city on a modern water bus, her sense of disorientation increased.

They'd been in Venice three days. Three long, interminable days, wandering the damp, chilly streets, riding the vaporettos until even Elizabeth's steady stomach threatened to rebel. She'd slept heavily in the narrow double bed in the tiny old *penzione* on a side canal, only to wake with Sam asleep beside her, his big hand entwined in her short-cropped hair.

In the daylight hours he didn't touch her. In the night they made love with a fierce, almost angry passion, as if they knew that time was running out for them, and they had to cram a lifetime of loving into a few short nights. She lay awake afterward, listening to the sounds of the motorboats on the canal outside the window, listening to the voices, wondering whether they'd survive.

At three o'clock that morning she decided to try to find out. Sam was asleep beside her, lying on his back, the sheet pulled up around his hips. She had touched him other nights, slept with his body wrapped around her, and nothing had come. But she hadn't been trying. This time she lay on the bed, watching him, watching the even rise and fall of his smooth chest, the silky fans of dark eyelashes resting against his high cheekbones. She counted his scars by moonlight, fascinated at the number and variety. One definitely had to be a bullet wound—the scar was neat and round on his shoulder and ragged on his back. There were knife wounds, burn marks, signs of pain that had somehow been incorporated into his relentlessly tough body. An armor of keloid tissue that kept his heart and soul protected, as well.

She reached out a hand and touched him, lightly, so as not to wake him, resting it against the smooth warm skin near his ribs. She could feel his heart beating, a slow, even pace; she could feel his blood pulsing. She watched him for a long moment, and then she closed her eyes and opened her mind, willing the visions to come.

Nothing. Blankness. Darkness as deep and murky as the canals surrounding them. She tried to conjure up the visions she'd glimpsed before, the red dress, the blood, but the pictures were curiously flat and two-dimensional.

Sam's hand covered hers, pressing it against his heart. She hadn't realized he was awake—there'd been no change in his breathing, his pulse rate. But his hand enveloped hers, trapping it between his own strong fingers and his steady heartbeat, holding her there. And blood spilled around them.

A moment later she was on the floor, in a corner, staring up at him with terrified eyes, not even knowing how she'd gotten there. He sat up, and wariness radiated through his body. "What is it? What did you see?"

"Blood."

"Damn," he said, flicking on the bedside light. "No house? No faces to lead us to where Shari is?"

"That's not what I was trying to see. I wanted to see whether you were going to survive."

His reaction was profane and impatient. "I don't give a damn about my survival. When the time comes I'll take my chances. Don't waste your energy on me. Find Shari Derringer!"

She looked across at his cold, emotionless face, at his beautiful, scarred body, and knew defeat. "Tomorrow," she said.

"It's that simple?"

"No. All I can do is wander around this city until something looks familiar. I just won't stop until I find the blue house."

"You'll be dead on your feet."

"You'll be dead *at* my feet," she replied, pulling herself off the cold floor and heading back to the too-small bed. "I don't think it matters either way. We'll find her tomorrow."

He had enough sense not to touch her when she climbed back into the soft, sagging bed. If he touched her she might shatter and break, and then where would he be? She was sending him to his death, and he was giving her no choice but to do so. There was no way she could fight him anymore.

Half an hour later his voice broke the darkness. "I don't think I'm going to die."

Elizabeth considered not answering. "No one ever does."

He took her hand in his, his long, hard fingers covering hers, and he brought it up to his mouth, kissing her soft palm. "I'll do my best not to," he said. "That's about all I can promise."

In the darkness of the moonlit room he seemed almost vulnerable. He wasn't a man used to giving, not of himself, and she had the sense to realize he'd made a major step. She turned in the bed, resting her short-cropped head against his shoulder. "That'll have to do."

Chapter 18

Elizabeth did her research carefully, waiting until just the right moment to make her move. It wasn't that Sam didn't trust her. She knew he did, inasmuch as he was able to trust anyone. But she didn't know how to explain to him that he was interfering with her abilities. She'd wanted that interference, welcomed it, even if it meant being haunted by visions of his bloody death, but last night she'd made a promise, and she always kept her promises. Refusing to help him find Shari Derringer and her cohorts would only postpone the inevitable, not change it. She had no choice but to use it for him. And no way she could use it unless she was alone.

She waited until he was in the bathroom. The *penzione* had all sorts of brochures advertising walking tours, motor bus tours, even gondola tours. She was heading for the vaporetto, this time equipped with Dramamine, and intended to spend the day seeing the sights of Venice, alone, hoping against hope that sooner or later they'd pass the seedy blue house that haunted her dreams.

And a vaporetto would be safer. Venice was the legend-
ary city of assassins. Not that anyone would suspect a
slightly myopic American tourist of being worth murder-
ing, but some of Sam's paranoia had worn off on her. And
if Shari Derringer's confederates were as thorough as they'd
proven to be so far, they wouldn't leave anything to chance.
They might already know that Sam and Elizabeth had made
it to Venice.

She hoped Sam would understand. She left him a note,
asking him to meet her in the *piazzetta* in the afternoon,
hoping she could bring him the information he wanted by
then. He was going to be furious when he found she'd taken
off without his protective custody, but it was the only chance
for her to give him what he wanted. She expected that if he
was faced with the choice, he'd opt for her running the risk.
She simply didn't want to give him that choice, since either
response would have torn her apart.

She had the sense to wear a raincoat, a silk scarf covering her too-short hair and an oversize pair of sunglasses as
she crowded into the sight-seeing motorboat and prepared
to tour Venice.

It was the first warm day in weeks, the multilingual tour
guide announced as her fellow tourists began to shed their
layers. The sun came out, gilding the canals, gilding the famous Ca'd'Oro, and even the gondoliers began to sing. Not
that anyone could hear them over the roar of the motorized
boat traffic, but the sight should have been slightly heart-
ening.

Not for Elizabeth. Despite the growing heat of the day she
kept her raincoat wrapped tightly around her, her mind
reeling with the scads of useless information the plump,
dark-haired tour guide was spewing forth in three lan-
guages. She didn't care about the doges, the history of St.
Mark's Cathedral, Titian, Tintoretto or the Bridge of Sighs.
Some other time, some other life, and she would have been
entranced. Now all she wanted was to see the blue house by
the canal.

Her fellow tourists were a friendly bunch from all over Europe, an American couple clearly on a second honeymoon, probably after their children had finally left the nest and before they returned, and a young black college student traveling alone. Elizabeth had done her best to ignore his friendly conversation, trying to concentrate on the houses and palazzi they passed, but he was clearly lonely and longing for another American to talk to, and she finally gave in, managing to partition still another part of her brain for him while she searched for the blue house.

In the end she might have missed the house if it hadn't been for him. They'd stopped for lunch at a small outdoor trattoria, part of the tour price, but Elizabeth, with her mild case of mal de canal, couldn't work up much enthusiasm for squid and liver in pasta. Her new friend had devoured his in no time flat, and she suspected that maybe his funds were limited and that any free meal was better than nothing. She wished there was some way she could gracefully offer her own untouched plate without hurting his pride, but she couldn't. She smiled at him as he tossed pieces of bread to the pigeons, and found herself oddly near tears.

"Something wrong?" he asked, smiling across the table at her. He'd shed his cotton sweater, and his standard issue college clothes—faded jeans and rugby shirt—seemed so familiar and safe and ordinary in a world gone haywire.

"Just homesick," she said, wondering if Sam was going to kill her when she got back. Particularly since she was having absolutely no luck. The day was only half over—she had three more nauseating hours on the vaporetto to go—but somehow her hopes were fading.

"Want to stretch your legs?" the young man—Martin, he'd said his name was—asked.

Elizabeth didn't even hesitate. This friendly fellow American was no danger to her, and she was tired of being alone with her thoughts and her fears. "Sure," she said, rising from the table and dropping her silk scarf. "Which way?"

They were in the midst of one of the tiny squares that abounded in the waterlogged city. "You choose," he said cheerfully, pulling his backpack on.

"You don't need that. We don't have time to go far," Elizabeth pointed out.

"Security. It contains all my worldly possessions," he said with a rueful grin.

"Okay." She looked around her and unerringly pointed down one of the narrow alleyways where a side canal glinted in the sunlight. "That way."

The city was teeming with tourists that golden day, even the backwaters and alleys. Martin was keeping up an entertaining patter about the rigors of Indiana State University, and Elizabeth listened with half an ear. The sun hadn't penetrated the dark alleyway, and she was suddenly cold. Very cold.

"Something wrong?"

She pulled her coat around her and began refastening it. "No. Just chilly."

"It's hot today," Martin said, and sure enough, there were faint beads of sweat at his dark temples.

"I must have caught a chill," Elizabeth said uneasily, moving faster down the dark alleyway toward the canal, only faintly aware of the man at her back.

She stopped short at the edge, teetering for balance for a moment, as she came to the side of the narrow canal. The sun penetrated the waterway, but no warmth came with it. The houses were smaller, seedier, than on the Grand Canal. And two houses down, on the opposite side of the canal, stood the blue house.

She stood, transfixed, ignoring Martin's presence. There was no question in her mind: that was the house. Beside it was an overgrown tangle of a garden, surrounded by an ornate iron fence that was orange with rust. Behind that fence, that tangled greenery, one could barely make out the paler color of a human. Elizabeth didn't need her glasses or her nearsighted vision to know that Shari Derringer was in that garden, alive and well.

She stared, transfixed, feeling the ice coat her body. She could see dark shapes at the windows, people watching. People watching her as she watched them. What a fool she'd been! Of course there would be people on guard! And while an American tourist staring at the old building should have seemed harmless, they'd known enough to send Kempton after her in Washington.

She took a step backward, stumbling against Martin's strong young body. "Sorry," she mumbled, and then her voice trailed off as she felt the unmistakable pressure of a metal gun barrel against her back.

"No problem," Martin said cheerfully. "Just walk with me, very carefully, and no one will even notice." He moved around her, taking her arm in his with a companionable gesture, and she realized the gun was tiny enough to be almost indiscernible in his large brown hand. She had no doubts as to its deadliness, however.

"What if I scream and run?" Her voice was harsh and strained. Why hadn't she known? Why hadn't she guessed this friendly tourist had sinister motives? What kind of wretched gift did she possess, that tormented her with scenes of death and failed to warn her of her own danger?

"You'd be dead before you even tried," he said, leading her back down the narrow alley. "You've got more sense than that, don't you, Elizabeth?"

She hadn't given him her real name. A sinking feeling of despair settled down over her heart. She should have known better than to strike out on her own. Finding the blue house had signed her death warrant.

And then she realized he hadn't taken her down the narrow walkway to the bridge across to the opposite side of the canal, the most direct access to the blue house. He was leading her away from that nest of vipers, and she allowed herself a brief hope that Martin might be one of the good guys. She cast a brief, furtive glance up at her captor and realized that despite the innocent youthfulness of his clothes and face, his eyes were old. Sam had the same kind of eyes, she thought. Eyes that had seen too much.

The tour group had left the tiny square by the time they returned, but Martin must have known that would happen. She followed him docilely enough, wondering if she could get away by jumping in a canal. It seemed unlikely, considering the fact that she'd never learned to swim, and the canals were both icy cold and polluted.

"What are you going to do with me?" She was proud of her self-control. Her voice sounded no more than casually interested in her eventual fate.

"That all depends."

"On what?"

"On how you behave. On Sam Oliver. And on my mood. Where are you staying?"

"Hotel Danieli," she lied instinctively.

"Sam wouldn't be caught dead at the Danieli. Where are you staying?" The snub nose of the gun poked a little harder at the underside of her breast, and for a moment she remembered that old poem, where the heroine had died warning the hero when a bullet shattered her breast in the moonlight. The image had always stayed in her mind, and she didn't fancy playing it out in living color. Even if she continued to lie, Martin could simply kill her and find Sam himself.

"Penzione del Zaglia," she said.

"That's more like it. And does Sam know where you are? He doesn't, does he? Maybe we'll go back there and give him a little surprise."

"I'm not going to tell you where it is," she said in one last show of defiance. Her faith in Sam's invincibility was almost limitless, but anything was possible. And she couldn't rid her mind of the bloody visions.

"Don't waste your time, Elizabeth. I can simply look it up in a phone book, and the delay might irritate me. You wouldn't want to irritate me, now would you?" His smile was dazzlingly innocent in his dark face. "Particularly since I might take out my irritation on Sam."

"Rio Banco," Elizabeth muttered gracelessly.

"Grazie," said Martin, his voice mocking.

The ride back on the public vaporetto seemed endless. The Dramamine had worn off long ago, and the tension from riding around with a gun pointed at her ribs was enough to upset anyone's stomach. The sun had disappeared, and the afternoon grew cold and gloomy. She waited, without hope, alert for the moment when his attention might falter. It never did. The only moment the gun left her side was when they'd returned to the cozy little room in the seedy *penzione* and he'd shoved her onto the bed.

"Now we wait," he said cheerfully, dropping down into the chair. "If I know Sam he won't be long in coming."

"Do you know Sam?"

"You could say so," Martin said, leaning back in his chair, the gun held with deceptive ease in his hand.

"You don't have a silencer on that gun."

"Don't need one. It's the latest government issue—silencer built right in."

"Which government?"

Martin grinned. "Curiosity killed the cat, Elizabeth."

"Are you part of the Spandau Corporation?"

"Sam told you about them, did he? You surprise me."

Elizabeth just stared at him. He didn't know about her talents. For all that he knew Sam, knew her name, he didn't know the most crucial thing about her, about *them*. And therein lay their only hope.

She knew when Sam entered the building. She could feel his footsteps approaching the second-floor room, even though the place was still and silent. She could hear him breathing outside the door, and she wanted to scream a warning. She could do nothing but sit there, numb with terror, as Martin crouched behind her on the bed, the gun pointed at her temple.

The knock startled both of them. She'd been so certain it was Sam, but he had his own key. "Ask who's there," Martin demanded in a fierce whisper.

"Who is it?" Elizabeth managed, her voice quavery as the barrel of the gun pressed against her throat.

"Room service," said Sam.

Martin chuckled. "Tell him to come in."

"No."

He cocked the gun. "Tell him."

She didn't need to warn Sam. He already knew. She had no choice—either she could tell him to come in, or Martin would put a bullet through her throat and Sam would come crashing through the door anyway. "Come in," she said, tears of despair running down her cheeks.

Slowly the door opened. Sam stood there, a gun three times the size of Martin's in his hand, a cold, deadly expression on his face as he surveyed the murderous tableau. Slowly, carefully, he stepped inside the room. Slowly, carefully, he shut the door behind him. And then he spoke.

"Danny, you turkey, what the hell do you mean by scaring us like that?"

The man behind her released her, moving off the bed and throwing his arms around Sam's taller, leaner body. "Just keeping you on your toes, old man," he said. "What do you mean by letting your woman out by herself in these mean streets?"

"Mean canals," Sam said absently, noting her pale complexion and the silent tears. "Serves you right, Elizabeth," he snapped. "You scared the hell out of me, taking off like that. What the hell did you think you could accomplish by yourself?"

"I...I..." It took all her strength to pull herself together, but she managed it, glaring at him, at Danny, at the world. "Go to hell," she said weakly, sinking back on the bed and wiping the tears from her face.

"Where'd you find her?" Sam demanded, turning back to his friend. "And what are you doing here, anyway?"

"I got assigned here."

"Damn, that's right, you're with the State Department. They can send you anywhere they please."

"Exactly," Danny said cheerfully. "I talked them into letting me follow you."

"They know I'm here?"

"No. They know you're in Europe, and they're hoping like hell I'm going to find you. I don't have to check in for three days. I expect you to come up with something by then."

"Or what? You'll tell them where I am? That won't do anyone any good."

"It could save your life."

"Come on, Danny, you know me better than that. And you know the government. When the time comes that I have to count on anyone but me for protection..."

"Hey," Danny protested. "You forget who you're talking to. Anyway, I was just wandering around St. Mark's Square, looking like a college kid on vacation, when your little lady friend comes hotfooting it by me and heads for the nearest tour boat. So I decided it was time to see the sights of Venice. Lucky thing I did."

"Why?" He turned to look at Elizabeth, who was sitting on a corner of the bed, white-faced and furious.

"She almost got her head blown off. She went tearing down some alley until she came to a house, and then stood there staring at it. And if that wasn't a gun barrel trained on her from the second floor-balcony, then I've been in the wrong business for the past fifteen years."

"The only gun barrel trained on me was yours," Elizabeth snapped.

"Not likely. If Danny says he saw a gun aimed at you, then you're lucky you're still alive. Where?"

"Where do you think Sam?" she asked, playing her trump card with all her finesse. "The blue house."

The room was filled with silence. She'd expected more enthusiasm, more excitement from Sam when he realized she'd found Shari Derringer and her cohorts, but he was surprisingly cool. "That's good," he said, his dark blue eyes so calm that she almost might have imagined the warning in them. "How did it look?"

"Tumbled down," she said. "With lots of people in it, even if I don't believe the gun part."

"What's this blue house?" Danny demanded.

"What are you really doing here?" Sam countered. "What's behind Shari Derringer's disappearance, and why the cover-up?"

"Why should I know?"

"You wouldn't be here if you didn't. I'd almost forgotten, you were assigned to the old man a few years back. Derringer knows how to command loyalty. Are you here as a private favor to him?"

"Sam, I told you why I'm here. And as far as I know, no one has any idea what Shari's up to. She's a loose cannon, and they're afraid all hell's gonna break loose if she's not caught and deprogrammed in time."

"Deprogrammed," Sam echoed. "Is that the plan?"

"Apparently. Stop her before she embarrasses the entire United States government with her antics. Get her in a top-security hospital and keep her there, doped up with Thorazine, until things cool down."

"And her father approves?"

"Hell, it's her father's suggestion. So what's the blue house?"

"I won't lie to you, Danny," Sam said. "For one thing, it wouldn't do me any good. You're the best there is, next to me. Someone in the blue house is connected to Shari's disappearance. I think she's in Beirut, but it would be impossible to find her unless I have some help. I think that help is in the blue house, but I'm not sure how I'm going to get it. Particularly if someone's packing a gun."

Elizabeth listened to those glib lies, spun for one of the few people Sam considered trustworthy, and felt even more confused and helpless.

"Who lives there?" Danny demanded.

"Riffraff. Disenchanted, overbred offspring of various wealthy European families," he said easily. "You know the sort, the ones who play at terrorism until they actually see someone die."

"Hell, yes, I know the type," Danny snorted. "They're almost more trouble than the real ones. What's this got to do with the Spandau Corporation? They're professional from the word go."

"Who says there's a connection?"

"Your girlfriend. When I was doing my best to terrify her, she asked if I was a member."

Sam's glance in her direction was far from benevolent. "We don't know. You haven't heard of any possible connection?"

"None," said Danny, his brown eyes shining with honesty.

"We only heard a rumor, and you know how rumors go in this business. So what's next?"

"What's next for you?"

Elizabeth almost started screaming. Sitting there on the bed, watching the two of them lie and spar and circle each other like angry dogs, she wanted to start beating on the wall and shrieking. If she ever got out of this mess she never wanted to hear another lie in her entire life.

"We're going to see if we can get near the blue house," Sam said. "We're going to get back in touch with our contact—"

"Who is?" Danny interrupted.

Sam's smile was feral. "You're an expert at this, Danny. See how long it takes you to find out."

"Bastard," he said genially. "In the meantime, I'll do my best to keep the big boys off your back."

"Why?"

"For friendship's sake. Why do you think I came up with the passports and dumped Kempton's body for you?" He cast a curious glance at Elizabeth. "She really did him in?"

"She really did. And I could have swallowed that explanation if you hadn't ended up here," Sam said coolly. "Your sudden appearance puts a real dent in my trust, buddy."

Danny shrugged. "These things happen. You let me know what you find out, okay? I'll keep busy tracking my own leads. But you'd better watch your lady friend. She could get into a lot of trouble."

Sam's expression was morose. "I know," he muttered.

He closed and locked the door after Danny's departure, leaning against it and staring at her, an unreadable expression on his too-handsome face. "Damn," he said softly.

"He frightened me," Elizabeth offered.

"Good. You frightened the hell out of me. Damn," he said again, sinking down on the bed beside her. "I'd forgotten about him working for Derringer."

"You don't trust him?"

"He was about the only person I did trust. And yes, if my life was on the line, I'd trust him. But I don't trust him to have the same goals in mind."

"What are our goals?"

He looked at her across the bed. "Beats me. Find Shari Derringer. Find the bastard who gutted Phil Grayson. Stop them before they stop us. You really found the blue house?"

"Yes. And Shari Derringer was there."

"You saw her?"

"Not exactly. But she was there, I'm sure."

He grimaced. "Now all we have to do is find out what the hell is going on. And the damnedest thing is, Danny knows."

"Can't you make him tell you?"

"No one can make Danny do a damn thing. You didn't pick up on anything when he brought you here?"

"I was too busy being frightened."

"Do you think if you were to touch him, open up..."

"No. It would be a waste of time. The only person more closed up is you." She stared out the window bleakly, knowing he wouldn't refute it.

"Then I suppose I'm just going to have to find out myself. Where's the blue house?"

"Why?"

"I'm going there tomorrow."

"They know who you are," she said with calm certainty.

"Probably. I don't think we can afford to sit around and wait any longer."

"Maybe, if you just gave me some time..."

"We don't have time. And I think you've done about all you can for now. At this point, it's up to me."

"Don't be ridiculous. Maybe if I just got close to her, touched her..."

"You aren't getting within spitting distance," he said flatly. "You're going to stay put. I'm going to have a hard enough time watching my back. I can't afford to waste any of my energy worrying about you."

"That's not what you said when we first came here."

"Well, I changed my mind. Where's the blue house?"

"I'm not going to tell you."

His smile wasn't pleasant. "Yes, you are," he said gently.

"Do you think I'm going to send you to your death? I won't do it. I can't...."

"You'll do it," Sam said, his voice like ice. "You don't have any choice in the matter. If you don't choose to tell me, I'll make you."

And looking at the cold, bleak expression on his face, she knew it was true. He'd hurt her for what he perceived to be the greater good, without a second's thought. So much for happily ever after. He might hate himself for it, but he'd do it, and deal with the aftermath later.

"Yes," she said wearily. "I suppose you would." And turning her back on him in the narrow bed, she closed her eyes.

* * *

"Where's everyone going?"

Muhammed Ali Reza was paring his fingernails with his knife, his unquestionably brilliant mind boiling with ideas as he watched the stupid, silly blonde. "Time for things to get moving," he said shortly. "Don't tell me you're afraid to be alone in this old house with me?" He knew perfectly well that she no longer comprehended fear as an emotion unconnected with excitement. And excitement meant eroticism, and eroticism meant pain. Silly bitch.

"I'm not afraid," Shari said breathily. "I just thought things weren't going to happen for another week."

"Something's come up. There are some people who've managed to follow us to Venice. A few stray threads that need to be snipped." He hadn't bothered to tell her about the woman with the haunted eyes and Oliver in the first place, and he saw no need in giving her any kind of explanation now. "As soon as we've taken care of them, we'll start in on the plan. In the meantime, I have a little job for you."

"You do?"

"You're going to serve as bait to pluck a rather mild pigeon. They're looking for you, and I intend to let them find you—once I'm there, ready to kill them."

"Will it be very nasty?" she inquired, her china-blue eyes wide and innocent.

"I expect so."

She flashed all her perfectly orthodontured American teeth at him. "Sounds delightful," she said. "When do we start?"

Chapter 19

It was a cold, blustery day. The sky was icy blue over St. Mark's Square, and the thick white clouds scudded above them. Elizabeth sat at the outdoor café, watching the pigeons and trying to control her shivers. The coffee should have warmed her up, but she'd already had two cups of the thick, strong stuff, and she didn't dare put any more caffeine in a system that was already overloaded with nerves.

Anyway, as she well knew, there were different sorts of cold. She much preferred the icy chill that bit its way through her thick cotton sweater to the inner chill radiating from things she didn't want to know, didn't want to see. Unfortunately, she was prey to both sorts right now, and the shivers reached so deep inside her bones that she thought she might shake apart.

She looked across the table at Sam, knowing he'd be staring into space, into his coffee, anywhere but at her. They'd slept side by side in the sagging bed last night, somehow managing not to roll to the middle and touch each other. Not until the first streaks of dawn had begun to reflect off the murky canals did he move, pulling her underneath his fully aroused body, sheathing himself in her damp, impossibly ready warmth. He took her with a kind of desperation, and she met his lost passion with a despair of her own, certain he was going to die, too afraid to let herself look too closely. When it was over he lay against her, his breath rasping in her ear, holding her as the tremors began to leave her body. And then he lifted his head, looking down at her, and once more asked the question she'd refused to answer. "Where's the blue house?"

Her sense of betrayal and hopelessness had been complete. She'd told him, knowing he'd force it from her through a pleasure that was somehow close to pain, and when she did, he simply nodded, dropping his head back to her shoulder. And reaching her hands up to push him away, she instead cradled him against her, staring up at the cracked ceiling and trying to memorize the water stains, trying to stop time.

He'd barely spoken to her since they'd risen that day, half his brain reserved for his own inner thoughts, the other half ever alert for the danger surrounding them. They'd been sitting at the outdoor café for more than an hour now, and what little body warmth Elizabeth possessed had long ago vanished.

"It's too cold to be at an outdoor café," she said, pushing the dregs of her coffee away.

He pulled his gaze back from the far side of the square and focused on her for a moment. "There are plenty of other tourists out," he said diffidently.

"That's because they've come to Venice on an expensive vacation and they don't want to let the weather stop them from experiencing any part of it. We, on the other hand, are not here to see the sights."

"No," he said, turning his gaze back to the columned portico across from them.

"Why are we sitting here?"

"I thought you wanted coffee."

"We could have had coffee in our room. Why are we sitting here? What are we waiting for?"

He lost interest in whatever had fascinated him and turned to her impatiently. "This is the safest place I could think of for you. There isn't any more public place in all of Venice. No one can sneak up on you. No one can stab you in the back. Everything's in the open."

"Including us. Which means, if someone's looking for us, they've found us."

"That goes without saying. Any number of people are looking for us, and they might be watching us right now." He glanced over at the imposing edifice of St. Mark's Cathedral with all the interest of a street cleaner assessing the litter.

"Then what are we doing here?" she asked again, getting impatient.

"Waiting for Danny."

"You've decided to trust him after all?"

"Not particularly. But at least I can trust him to a greater extent that I can anyone else. I know how his mind works, we were trained by the same people. The problem with that is that *he* knows how *my* mind works. I'm going to be hard put to keep one step ahead of him."

"But you're going to?"

"I have no choice."

"Then why are we waiting for him? Why don't we just take off?"

"Because we aren't going anywhere," he said flatly. "He's meeting us so that he can watch you. Keep you safe. While I go after Shari."

"Damn you, Sam, you can't do that."

"Try me," he said.

She shut her eyes for a moment, thinking of all the pleas, the bribes, the reasonable excuses, she could come up with. All she could see was his blood.

He took her limp, cold hand in his, and her eyes flew open to meet his, hoping to find tenderness, love, reluctance. All she saw was a certain rueful determination. "I don't want you to die," she said clearly.

He shrugged, but for a moment she felt a shaft of remembered pain sweep through him, pain and guilt. "Better me than you," he said with an attempt at lightness. "I don't want to have your death on my conscience. It's heavy enough as it is."

She felt the warmth pulsing through his hand, felt the pain and withdrawal, and she wanted to cling, to pull him back to her. But he was going, fading, and if she didn't stop him, he'd be gone. "I'm not going to die," she said.

"Not if I have anything to say about it," he said, gently pulling his hand away from hers. He glanced around the square, searching for Danny. "Damn it, where is he?"

She knew she only had moments. Once Danny arrived to take over guard duty, Sam would disappear. "Don't leave me behind, Sam," she said desperately, but he ignored her. "Sam, please." He made no response.

She had one weapon left, and she had no idea how powerful it might be. "Sam," she said, suddenly very calm. "Who was Amy Lee?"

She had his full attention now, and his eyes were dark with pain and rage. "The reason I'm leaving you behind, swami," he said. "She was my wife." And without another word he pushed himself back from the table and walked away from her.

She let him go, sitting back in the wire chair and absorbing the blow, waiting for the pain of betrayal to rip away at her. It never came. *Was* his wife, he'd said. She was dead, along with Phil and a hundred others, and in that death was a gut-wrenching betrayal. But whose betrayal had it been?

Sam was out of sight. He'd walked away from her without a backward glance, moving at something close to a run. She knew perfectly well that he hadn't been running from her, but from memories too painful to face. She glanced around her, over her shoulder, for Danny's deceptively guileless face. He was nowhere in sight.

Sam had left a pile of lire on the table, and she could only hope it was enough to cover the exorbitant cost of the coffee. She shivered, wondering if she dared follow Sam, then decided against it. Sam was on a wild-goose chase on the right bank of the Grand Canal. The blue house was tucked in a seedy old neighborhood on the left. She'd lied to him, still trembling with the aftermath of his lovemaking, still holding his body tight within hers. She'd looked up into his implacable face and lied, to save his life. She'd only bought a little bit of time, a day at the most. When he returned to the *penzione* he would know she'd lied. And this time she wouldn't be able to hold out against him.

She glanced around the huge, crowded square, wondering if Danny were watching her from a distance. The black tourists were few and far between, and they seemed to be in family groups. There was no sign of her dangerous nursemaid; no one paid the slightest bit of attention to her.

Her eyes drifted over a dark-eyed, slender man at a table near hers, moved on and then stopped. She didn't look back at him—she didn't dare. She knew she had never seen him before in her life. And she knew who he was.

She allowed herself a brief glance as she once more surveyed the piazza. He was looking to her left, paying no attention to Elizabeth at all, and she breathed a tiny sigh of relief, wondering if she'd somehow sent her odd talent into a tailspin by trying to force it. Wondering if she was imagining monsters in the closet, murderers in every stray tourist. Shifting in her chair, she followed his intent gaze. And looked directly into Shari Derringer's placid blue eyes.

She was sitting alone, seemingly unaware of the man's inimical gaze, or of Elizabeth's shocked expression. Her mane of golden blond hair was shorter than the photographs, closer to Mary Nelson's. Her face was as open, as cheerful, as guileless, as an innocent child's, and Elizabeth wondered if they'd made a very grave mistake. If Shari Derringer was simply one more victim of some monstrous plot.

There was only one way to find out, a way she dreaded. But she couldn't hide from her responsibility any longer. She couldn't leave it up to Sam, or Sam would die. She had to make a move on her own, and quickly, before the dark man made his, before Shari Derringer disappeared, this time never to be seen again.

Elizabeth rose, dropping her napkin on the table, and headed over to the woman, half expecting the blonde to run. She didn't. She greeted Elizabeth's steady approach with nothing more than mild curiosity.

"This seems awfully rude," Elizabeth said, her voice huskier than usual with the strain, "but you look like you're an American. I'm alone here in Venice, and I haven't had anyone to talk to for days. Would you mind letting me buy you a cup of coffee and giving me a chance to talk to someone from home?"

God, it sounded lame, even to her own ears. But Shari Derringer simply smiled at her and gestured toward the wire chair opposite her. "I'd like that," she said, her voice softly accented from her native Virginia. "I've been here for ages with no one to talk to." She leaned forward, her blond hair brushing her pretty face. "Do you see that man over there?"

Elizabeth squirmed in the chair, not having to look. "You mean the one staring at you?"

"That's it. Does he look familiar to you? I can't get over the feeling I've seen him before. At first I thought he was just one of these Italian Romeos, but now I'm not so sure." The waiter arrived with two cups of coffee, and she accepted hers with a flirtatious smile that sent the waiter off in a daze.

Elizabeth allowed herself a glance backward. The man was still watching Shari, watching her, and that definitely wasn't lust in his dark eyes. "Never seen him before," she said, taking a sip of her coffee. It was sweeter than the stuff Sam had ordered for her, but just as potent. "He's handsome enough."

"In a creepy sort of way," Shari said. "My name's Mary Nelson."

Elizabeth spat out her coffee, then tried to cover it with a fit of coughing. "Sorry," she said, dabbing at her coffee-stained sweater. "It must have gone down the wrong way. I'm Amy Lee Oliver." It was the best she could come up with on short notice, but Shari just smiled at her, that sweet, otherworldly smile.

"Hi, Amy Lee," she said. "God, this coffee's good. Almost worth being in Venice."

Elizabeth took another tentative sip, concentrating on the woman opposite her, wondering if she really didn't know who she was. There were all sorts of mind-altering techniques, from drugs to hypnosis to things she couldn't even begin to imagine. If Shari *were* a victim, she could have been subjected to one of those techniques.

She took another drink of her coffee, hoping the hot stuff would warm the deep chill that had settled in her bones. She could only be glad they were in the midst of St. Mark's Square. She wouldn't want to be anywhere more remote with that man watching them. "Why are you in Venice?" she asked, hoping she sounded casual as she drained her cup.

"Beats me," Shari said cheerfully. "I was traveling around Europe with a bunch of friends and ended up here. The rest of them went on to Marrakech and were supposed to pick me up on the way back, but I think they might have run into trouble. Want some more coffee?"

She was going to have to touch her. Elizabeth didn't want to—she'd rather touch a snake, but she couldn't quite convince herself why. Shari Derringer might be completely innocent, and all Elizabeth had to do was reach out and put a casual hand on her arm. There were bruises on that slender arm, nasty bruises, not the sort an innocent tourist might acquire, but there was no fear, no deception, in those beautiful blue eyes. Just limpid friendliness.

Damn, she was so cold her head was throbbing. Her veins were turning to ice; even her heart was struggling with the strain of fighting the chill. She held out a hand toward Shari, but it didn't reach, it flopped uselessly on the table, and she knew she was going to slide out of the chair, onto the pavement, and where was Danny, where was Sam, where was anyone . . . ?

"Al," Shari said to the dark man who'd come up behind them. "I think Elizabeth is ill. We'd better get her home to bed."

Elizabeth opened her mouth to protest, to scream for help, but nothing came out. The man picked her up effortlessly, his arms tight, like those of an octopus, and she knew she was being wrapped in a shroud. Sam wasn't going to die, she was, and there was nothing she could do about it. No sound came out of her mouth, much as she tried.

She could see the faces around her, the concerned faces of strangers. And she could see Shari, a smile wreathing her pretty face, as she put a solicitous hand on Elizabeth's face and carefully closed her eyes. And then everything was dark, and silent.

Elizabeth wasn't sure when she awoke. The darkness was still all around, but she could hear faint noises. The lapping of water against the house, the distant sound of a catfight, the scolding voice of a mother and the whine of a child. She tried to shift, but her arms were bound so tightly that the pain was almost unbearable. She put it in a tiny compartment of her mind, knowing there was nothing she could do about it, and tried to roll over.

She was on some sort of makeshift pallet on a stone floor. Her hands were tied, her feet were tied, and her mouth was gagged with something foul. For a moment she thought she was blindfolded, too, but as she twisted her head around she could begin to make out shapes in the inky dark room.

She knew where she was, of course. It didn't take a psychic to know she was a prisoner in the blue house. What she couldn't understand was why it was so silent. It had been teeming with people yesterday. Now it felt empty. Deadly. Like a tomb.

She managed to sit up, ignoring the pain in her arms, and leaned back against the wall, trying to ease the pressure in her body. As she pulled her feet beneath her she realized with sudden horror that she wasn't wearing the same clothes she'd been taken in. At some point when she'd been unconscious from whatever filthy drug they'd put in her coffee they'd stripped her clothes off and dressed her in something long and flowing. She didn't need to peer at it in the dark to know that it had to be dark—blood-red.

She started to cry, letting the tears roll down her face and soak into the gag binding her mouth. It seemed silly, childish, but there was no one there to watch. She sat there, alone, and waited.

The light that flooded the room was blinding, and she shut her eyes tightly against it, against the slender, scantily dressed figure that sauntered into the room. She kept them shut for as long as she possibly could, until she felt a slender hand stroking her tearstained face, and she shuddered with real horror.

"Poor baby," Shari crooned, kneeling in front of her. "Don't cry."

At that inanity Elizabeth glared at her, her expression contemptuous. But Shari simply slid her arms around Elizabeth's body, pressing her against her silk-covered breasts, smothering her in perfume. "You'll see, darling. It won't be so bad. You'll grow to like the pain. You'll want him to keep on, and on, and on...." She smiled down at her, a dreamy, doped-up smile. "Al's very good at it. I promise. You won't even mind when he kills you."

Elizabeth shut her eyes in horror. Not at the thought of her own death at Al's evil hands. That had been a foregone conclusion from the moment she'd felt her consciousness fading in the outdoor café. No, she was reeling from something far worse. Shari's weird, scented embrace had opened doors that had remained tightly closed, and she now understood what Shari was doing. Why she was important enough to a group of international criminals to make them go through the elaborate charade of the Colorado Slasher.

Inside that vapid, drug-soaked brain was detailed mathematical knowledge that was going to kill thousands of people. Perhaps hundreds of thousands of people. Inside a brain that held only a minimal IQ were the secret locations of a dozen missile silos all over Europe and Latin America. Not only the secret locations, but the means of overriding the security to enter them. In the next few days the Spandau Corporation was going to tap into Shari Derringer's limited mind and use that information to set off nuclear warheads in a series of accidents that would trigger world chaos. And there was nothing to stop them. Unless someone stopped Shari.

"I know you don't understand," the woman crooned, rocking her body back and forth. "But try not to worry. Don't cry, baby. It won't do any good. There's nothing you can do to stop it—it's too far along. Just try to relax."

"Shari!" The man she called Al was standing at the door, bristling with rage. "Get away from her."

Shari sat back, releasing her reluctantly, her head bowed like that of a naughty little girl. "I was just trying to comfort her, Al," she said softly.

"There's no comfort for her," Al said flatly. "She's going to die, and painfully. She knows that. It's no wonder she's crying like a baby. Come back downstairs."

"Al!" Shari wailed. "You promised I could watch!"

"I'm not going to do anything now, bitch," Al snarled. "Get away from her. I don't trust her."

"She's tied up. What could she do?"

"Have you looked in her eyes? They're devil's eyes. She sees things no one should see." He crossed the room, caught Elizabeth's cropped hair in one rough hand and jerked her face up. "See? She knows things. She knows what we're doing, and no one could have told her. Unless you . . . ?"

"No, Al! I promise, I didn't—"

"It wouldn't do any good." He released her, but she turned her head, staring at him, putting all her rage and despair into her gaze. "She can stare at me all she wants with those witch's eyes. It won't do her any good. She's going to die, and if any of her friends are lucky enough to find where she is, they'll die, too." He took Shari's arms, his long cruel fingers digging in painfully, and Elizabeth knew where those bruises had come from. "Come on," he said, yanking her to her feet. "There'll be time enough to play with your new toy."

He flicked the light off as they left, shutting her back in the darkness, and through the heavy door she could hear their footsteps disappearing. She sank back, exhausted, horrified, shaking with reaction. She had never felt so helpless in her entire life. It made no sense that Shari could know those things, but she did. It made no sense that a group of crazy terrorists would be able to pull off such an atrocity, but she knew that they were very close to doing just that. And there was nothing she could do about it.

Her only comfort was that Sam wasn't going to die. He'd be half-crazy by now, combing Venice for her, but he'd never find the house. In the darkness the faded blue paint looked muddy, and tomorrow she'd be dead, and Al and Shari would be gone. The best Sam would come up with was vengeance. But vengeance would keep him alive, would keep his blood from staining this horrible red dress they'd put her in....

Minutes passed into hours, and time ceased to exist in the numbing-cold darkness of that room. It wasn't until the first pale streaks of dawn lit the sky that she could see they'd left the window open to the chilly night air. She shivered, looking out at the disappearing stars, and wondered whether she ought to try to cross that expanse of room and end up in the canal. She couldn't even try to swim with her arms and legs bound, but at least she'd be spared the treats Al had in store for her. And if he wanted to find out where Sam was, there would be no way she could keep that information from him if he was determined. She wanted to be strong, indomitable, but she'd never been good where pain was concerned. And Al appeared to be an expert.

She'd have to think about it. Have to consider it from all angles before she did something as desperate as taking her own life. It might be the only form of revenge she could have against the two ghouls who'd left her tied up in this room. Depriving them of their sadistic thrills seemed a small enough triumph, but it might be all she could hope for. She inched forward, testing her mobility, when a shadow darkened the window opening.

She held herself motionless. Whoever had come in the window couldn't be any worse than Shari and her murderous companion. If someone wanted to dispatch her sooner, then it would probably be all the better. That way the choice wouldn't be up to her.

She thought of making a noise, but couldn't bring herself to do it. The room was still shrouded in shadows, so dark that whoever had climbed over the balcony probably wouldn't be able to see her. Whoever it was dropped lightly onto the floor, moving across the empty room with a disturbingly familiar grace. Moving directly toward her, with dark blue eyes that could see in the dark, and she wanted to scream in rage and despair as Sam's hands reached her face and pulled the gag from her mouth.

"I ought to let them kill you," he said coldly. And then his mouth replaced her gag, kissing away the dry, dead taste of silence.

Chapter 20

Elizabeth's mouth came alive beneath his. She wanted desperately to reach for him, but the numbing bonds on her wrists kept her still. She wanted to scream at him, to tell him to run, to leave, before they killed him, too, but her mouth was too busy answering his. She was balanced on her knees, leaning into him, when suddenly her tenuous balance disappeared, and she toppled back on the thin pallet, taking him with her.

His big body covered hers, and there was a light of amusement in his eyes. "This really isn't the time or place, Elizabeth," he said, pressing into her. "Though I grant you, danger can be an erotic stimulant."

Outrage kept her silent as he quickly cut through her bonds. And then the pain as the blood rushed back through her arms was so great she almost passed out, biting her lip hard enough to draw blood. He held her then, his arms infinitely gentle, knowing her pain, but helpless to take it from her. His words were soft, soothing, silly words, and she drank them in in a pain-drugged daze, too weary to tell him he was going to die.

As soon as she'd managed to catch her breath he cut the bonds between her ankles, cursing as he noticed her bare feet. "You're going to have a hell of a time getting around Venice without shoes," he muttered under his breath. He pushed her shoulders back gently, looking into her face. "Are you okay?"

"So far. Get out of here, Sam. It wasn't my death I saw in my visions, it was yours."

"Which doesn't mean you're safe. And doesn't mean I'm going to die," he said flatly.

"Sam, I saw your blood, covering my red dress."

"Then what the hell did you put on a red dress for?" he demanded with some asperity.

"I didn't have any choice in the matter," she said. "I was out cold at the time. Sam . . ."

"So someone here has lousy taste in clothes. That doesn't mean I'm going to bite the big one, Elizabeth. Can you stand?"

"Of course," she said, letting him help her up and promptly collapsing against him. "Sam, you don't know what they're planning to do," she said urgently, remembering that horrifying flash she'd had when Shari had put her arms around her.

"Yes, I do," he said grimly. "I was able to persuade Danny to tell me."

"You were? How?"

"For one thing, he felt guilty as hell for letting them get you. For another, I would have killed him if he hadn't. He's known me long enough to know I wasn't bluffing."

"Weren't you?"

He looked down at her, his eyes bleak and cold. "They had you. The only chance I had of getting you back was to find out what was going on. The only person who knew was Danny. He'd seen the blue house, and he knew what was going on here. Yes, I would have killed him. Maybe because it was just as much my fault for leaving you as it was his for not getting there on time. You could have been killed. And the damned thing about it is I can't even afford to think about that right now. I can't even take the time to get you out of here. I've got to find Shari Derringer and stop things before they get completely out of control."

She shivered in the predawn darkness. "Maybe it's not as bad as we think. I can't imagine how the Spandau Corporation could manage to circumvent the security of all those missile bases. If the government knows, they must have beefed up security. Surely—"

"The government knows. They just haven't managed to tell NATO, or the countries where the bases are housed. Too embarrassing, apparently. They're still hoping they'll be able to minimize the disaster, or cover their butts." He shook his head. "It's probably already too late to stop at least half of the saboteurs." He started pulling her toward the window, but she held back, stubbornly.

"No, it isn't. She hasn't told them yet."

He stopped, a grim sort of hope forming in his eyes. "What makes you think she hasn't?"

"I looked in my crystal ball."

"Damn it, Elizabeth . . ."

"I don't know, Sam. I touched her, and I saw it. She doesn't even seem to understand what she knows. I don't know if she's just incredibly dull-witted, or too drugged, or what. But she hasn't told them everything they need to know. Otherwise Al would have killed her."

"Al?"

"The man who killed Phil. The so-called Colorado Slasher. He's a man she calls Al."

"What are they waiting for?"

"I don't know."

"We're waiting for the proper drug." They hadn't heard him come in. He moved very silently, like a cat, standing between them and the window. The knife at his waist glinted in the first rays of dawn, but the compact Uzi in his hand looked even more efficient. "You can't imagine our frustration," he went on, pulling the window shut behind him and latching it. Locking their best avenue of escape. "This has been in the planning for more than five years. And it's teetering on the brink of disaster because of a few careless mistakes."

"Al," Sam said under his breath. "Muhammed Ali Reza."

Al's smile was wide and terrifying. "You've heard of me. Very thorough of you, since I've managed to keep a very low profile over the past few years. I've heard of you, of course, but then, your country doesn't know how to keep a secret. Look at that stupid American bitch downstairs. In most countries the spoiled, stupid daughter of a politician would never have been allowed anywhere near such dangerous information."

"What can I say?" Sam said, shrugging his shoulders, his hands still tight on Elizabeth's arms. "Her father has a number of problems that no one seemed to be aware of. My government has an unfortunate habit of covering up embarrassments, and MacDonald Derringer was one of those embarrassments. His weakness for alcohol and young boys made him a security risk. And the last person he'd be wary of was his own daughter."

"He's a fool, like all the other fools," Al said, dismissing him. "His daughter was a gift from Allah, however. She already had a taste for drugs. She was introduced to a new one, with special properties. A very experimental drug, one that enabled her to carry vast amounts of information tucked in the back of her brain. Unfortunately, it overloaded other parts of her already limited intellect, but these things can't be helped."

"I wondered how you did it," Sam murmured, his fingers flexing gently against Elizabeth's soft skin. She knew what he intended. When his moment came he was going to thrust her out of the way and go for Reza. Despite the Uzi, despite the bright silver knife, he was going to try to kill him. And right then and there Elizabeth decided she wasn't going to let him shove her to safety.

"Yes, the little American couldn't remember her own telephone number if it weren't for the help of drugs. The problem is, she needs another dose to bring all that lovely information out in accurate detail. And we've been having trouble manufacturing it. One of the ingredients is notoriously unstable. Three women have been killed testing it."

"Pity," Sam said briefly. She could feel the tension thrumming through him. He had a small knife; she knew that much. He'd cut her bonds with it. And she thought she'd detected a small bulge beneath his waistband, one that could be a gun similar to Danny's miniature. Even with both weapons, he'd be no match for Reza, though.

"We think the last batch is it, though. The last person to test it survived, though she's just now come out of the coma. We'll test it one more time, and then give it to Shari. I doubt she'll have any mind left at all once she's emptied it of all her wonderfully useful information, but that's of little consequence. We'll make sure she survives long enough to be a great embarrassment to your country and then dispose of her."

"Very well thought out. What makes you think her security information will still be correct?"

Al smiled. Several teeth were dark and crooked, and he no longer looked like the handsome, somewhat dangerous tourist from St. Mark's Piazza. He looked like a hideous, flesh-eating beast, ready to rip their throats out. "A number of things, the sorts of things that have made the Spandau Corporation so successful over the past few years. A knowledge of the way the enemy's mind works, for one thing. Luck, for another. The knowledge that we are in the right and you are decadent and evil."

"You'll kill a lot of children if you carry out your plan. Are they decadent and evil?"

"Blood must be shed for the greater good," Al said, and Elizabeth could feel his hand tighten on the Uzi. "Everything must be purged in the fire."

It seemed to happen in slow motion, yet very, very fast. Too fast for conscious thought, too fast for safe decisions. As the Uzi prepared to spit out its deadly fire, Sam gave her a sudden thrust. Not to the floor, as she had expected, but directly at Al.

The man acted instinctively, throwing the gun upward as he tried to ward her hurtling body off. She knocked him over, the Uzi went scudding across the floor and the two of them were locked together, Reza's face insane with rage, as he yanked his knife out and started slashing toward Elizabeth's throat.

She kicked at him helplessly, and then went spinning backward, hard, against the stone floor, the breath knocked out of her as Sam leaped atop Reza's body, seemingly oblivious of the deadly knife.

Elizabeth screamed then, terror and despair slicing through her as thoroughly as Reza's knife would have. She struggled to her knees, oblivious to the stinging pain in her neck, oblivious to Sam's panted orders to run. She knelt there, in the warmth and dampness, and waited for Sam to die.

It was over so quickly. One moment a man was alive, fighting and full of hatred. In another he was dead, blood seeping from his lifeless body, his dark brown eyes open and sightless. And Sam extricated himself from the dead man's embrace and turned to Elizabeth, pulling her into his arms, kneeling there in the early-morning sunlight, with the smell of blood all around them.

It took a moment for him to pull back, and when he did he was covered with blood. "You're hurt," she moaned. "I told you. I warned you...."

"It's you, darling," he said gently, touching her neck. "He managed to nick you with that butcher knife of his. You're bleeding like a stuck pig."

She reached up and touched her neck, and her hand came away bright red with blood. Her own blood. She stared at it, dizzy with relief. "How wonderful," she said faintly.

"Yeah, great," he muttered, looking around him for something to stop the flow. He settled for her tattered red dress, ripping a strip off the bottom and winding it around her neck. "I don't think he hit anything vital—you wouldn't be looking so cheerful if he had. But I want to get it looked at anyway."

"Sam," she said. "What about Shari?"

Sam's response was instant. "I've got to get out of this business," he said. "I'm so damn worried about you that I'm forgetting what I'm doing." Pulling away, he leaped over Reza's prone body without a backward glance and headed for the hallway, with Elizabeth close behind him. "We can't let her get away. If she meets up with the other members of the Corporation they can administer the drug. We've got to get her back to the United States, back in treatment with people who know what they're doing. God knows what sort of quacks devised that drug in the first place."

The blue house was deserted. The front door was open, leading onto a narrow alleyway, and Elizabeth knew with sudden, shattering certainty that it had been her terrified screams that had alerted Shari. "Stay here," Sam said, pulling away from her and staring down the deserted alleyway.

"No."

"Damn it, Elizabeth . . ."

"She didn't go that way," she said with sudden certainty. "She's out by the canal."

"There's no walkway on that side," he said. "I should know. I had to scale the damn building to get to your balcony."

"She's on the canal side," Elizabeth said flatly, turning and heading back through the house, not even bothering to see if he'd follow her.

He passed her before she got to the canal side, pushing ahead of her onto the narrow balcony. "You see," he said with bitter triumph. "She's nowhere in sight."

Daylight had broken over Venice, a fitful, murky daylight promising more cold, more rain. In the distance Elizabeth could just make out a pale figure edging along the narrow ledge, four or five houses down.

"There she is," Elizabeth said, pointing.

Sam was over the balcony and following the blonde in a matter of seconds. He was much faster than Shari was, moving along with the grace and speed of an experienced climber, and within less than a minute he was almost in reach. Shari looked back at him, terrified, and kept struggling across the narrow ledges.

"Go away," she spat at Sam. "Leave me alone."

He paid no attention, moving steadily closer. He grabbed for her, catching her arm, but she fought him off, mouthing obscenities, beating at him. He tried again, but she scratched him, and even from a distance Elizabeth could see the stripes of blood across his face.

She leaned over the balcony, her hands clenched around the iron railing so tightly they were almost numb, as she watched the silent battle, and when Sam lunged for Shari the next time he managed to keep his grip, hauling her toward him.

The next few moments passed in a blur. One moment Shari was caught tight in Sam's furious grip. In the next she was gone, sinking beneath the dark waters of the canal, dark red matting her golden blond hair before she sank.

Without a moment's hesitation Sam dived in after her, and for a moment Elizabeth was terrified that he'd been hit, too. He came up for breath, then dived back down again, and this time he was gone for endless moments, lost in that filthy, murky canal with the dead socialite.

Elizabeth had just started climbing over the iron railing, ready to jump in after him and drag him to the surface herself, despite her inability to swim, when he reappeared, alone. There was no boat traffic on the tiny side canal at that hour, and he swam toward her balcony with long, easy strokes, hoisting himself up over the side with weary ease.

Elizabeth flung herself into his arms, weeping, and the force of her embrace pushed him back against the peeling blue paint. "I thought you were dead," she murmured. "I thought he'd killed you, too."

It was a moment before he said anything. "No," he said finally. "He knew what he was doing. One single shot into Shari Derringer's tangled brain and the threat was gone. There was no need to kill me." He looked up, across the silent canal to the man on the other side. The man with the gun, his dark face impassive, waiting. "Damn him," Sam muttered. "She didn't have to die."

Pushing Elizabeth behind him, he moved to the edge of the railing. "Perfect shot as always, Danny," he called softly, the sound carrying across the water. "She's dead."

"You going to leave her that way, man?" Danny inquired affably, still cradling the gun.

Elizabeth held her breath, watching. For an eternity Sam didn't answer, and she closed her eyes, waiting for the shots, waiting for the end.

"Doesn't make much sense to do otherwise," he said finally.

Danny lowered the gun. "You always were a reasonable man, Sam," he said. "See you in Washington." And he walked away without a backward glance toward the canal and its pitiful victim.

"Let's get the hell out of here," Sam said as a faint shiver washed over his soaked body.

"You're freezing. Shouldn't we try to find some clothes . . . ?

"I don't want anything from that house. The sooner we're out of here the sooner Danny can clean up the mess." He took Elizabeth's hand in his and dragged her through the house, out into the narrow alleyway. The paving stones were icy and painful beneath her bare feet, but she said nothing. She had no more arguments—she wanted to get away from the blue house as much as Sam did.

"Danny will clean up the mess?"

"He's good at that, remember? It wouldn't do to have Shari's body surface in any recognizable condition, now would it? Remember, she's already dead. And Muhammed Ali Reza might be a little difficult to explain. I imagine he'll just disappear, too." He stopped for a moment in the deserted alleyway and pulled Elizabeth into his arms. "Damn," he muttered against her cheek. "You feel so damn good."

"I'll feel better when you're warm and dry," she said prosaically.

"You'll never feel better to me," he said. "Let's get out of here." And he took off down the alley at something close to a run, ignoring her bare feet.

They had their choice of a garbage barge or a gondola, the only two boats moving on the wider secondary canal. She knew which one he'd pick, and she didn't blame him. His water-soaked clothes smelled like the garbage scow anyway.

To her amazement he signaled the gondola, helping her in with all the deftness of an ancient courtier, following her into the gently rocking boat as if he weren't drenched in canal water, as if she weren't tattered and barefoot and bloodstained. Pulling her into his arms, he looked up at the astonished gondolier. "Penzione del Zaglia. You know it?"

The gondolier nodded his assent. "And take your time," he said. "It's a beautiful morning." He dropped a kiss on Elizabeth's upturned mouth.

She looked around her in belated shock. The sun had risen, gilding the murky waters surrounding them, bathing the ancient city in a warm, flattering glow. Leaning back, she rested her head against Sam's damp shoulder, oblivious to the wet chill of the cotton. "I don't understand it," she murmured. "I was so certain it was your blood on me. That you were going to die. How could I have been so wrong?"

"Let's face it," he said, and there was a definite smirk in his voice. "You aren't infallible. You must have seen a possibility, a possibility we managed to circumvent. I still wish it *was* my blood." He touched the strip of material wrapped around her throat with gentle fingers.

"I don't," she whispered. "You have too many scars as it is. This way maybe I'll start to match." She angled her head painfully to look up at him, at the distant expression in his blue eyes. "What are you thinking?"

"That Shari Derringer didn't have to die. That too many people have died. And that you might have died, too, all because of my stupidity." He shook his head in disgust.

"But I didn't," she said gently. "We both survived, and it's a beautiful morning."

He looked at her in surprise. "Beautiful," he agreed, pulling her tightly against him.

"And I love you," she said, waiting for the reply that still wouldn't come. He said nothing, resting his head against hers, and with that she had to be content. She closed her eyes, accepting it, and leaned against him. And there were no more dreams of blood.

A light snow was falling when Sam and Elizabeth left Venice. It was drifting over the gondolas, melting in the canals, pausing for a moment on top of St. Marks' famed spires before dissolving. For the first time in weeks Sam no longer felt as if someone was watching him. Danny hadn't been anywhere around, the blue house had been closed up tight, and no extraneous bodies had emerged from the canals. The cover up was efficient and complete, and MacDonald Derringer appeared at public functions in a dark suit, still mourning his wayward daughter's death and his own close brush with disaster and disgrace.

The flight to New York was long and tiring, and both of them slept. Sam had so many things he wanted to tell her, so many things he was afraid to tell her—he, who was never afraid of anything or anybody. He waited until they landed in New York, waited until they went through customs and he left her for a moment to make a phone call. He waited until they were walking through the terminal, chewing on croissants from one of the wagons that lined the hallways.

"I'm in love with you," he said, just like that, surprised that the croissant didn't stick in his throat.

"I know," she said serenely.

He stopped, staring at her in outrage. "Then why did you make me say it?" he demanded, affronted. All that agonizing, and she already knew it.

"Because it's good for you," she said. "As a matter of fact, I'm in love with you, too. Are you going to make an honest woman out of me when we get back to Washington?"

"We're not going back to Washington. I quit my job."

That surprised her. She looked up at him curiously. "I didn't know you could quit Army Intelligence."

"I can. I know too much for them to make things difficult. I thought we'd go back to Virginia for a while. I've had half a dozen job offers over the past couple of years—one of them is bound to work out. Or we could raise turnips."

"Or we could raise babies," she said, her eyes wary.

He didn't even blink. "Or we could raise babies," he agreed. "Maybe babies and turnips. Do you want to go back to Colorado?"

"Never."

"We don't know each other very well," he temporized. "We only met ten days ago."

She snorted. "We know each other better than most people do in their whole lives. We have no secrets."

He hesitated. "I have one. Amy Lee. I should tell you about her." The moment the words were out of his mouth he felt a huge weight leave him. All the guilt finally dissolved and vanished, along with that part of his life.

"You don't need to," she said gently. "I already know."

"How...?" He shook his head. "Stupid question. Of course you know. I think I need to tell you anyway." He took a deep, shaky breath. "I never had much of a family. I was an only child, and my parents were older when I was born. They died when I was in college, and I joined the Army soon after. It wasn't until I met Amy Lee that I ever thought I could fall in love. And then I failed her, and she died. I didn't think I could ever forgive myself for that. Ever allow myself to feel that way for someone again."

"And you feel that way for me?"

He shook his head. "No. Loving Amy Lee was something safe and young, from another lifetime. Loving you is forever." He took her in his arms, oblivious to the amused stares of the passersby. "Will you?"

"Will I what?"

"Marry me. Raise turnips and babies and hell on occasion?"

She smiled up at him. "I thought you'd never ask." And as busy travelers threaded their way around the entwined couple blocking the middle of the busiest corridor in the building, she gave him all the answer he needed.

* * * * *

Silhouette Intimate Moments®

COMING NEXT MONTH

#325 ACCUSED—Beverly Sommers

Anne Larkin was assigned to defend her former law professor, Jack Quintana, on a murder charge. Jack was innocent, but Anne was guilty—guilty of falling in love with her client. When the verdict was handed down, would it be life without parole—in each other's arms?

#326 SUTTER'S WIFE—Lee Magner

When Alex Sutter and Sarah Dunning met, the air crackled with electricity. If only they could find a way to merge their lives.... Could a cynical, semiretired intelligence agent who was accustomed to a no-strings-attached lifestyle and an independent, settled young woman find permanent happiness together?

#327 BLACK HORSE ISLAND— Dee Holmes

Keely Lockwood was stuck between a rock and a hard place. She was determined to fulfill her father's lifelong dream to work with troubled boys, but she got more than she bargained for when she hired Jed Corey. Could she mix business with pleasure and succeed at both?

#328 A PERILOUS EDEN— Heather Graham Pozzessere

What do you do when the man you've fallen in love with may be a traitor to your country? That question haunts Amber Larkspur when she finds herself held hostage in a terrorist plot. Suddenly she has to trust Michael Adams, not only with her heart but with her life.

AVAILABLE THIS MONTH:

Silhouette Special Edition

proudly presents

Taming Natasha
by
NORA ROBERTS

In March, award-winning author Nora Roberts weaves her special
brand of magic in TAMING NATASHA (SSE #583). Natasha
Stanislaski was a pussycat with Spence Kimball's little girl, but to
Spence himself she was as ornery as a caged tiger. Would some
cautious loving sheath her claws and free her heart from
captivity?

TAMING NATASHA, by Nora Roberts, has been selected to receive
a special laurel—the Award of Excellence. Look for the
distinctive emblem on the cover. It lets you know there's
something truly special inside.

You'll flip . . . your pages won't!
Read paperbacks *hands-free* with

Book Mate·I

The perfect "mate" for all your romance paperbacks

Traveling • Vacationing • At Work • In Bed • Studying • Cooking • Eating

Perfect size for all standard paperbacks, this wonderful invention makes reading a pure pleasure! Ingenious design holds paperback books OPEN and FLAT so even wind can't ruffle pages – leaves your hands free to do other things. Reinforced, wipe-clean vinyl-covered holder flexes to let you turn pages without undoing the strap . . . supports paperbacks so well, they have the strength of hardcovers!

Pages turn WITHOUT opening the strap

SEE-THROUGH STRAP

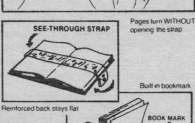

Reinforced back stays flat

Built in bookmark

BOOK MARK

BACK COVER HOLDING STRIP

10 x 7¼ opened
Snaps closed for easy carrying, too

At long last, the books you've been waiting for
by one of America's top romance authors!

DIANA PALMER

DUETS

Ten years ago Diana Palmer published her very first
romances. Powerful and dramatic, these gripping tales
of love are everything you have come to expect from
Diana Palmer.

In March, some of these titles will be available again in
DIANA PALMER DUETS—a special three-book collection. Each book will have two wonderful stories plus an
introduction by the author. You won't want to miss them!

Book 1
SWEET ENEMY
LOVE ON TRIAL

Book 2
STORM OVER THE LAKE
TO LOVE AND CHERISH

Book 3
IF WINTER COMES
NOW AND FOREVER

 Silhouette Books®